S0-BIQ-666

DEVIL'S CHILD

A NOVEL BY
MARGARET BINGLEY

POPULAR LIBRARY

An Imprint of Warner Books, Inc.

A Warner Communications Company

Acknowledgements
My grateful thanks to
Ros Anderson and Dr Jill Baumber
for their advice and encouragement

Dedication
For Alan

POPULAR LIBRARY EDITION

Copyright © 1983 by Margaret Bingley
All rights reserved.

Popular Library® and the fanciful P design are registered trademarks of
Warner Books, Inc.

This Popular Library Edition is published by arrangement with Judy
Piatkus (Publishers) Limited, 5 Windmill Street, London, England.

Cover illustration by Richard Newton

Popular Library books are published by
Warner Books, Inc.
666 Fifth Avenue
New York, N.Y. 10103

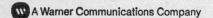 A Warner Communications Company

Printed in the United States of America

First Popular Library Printing: December, 1987

10 9 8 7 6 5 4 3 2 1

He looked into the eyes of the woman he loved, the woman who had just tried to stab him to death.

☐   ☐   ☐   ☐

"Why?" Adam's voice was a whisper. "Laura, why did you try and kill me?"

"It's all your fault," she said, her voice strangely pure and childlike. "You gave mummy help. Without you she wouldn't dare oppose me."

The hairs on the back of his neck prickled, and he took a few steps away from whomever it was who sat on the chair.

"Where's Laura?" he asked it.

Laura's mouth opened, her eyes tried to focus on his face.

"I'm Laura." The voice was the same. Too light for Laura.

"No, you're not. You're Edward."

"I'm not. I'm Laura!" The voice was stronger now, changing back to Laura's.

Suddenly, desperately, he wanted to get away . . .

DEVIL'S CHILD

ATTENTION: SCHOOLS AND CORPORATIONS

POPULAR LIBRARY books are available at quantity discounts with
bulk purchase for educational, business, or sales promotional use.
For information, please write to: SPECIAL SALES DEPARTMENT,
POPULAR LIBRARY, 666 FIFTH AVENUE, NEW YORK, N.Y. 10103.

**ARE THERE POPULAR LIBRARY BOOKS
YOU WANT BUT CANNOT FIND IN YOUR LOCAL STORES?**

You can get any POPULAR LIBRARY title in print. Simply send title and
retail price, plus 50¢ per order and 50¢ per copy to cover mailing and
handling costs for each book desired. New York State and California
residents add applicable sales tax. Enclose check or money order only,
no cash please, to: POPULAR LIBRARY, P.O. BOX 690, NEW YORK,
N.Y. 10019.

Prologue

July 1957
It was the end of the summer term at the exclusive private school for girls between the ages of five and eleven that nestled deep in the heart of the Surrey countryside. For the two children walking hand-in-hand down the sweeping gravel drive it was the end of their stay there. In September they both moved on to boarding school in Brighton, and because they were acutely aware of their lofty positions in the present environment, and their forthcoming insignificance at Brighton, they walked slowly and with dignity. Smaller girls, not yet self-conscious enough to care about impressions, ran past them chattering loudly.

Both of the girls were attractive in their own way. The smaller of the two had long, dark hair neatly tied in two plaits and grey eyes with thick lashes that even now surveyed the world with a slightly cynical air. Her companion was tall and slender, already showing promise of the beautiful young woman she would one day become. Ash-blond hair, large dark-brown eyes, and a porcelain complexion.

'What shall we be, do you think, when we grow up?' queried the dark girl as they approached the school gates. 'I want to be a doctor,' she continued; 'and mend broken bones and things.'

The fair-haired girl widened her eyes a little. 'You won't get very rich,' she commented. 'I'm going to marry a rich man and have four children.'

'Bet you don't!'

'Bet I do!'

'It will be pretty boring if that's all you do.'

'I don't mind if it is. I don't want to spend my life rushing around like my mother.'

'Well, that's different; she's an actress. There are plenty of jobs apart from that.'

'I don't want a job, I just want to get married.'

At that moment their respective mothers drew up outside the school and the girls paused for a moment before parting for the holidays.

'You'll change your mind,' continued the dark girl. 'It's just a phase.'

The fair hair was tossed back in a small fit of pique. 'I won't. Just you wait and see,.Victoria Tyson. I'll be happily married long before you set any stupid old bones!'

An impatient toot on the horn by Victoria's mother terminated the discussion. Victoria ran off with a final wave to her friend.

Slowly the other girl wandered to the waiting Rover. Inside her immaculately made up and incredibly youthful-looking mother was waiting.

'Don't scowl Laura, you'll get worry lines,' she said automatically. Laura's mouth tightened.

'I'll show Victoria,' she muttered. 'One day she'll be sick as a pig when she's up all night with moaning patients and I'm sitting happily at home with my children safe in their beds.'

'Did you say something, Laura? I wish you wouldn't mumble so, dear.'

4

'Don't scowl; don't mumble; always sound the ends of your words,' thought Laura to herself. 'When I'm a mother I won't ever nag at my children like that. We'll be one big, happy family.'

For the first eleven years of her life Laura Kenley had managed to get everything that she wanted, with the exception of her mother's time, and she had no reason to think that provided she was sensible she would not achieve her relatively modest ambition. After all thousands of women raised large, happy families, and she knew that she would be a wonderful mother.

The years that followed only served to strengthen both girls in their ambitions. While Victoria shone academically at the new school, and devoted every spare moment of her time to reading medical books and pursuing her goal with single-minded determination, Laura found it difficult to remain in the top half of her class for most of the subjects on the curriculum. Her work was always neat, and carefully thought out, but she lacked flair and initiative. She worked twice as hard as most of the girls who were placed above her, but she knew only too well that while many of them were capable of better things she was working to the limit of her capability.

She continued to drive herself hard, not because of her parents, for providing that she seemed happy and well fed they were not concerned about class placings and form prizes, but because she had to do everything that she undertook to the very best of her ability. She even wished, however unreasonably, that her parents did care more. She wouldn't have minded their disappointment when the end-of-term report was sent home; she could have stood up to criticism and parental urging to do better, if only they would show that they cared.

If term-time was difficult, then the school holidays were intolerable. Every time she hoped that it would be different, that for once she would not be left alone with only the housekeeper and her mother's secretary for company, but every time she was disappointed. Her birthday and Christmas gifts were lavish, even by the high standards of her contemporaries, but to Laura's sensitive spirit they only emphasized the terrible emptiness of her home life.

Her own father never came to see her, indeed he was rapidly becoming nothing more than a fleeting memory, and the stepfathers were busy men travelling abroad in their complicated efforts to make more money and offer Laura's mother, and therefore Laura, more security. It wasn't this kind of security that Laura craved, but because she was a polite child and also an inhibited one she kept such thoughts to herself.

Her mother, to whom every holiday meant a reminder of the passing years as Laura grew taller and more attractive and less and less a daughter with whom she would wish to be photographed, was always away. Sometimes it was a play, touring the provinces with the possibility of ending up in the West End. It never did, but her mother continued to talk as though the West End was just around the corner. Then, when she became too old for young parts but was unwilling to start playing older women, she was given a role in a television soap opera that occupied her for five years and allowed her to play a *femme fatale* who took men away from younger women because of her sophistication, and who certainly did not have a teenage daughter lurking in the background as a reminder of the passage of time.

She wasn't an unkind woman, just a self-centred one. She imagined that Laura was happy enough left to her own devices. After all, most girls complained that their parents cramped their style whereas Laura was free to do as she chose. On the rare occasions that they actually communicated and Laura expressed her wish, now rapidly dying, for a brother or sister, her mother would laugh her tinkling laugh and point out the disadvantages. How it would interfere with Laura's pleasures – whatever they were, Laura thought bitterly – and how presents would become less frequent and less opulent because there were two sets to be bought.

Laura listened, but she knew the truth. She knew that her mother deeply regretted having one child, and would never never willingly produce another. She understood her mother's insecurity, and at times she pitied her in her frantic search for perpetual adoration from husbands and audiences, but she could not forgive her.

By the time that she was fifteen Laura had given up hoping for things to change. She accepted her home life for what it was, but her resolve to raise a large and happy family of her own hardened with every hurt that she experienced. 'I'll never do that to my children,' she would mutter as she was brushed aside because visitors were coming and she was in the way. 'I'll always listen to them; I'll remember how important things are to children.' Her image of a sprawling, happy family sustained her, and became clearer in her mind. She would have three or four children; a boy first of course (men usually wanted sons) and then a daughter, and after that she didn't mind as long as they were healthy. In her daydreams the boy was blond, sturdy and laughing as he climbed trees and teased his younger sister, but she knew that if he turned out to be brown haired, or even auburn, she wouldn't mind. It was just that blond children looked so lovely in the summer, when they were tanned.

For the last two years at school she was able to study Domestic Science, and here at last she excelled. Unlike most of her classmates she had never had the opportunity to watch her mother cooking and sewing, and it was all new. Not only was it new, it related to her plans for a large family, and she set to work with a will. The hours spent in the cookery rooms were the happiest that she had known, and to her great delight her talent matched her enthusiasm. She also did typing and shorthand, and was competent at both. Competent, but not exceptional.

She left school a year before Victoria; after all what need did she have of A levels, even supposing that she had the ability to gain any? She had her future firmly planned. She would find a good secretarial job, and then within a couple of years she would get married. After that her life would really begin. She knew, knew beyond any shadow of doubt that she would make an excellent wife and mother, and she could hardly wait for that stage of her life to begin.

Fortune had favoured her in some respects that she did not, as yet, appreciate. She had a natural grace of movement that made her stand out among a crowd of girls, and she was truly beautiful. Victoria sometimes worried about Laura, it frightened her to see how susceptible her friend was to affection. Beauty and vulnerability combined were a frightening combination, and she could only hope that the man whom Laura finally did marry would be a kind one, someone who appreciated her good points, and did not take advantage of her naïvety. It was strange, she thought, that the daughter of an actress could grow up so unsophisticated.

Strange, and a little perturbing. Victoria would hate to see Laura hurt.

Armed with her innocence Laura had no such fears. 'I'll think of you studying away next term, Vicky!' Her eyes danced with happiness. 'Don't you envy me, going out to work? Real life at last!'

Real life, thought Victoria, and hoped that Laura would be able to cope with real life.

'Of course I do,' she said aloud. 'Never mind, I'll be there, readly to help at your first confinement!'

'I do hope you get what you want, Vicky. I hope we both do.'

'Why shouldn't we? After all, we're not asking for the moon!'

'Don't forget to write,' reminded Laura. 'I shall want to hear all the school news next term.'

'Don't worry; I'll keep you well informed. Hope you find a nice job, and a nice boss of course!'

And so they parted: Victoria with years of study ahead of her, but willing to make sacrifices in her personal life to achieve her goal, Laura free now to begin her life, her life as she wanted it to be. Perhaps her expectations of marriage were a little too rosy, her images of children just too perfect, but there was no harm in that. If anything it would make her strive all the harder, and a good marriage, as Laura knew only too well from years of studying bad ones, needed constant work if it were to succeed. Failure was inconceivable. Her marriage would be as near perfect as was humanly possible. Then, and only then, would her solitary childhood have any point at all. For the first time that she could remember she left the school grounds and started her journey home with a light heart. From now on life would be good.

'This time next week you'll be Mrs. Nicholas Wells. How does it feel?'

Laura fiddled with the diamond- and-sapphire engagement ring on her left hand. 'Well, it's wonderful of course. I can hardly believe that it's true, to tell you the truth. But, when I stop to think, I suppose that apart from being excited I feel a bit scared.'

'Scared?' Victoria pushed her long, dark hair behind her ears and raised her eyebrows quizzically. 'Scared? It's what you've always wanted, Laura. Don't you remember, even at Ambleside, you only ever wanted to get married and have a family?'

Laura raised her large brown eyes until they met those of her friend. 'I know. I suppose that's why it's scaring me. I can't believe that I've been so lucky, and I'm frightened that something will go wrong.'

'What on earth could go wrong?'

'I don't know.'

'You must have something in mind.'

'Promise you won't tell?' Victoria nodded. 'Well, I'm terrified that I won't be able to have children.'

'Would that matter so much, Laura? After all,

Nicholas does have a son by his first marriage. Would he be devastated if he never had any more children?'

'No, I don't think so. Disappointed perhaps, because we have talked quite a lot about having a large family, but not devastated. No, I'm the one who would be devastated, Vicky. I just don't think I could go on living if I knew I was unable to have children.'

Victoria surveyed her friend carefully. She had lost weight during her courtship, but that was hardly surprising. Nicholas Wells was rich, handsome and since his divorce one of the most eligible men on the London social scene. It must have been a terrible strain for Laura reading about his alleged affairs in recent months, and hearing the speculation as to whether he would indeed marry her or whether she would find herself politely dropped after the relationship lost its initial attraction, a fate already endured by several attractive debutantes. However, this time it appeared that Nicholas Wells had lost his heart too.

'You shouldn't think about it so much,' remarked Vicky bluntly. 'The only reason you're likely to fail to conceive is mental. There is such a thing as wanting something too much, you know. It's best to adopt a relaxed attitude towards that sort of thing. The mind can play funny tricks on the body if you're not careful.'

'Thank you doctor!' Laura laughed lightly.

'I'm serious, Laura. After all, there is more to marriage than babies. Surely you and Nicholas want some time alone together before you hear the patter of tiny feet?'

'We want a family straight away,' said Laura firmly. 'He knows exactly how I feel about it, and is in complete agreement with me.'

Having noticed how every male in the restaurant had been covertly eyeing Laura ever since they had come in

12

Victoria accepted this. Tall, slim, her blond hair in a stylish pageboy and her perfect complexion giving off an almost ivory sheen, Laura would have most men in complete agreement with whatever she said. Victoria felt a pang of envy. She had none of those attributes, and while she had never desired the lifestyle of Laura it would have been nice to have had one or two men falling over themselves in their haste to take her out wining and dining.

They left the restaurant shortly after 11 pm, and found Nicholas waiting a hundred yards down the road. 'It's Nick!' cried Laura, and Victoria watched as she flew along the pavement and threw herself into the arms of the man standing by the side of the silver Mercedes.

Yes, she mused, he is very handsome, and he looks a kind man. Laura needed a kind man, and preferably someone who was down to earth as well. Her highly strung disposition did not react well to stresses and strains. Marriage to this man should ensure her a relatively smooth passage through the matrimonial waters.

Nicholas smiled over Laura's head as Victoria approached.

'Good evening, Vicky. A pleasant girls' night out?'

'Yes, thank you. I'll see you at the Register Office next week.'

Laura disengaged herself long enough to wave farewell before being assisted into the passenger seat of the car. Victoria walked round the corner to where she had left her own, rather battered Austin. It all seemed so perfect; a beautiful girl, a sophisticated man, and an apparent abundance of love. Why then did she have such a strange feeling when talking to Laura this evening? Was it merely that her friend's frantic, nervous excitement troubled her medical mind? Perhaps. But somewhere in the deepest corner of her brain there had stirred that night a flickering of fear for Laura's future.

'I'm jealous,' she told herself firmly. 'I'm envious, and I can't bear to think that she'll always be so lucky. That's all it is, the proverbial green-eyed monster!' She turned on her radio and sang along with it. It was the only logical explanation, and she was a very logical young lady. She did not believe in strange presentiments, however strong, and even if she had there would have been nothing that she could do now. After all, if anything did go wrong Laura could always count on Victoria for help. That was what friends were for.

Nicholas arrived at the Register Office ten minutes too early. It was a particularly perfect June day, but then it was impossible to imagine Laura having the misfortune to marry in the midst of a summer downpour. He sensed that life had not always been kind to Laura, but from the first time he had met her he had resolved that as far as it was in his power, he would make it good for her from then on.

He exchanged a few words with his parents when they arrived, and then watched as Laura's mother accompanied by her third husband, made a grand entrance. She was a woman who could create the illusion of beauty through skilful make-up, and much animation and energy. Nicholas admired her, but did not particularly like her. She seemed a cold woman, and not in the least like her beautiful, affectionate daughter. Laura had so much love to give that at times it frightened Nicholas. To be the recipient of such love was in itself a responsibility, and he thought that it would be healthier for both of them once there were children to share her affection.

14

At exactly 10.30 am Laura arrived. She wore an Edwardian-style skirt and blouse, and carried a spray of red roses. Her hair was flicked behind her ears, and small diamond ear-rings, a gift from Nicholas, glittered in the shaft of sunlight from the small window. He smiled at her, and she warmed beneath the appreciation in his glance. As he stepped towards her the Registrar signalled for them to enter the Register Office, and in the general exodus mother and daughter stood for one brief moment side by side in the doorway.

The contrast between them was sharp, and Nicholas imagined painful to the older woman, if she was aware of it. She was. She flicked her gaze from the tip of Laura's head to the toes of her white suede shoes, took her husband's arm and walked by. Nicholas saw the momentary droop of Laura's shoulders before she quickly straightened and looked across to him. How fragile her self-confidence was, he realized, and he hoped desperately that in time he could strengthen her.

As he listened to the words of the marriage service he noticed Victoria out of the corner of his eyes. She was wearing a light blue suit, but even dressed up for a wedding she gave the impression of a down-to-earth career woman forced into a day of frivolity that she had little time for. He quite liked Victoria, but never thought of her as a woman. She was simply a good friend for Laura, a steadying influence.

Quickly, very quickly compared with the church service that his first marriage had entailed, it was over, and he was invited to kiss his bride. Her lips were full and soft beneath his, and he experienced a swift surge of desire. They had not yet slept together, and he longed now for the reception to be over so that they could be on their way to Corsica and a two-week honeymoon in the sun.

There were seventy-five guests at the reception, and it seemed to Nicholas that it took hours for each one to be spoken to and thanked. Now that he was so near to possessing Laura every moment's delay annoyed him. At last Laura slipped away to change into a peach-coloured chiffon dress and large straw hat ready for their going-away. Finally they were in the car, calling out last goodbyes, and listening to the clanging of the tin cans tied to the boot.

When they finally arrived at their hotel Nicholas, glancing at Laura's pale travel-weary face, felt a brief fear that in some way he would ruin the honeymoon for her. He was so anxious to make their first night together a perfect one that he even worried about his own abilities, and such a thought had never crossed his mind since he was a shy boy of sixteen. Once they were alone together all his worries disappeared. She revealed a gratifying streak of sensuality that he had not really expected from her, and the honeymoon passed off in a glorious sensual blend of warm sun, excellent food and physical satisfaction.

On the flight back to England Nicholas glanced at Laura's tanned face and marvelled that she was truly his. He touched her lightly on the knee.

'Who knows? Perhaps we've managed to create a perpetual reminder of our honeymoon for ourselves!'

Laura put her hand over his. 'Really Nick? I suppose we might have done! What bliss that would be. I can't wait to become a mother!'

Ten weeks later, when they were comfortably settled in their London flat, and Nicholas had filled the vacancy of Deputy Managing Director at his father's industrial firm that operated under government licence and was therefore ensured of a perpetual flow of work, Laura had her pregnancy confirmed. They were both very pleased with themselves; and apart from ceasing to smoke or drink alcohol Laura did not change her lifestyle. She was too aware of the admiring looks that her tall, broad-shouldered husband received from other women at social functions to allow herself to give in to the waves of tiredness that assailed her from time to time.

In March the following year they purchased a six-bedroomed house with potential nanny-flat in the Sussex countryside. On the morning of 14 April 1967 Laura experienced her first contractions, and was admitted to the local maternity hospital. She only had a few more hours to wait before her greatest ambition would be fulfilled, and she became a mother at last. As she left her home, driven by Nicholas with great care along the short route, she reaffirmed to herself her intention of becoming the best possible mother. She would provide a childhood that would never be forgotten.

Only eight hours after her admittance Laura gave birth to an eight-pound baby boy. She was delirious with delight, and she and Nicholas gazed with pride on this, their firstborn child. They decided to call him Edward Nicholas, and when Laura was finally wheeled down from the delivery floor and into the four-bedded ward where she would spend the next six days, she looked at him sleeping peacefully in his cot beside her and felt that he set the seal on her perfect marriage. Nicholas, if asked, would have voiced the same opinion. For the rest of that day Laura was almost intoxicated with delight. She now had a husband and a fine young son, the nucleus of her own happy family.

It was the next day when she experienced her first pang of anxiety, for in contrast to the other three babies in the ward Edward never cried. He lay quietly on his stomach, where a nurse would carefully place him after his feeds, and there he remained until lifted for the next feed. Wet and dirty nappies did not trouble him, he remained serene. At first, noticing how harrassed the other mothers became when their babies cried, Laura had been pleased by this good behaviour. After a time, when he did not even utter a whimper, she began to worry. It wasn't as though he were sleeping; a lot of the time his eyes were open, gazing into the distance, although Laura knew from her ante-natal literature that he couldn't possibly be seeing anything clearly. She waited, and she waited for him to cry and release her from her fear, but she kept her worry to herself. She was afraid of sounding ridiculous.

On the third day he did produce a small fit of crying when Laura took a shower and was late feeding him. Although penitent she felt relieved. At least he could cry. Her relief was short-lived. After lunch the paediatrician came round to check all the babies thoroughly. The quietest baby in the ward apart from Edward was a tiny girl called Jessica. Jessica did cry, but weakly and far less frequently than the other two. The paediatrician spent a long time with Jessica, and his face lost its original cheerful hue. When he moved on to the other babies he appeared distracted, and Laura was afraid to mention Edward's unusual tranquility. She held her breath when the doctor straightened from Edward's crib, but he smiled briefly at her.

'A fine, strong boy, Mrs Wells. Any problems?'

'Well, no. Not really . . .'

'Fine. That's the spirit.' Another brief smile and he was gone.

A few minutes later Jessica's mother went out of the ward with the staff nurse, and later still a junior nurse came and wheeled Jessica away. They did not return.

The three remaining mothers talked and speculated, but could come up with no solution. It wasn't until after the evening visiting that they learnt the truth. Little Jessica was a mongol child, and her mother had become hysterical at the news and was now in a side ward heavily sedated.

That night Laura lay awake in a blind panic. In all her daydreams she had never envisaged having a child that was anything but physically and mentally perfect. Not necessarily brilliant, but certainly of adequate intelligence. A child who would at least be able to grow up properly, developing over the years into a well-balanced teenager. If Jessica were mentally retarded, then what, she wondered hysterically, was the matter with Edward? At least Jessica had cried a little, and there had been no obvious physical signs on the little girl. She had appeared normal to Laura's unpractised eyes, just as Edward appeared normal.

She tried to calm herself with the thought of the doctor. He would have known. Certainly he had been quick enough with Jessica. But then he had looked at Jessica first. He wouldn't have expected to find two mentally sub-normal babies in one ward, would he? Perhaps that had made him careless; after all he hadn't let Laura tell him her worries, had in fact brushed her hastily to one side. What should she do? Should she tell Nicholas? She rejected the idea instantly. She would wait. She would wait and see how Edward progressed. Perhaps once she got him home he would cry more, he was bound to. All babies sensed when their mothers were nervous or unsure, and Laura was certainly that. Away from the competent nurses and their efficient bathing and changing of him, Edward would soon raise his voice in protest. Until then she must try and keep calm. She didn't want anyone else to suspect there might be anything wrong.

Nicholas noticed that Laura's first delight had disappeared, but he knew enough about post-natal blues not to be too concerned. He was glad when he was able to take his wife and son home with him, and they were all under one roof for the first time. He had managed to engage a nanny, Sandra Lucas, during the last week and felt proud of this achievement. Nannies were like gold dust at the moment, and Sandra had excellent references.

As Laura had decided to breast-feed Edward, Nicholas had been prepared for very disturbed nights for the first few weeks. He was agreeably surprised by the baby's placid temperament. As long as Laura set the alarm so that she fed him regularly at four-hourly intervals then their nights were uninterrupted. Even Sandra commented on how good the baby was. Sometimes Nicholas would look at his son lying open eyed in his cot and wonder what the child was thinking. Probably nothing at all, but he had such an adult expression on his tiny features that it was impossible to believe that he lay there without thinking about something.

To Nicholas's amazement Laura was not pleased by the baby's behaviour. She kept asking him how often his first son had cried when he was a baby, and whether or not he had slept more.

'I can't remember,' laughed Nicholas. 'At the time he seemed incredibly noisy when he was awake, but yes, he did sleep more than Edward. What does it matter? They're all different.'

One evening he found Laura crying hysterically in the downstairs cloakroom, muffling her sobs in the hand-towel. Horrified, he led her gently into the living-room, and there she confessed reluctantly to her fear, a fear that was gradually growing into certainty.

'He's too good,' she sobbed. 'I know there's something wrong with him. It isn't normal. All the babies in my ward cried more than he does, except for Jessica.'

'There you are then,' soothed Nicholas. 'Why all the worry if there was an even quieter one in with you?'

'She wasn't normal,' blurted out Laura. 'She was a mongol.'

There was a short pause, and Laura held her breath. Suddenly, and to her shockingly, Nicholas started to laugh.

'My dear Laura, you don't seriously imagine that our son is retarded? Good grief woman, the doctor would have picked that up quickly enough. Besides, he looks extremely alert to me. I think he's a sharp little chap, conserving his energy for the future!'

Laura pulled herself away from her husband. 'I knew that I shouldn't have told you, but I never expected you to laugh. How insensitive can you be?'

Nicholas looked carefully at her. 'You're serious about this, aren't you?'

'Of course I am.'

'Well you're being utterly ridiculous, and the sooner you put it out of your mind the better. You're missing all the pleasure of a first baby with this outlandish theory of yours, and I for one don't want to hear any more about it. He is perfectly normal, Laura, a contented baby with a placid nature. We're very lucky.'

Laura knew from the note in his voice, a note that had never been there in conversations with her before, that he meant what he said.

As a result she never mentioned it again. For the next four months she watched her son anxiously, waiting for an outburst of crying to calm her fears, but it never came. He grew plumper, and he even produced a tooth, but still he lay for hours at a time in pram or cot gazing at the sky or the ceiling without a sound. Once or twice, when she approached him very quietly in the garden, she would hear small gurgles of sound but they always ceased when she appeared in his line of vision and after a time she began to suspect that she was imagining them.

She became tense, anxious, and she lost far too much weight. Once, pushing her pram through the village, she saw a mother with a mongol child in a pushchair and her heart began to thump in fear. She hurried by, almost as though she feared Edward could become contaminated. That evening she studied his features carefully, but his eyes were large and round; there was no hint of that distinctive slant. Nevertheless she continued to worry.

At last Nicholas lost patience. Waking one night to find her crying into her pillow, and knowing full well what the trouble was he went off the next day and without her knowledge made an appointment with the best paediatrician in London. In the evening he told Laura what he had done, but was unprepared for her reaction.

'Why?' She was almost shouting. 'You said he was all right, so why the appointment?'

'Laura, calm down, I thought you'd be pleased. It's so that you can get some peace of mind at last. I don't like seeing you worn out with worry, forever listening, wanting him to change. I want you to hear from the best authority there is that our son is a normal, healthy child. Then, and only then, will you be well again.'

'You believe that? You truly believe that he's all right? This doctor won't find anything wrong? Only if he does, and says so, then it's final, isn't it? It can't be unsaid.'

'Poor Laura,' said Nicholas softly as he wrapped his arms around her. 'You didn't realize what a responsibility another life would be, did you?'

'Is that all it is? First-time fears?'

22

'That's all, Laura.'

'You think I'm being silly?'

'I think you're suffering from depression. Once this Dr Castle gives Edward the all-clear we'll trot you along to Dr Anderson and see if he can calm you down a bit. Agreed?'

'If Edward's all right then anything, anything at all.'

Nicholas gently stroked her silky, blond hair and kissed her lightly on the temples. All that he wanted was the old Laura back, and this was the only way that he could think of to achieve this. Dr Adam Castle had a wonderful reputation, and he had complete confidence in the outcome of the appointment. Soon everything would be well with Laura again, and she would begin to appreciate their splendid son.

Dr Castle was short, slight and surprisingly young. His light-brown hair kept falling over his forehead as he listened intently to Laura's fears, his grey eyes flicking occasionally to Nicholas before resuming their steady observation of Laura. She didn't like him, felt no warmth in him at all, but she knew that he was the very best and that was all that mattered. He had a pen and pad before him, but took no notes, keeping his hands clasped on the desk top.

'In other words, Mrs Wells, you feel that Edward is too passive.' His voice was harsh and clipped. He sounded impatient.

'No, not passive, more placid.'

'Too placid? I see.'

'If only he would cry more, or laugh.'

'Anything at all except keep quiet?'

'Yes, that's right.'

The specialist rose from his seat and took Edward from Laura's arms. The baby uttered no sound, but when Laura turned to watch the examination the specialist was blocking her view completely. He was quick and deft, and there was not even a protesting murmur from Edward. Laura found that her hands were gripping each other tightly. This was the moment she had dreaded all the past weeks.

She heard rattles being shaken and bells tinkled softly by a pretty Malaysian nurse, but Edward remained steadfastly silent.

'I'll take a blood test,' murmured Dr Castle, and Laura saw Nicholas tense for the baby's cry which she knew would not come. In her mind the silence was deafening.

After a time they took Edward away into another room for 'a few more complicated tests', in the specialist's words. Left alone they glanced at each other, and Laura saw that at last Nicholas was worried.

'He is pretty silent,' he admitted reluctantly, 'but this chap is supposed to be very good with children. Probably that's why.'

'During a blood test?'

He could think of no reply.

At last Dr Castle returned, but without Edward. He sat down and wrote a few lines before meeting Laura's anxious gaze.

'Now then mother!' His attempt at a jocular vein chilled her; he was not a jocular type of man.

'Yes?'

'Have you always worried a lot, before this little fellow came along?'

'What do you mean? Don't you think that I've got something to worry about?'

'Not at all. He's a grand little fellow. Unusual I'll

24

admit, but away from you we managed to get some more normal responses out of him. One or two smiles, and a quick howl when he got rather damp.' Laura felt her hands go clammy with perspiration. 'What do you mean, away from me? Do you mean it's my fault he's so quiet?'

Again that quick flick of his eyes to Nicholas. 'Fault? I wouldn't put it quite like that. Babies are very sensitive. If you're a highly strung, first-time mother a bright baby can pick up the vibrations and react in its own way. In your son's case he goes quiet. Better than howling twenty-four hours a day of course!'

Nicholas cleared his throat. 'You mean, there is absolutely nothing wrong with him?'

'Nothing at all. All absolutely normal. In fact he's brighter than average, at this stage, which is all one can say with babies. You have nothing to worry about, nothing.'

Laura looked straight into the cold grey eyes: 'You found him normal? Just like other babies you see?'

'My dear, Mrs Wells, all babies are different, and most of those that I see are far from normal, which is in any case a misleading term. Who decides this so-called "norm"?'

'I don't know and I don't care,' snapped Laura. 'I still think you were surprised when you first examined him.'

For a moment a brief smile crossed Dr Castle's features. 'I admit that he was unusually well behaved; impassive almost. However, I managed to break through his barrier later on. We became firm friends.'

Laura had never heard such rubbish, and was relieved when another nurse entered and placed Edward back in her arms. 'All dry now, mother!' she said.

Laura held him close, then settled him on her lap facing the desk. His eyes, already turning from baby blue to a darker shade that suggested they would one day be brown, fastened immediately on the specialist. Slowly, very slowly, his mouth opened in an enormous smile and he gave a loud chuckle of delighted pleasure such as Laura had never heard from him in the four months since he was born. One of his chubby fists was extended towards the specialist, who lent foward to place an index finger carefully inside it.

'There, as I told you, firm friends.'

She looked down on the tiny head and felt a spurt of rage. He had made her look a complete fool. Instead of relief she felt foolish, humiliated. If he had been older she would have felt certain that he had done it on purpose. As it was, she had to accept that by some strange quirk of fate her son felt an affinity towards this cold but brilliant doctor that he had never experienced in his contact with other people; for she knew, even if no one believed her, that he had never made such a sociable gesture before in his short life.

She and Nicholas scarcely talked on the drive home. After Sandra had taken Edward away Laura went and had a bath before changing for dinner. When they were alone eating she spoke before he had time.

'I'll see Dr Anderson as quickly as you can make an appointment. I'm sorry that I've been so neurotic.' She wasn't, but she knew that she had to make the gesture, there was nothing to be gained now by harping on the past. Whatever it was that kept her son so silent had escaped the doctor, for all his brilliance. She was right. She knew she was right. There was something wrong with Edward, but she would not speak of it again. They would all see in time, and then the laugh would be on them. She could wait.

'Fine, Mrs Wells. Now, if you take these green ones three times a day, and the small yellow ones four times a day, and the red capsule at bedtime, then you'll soon feel much better. Come back and see me in four weeks, and enjoy your stay in Scotland. A lovely country, I always think.'

Laura smiled gently at him. 'Thank you so much, doctor, I'm sure I will.' Stupid old fool she thought to herself, I shall be too doped to enjoy anything except bed if I swallow all those.

Nicholas was pleased with her account of the consultation, and even more pleased at the ease with which he prized her away from Edward to give her ten days on the east coast of Scotland. What he did not realize was that Laura no longer felt so acutely protective of their son; she had decided that at four months old he was clever enough to fend for himself. To her way of thinking the interlude with the paediatrician had proved that. She did not tell her husband, knowing that he was already worried about her mental state of health.

Nicholas golfed a lot during the holiday, and Laura walked round with him, frequently pulling his trolley for some of the way. Once she was separated from Edward she quickly began to regain her spirits. She and Nicholas spent long evenings in quiet pubs, and would return to heir hotel room and make love with all the enthusiasm of their honeymoon. Delighted by Laura's quick recovery, Nicholas suggested that they should entertain more once they got home, a suggestion greeted with enthusiasm by his wife. They were both sorry when it was time to return to Sussex.

As they drove up to their front door, Laura felt the old sickness in the pit of her stomach, the fear that she now associated with close proximity to her baby. She

27

fumbled in her handbag and swallowed a yellow pill, relieved that Nicholas was too busy to notice.

Sandra was waiting in the hall, baby in her arms. Nicholas put out a hand and poked Edward's rounded stomach.

'Hi there, podge!' The baby did not even blink; he looked as though it were all beneath him. Laura approached softly, and gently touched him on the cheek with the tips of her fingers. 'Did you miss Mummy?'

'Of course he did,' retorted Sandra; 'but he was very brave!'

'No trouble?' Laura sounded, to Nicholas' pleasure, almost disinterested.

'No, Madam, none at all. He's been as good as gold.'

'I'll come up when he's settled for the night then.'

She and Nicholas stood side by side at the foot of the stairs watching Sandra as she ascended. Nicholas placed an affectionate arm round Laura's waist.

'There! All those months of worry and now you can happily leave him to Sandra after ten days away. I told you Dr Anderson was good!'

Laura threw him a brilliant smile. How fortunate, she thought, that he doesn't realize I no longer care. I don't believe that I even like Edward very much these days.

Much later, after a lot of wine and brandy, Laura and Nicholas went into the nursery together to say goodnight to their presumably sleeping child. The nightlight gave off a soft glow. Edward lay on his back, eyes wide open, watching his mobile as it turned gently above the cot.

'You know, I may be biased, but he is in my opinion incredibly good looking,' said Nicholas, recalling his first son's smudgy baby features.

'He takes after me!' laughed Laura, and suddenly Edward gave a low gurgle and smiled.

'He agrees!' snorted Nicholas. 'Come on, let's go to bed.'

'I'm quite sure he understands us,' said Laura, rather too loudly.

'Naturally!' said Nicholas.

He took her hand, anxious to be alone with her again. She cast one last look back at the cot where Edward lay, again gravely watching the small animals as they dangled above him. To Laura it looked as though he was not only watching but also listening, either for their voices to resume or for something else. The nursery clock perhaps? She felt the strange fear beginning again, rising in her throat like a physical constriction. She quickly followed Nicholas, and remembered to take her red capsule before undressing.

In Scotland she hadn't needed to take them, but now that she was back here nothing had changed, and she knew that she must keep taking all the pills in case Nicholas noticed. She wondered how she was going to cope, but she knew that there was nothing wrong with her. It was Edward, only no one else realized that as yet.

Victoria was bored. She hadn't wanted to come in the first place; but since she was Edward's godmother she felt that to refuse every weekend invitation down to Sussex was socially impossible. It wasn't as though Laura and Nicholas didn't make her feel welcome. No two people could have been better hosts, it was simply that she would have been happier in her small London bedsit. There she could work or go out and socialize as she wished. Here she was obliged to accept all the entertain-

29

ments put on by Laura, whose tastes she had never really shared.

Upon her arrival the previous evening she had found herself immediately in the centre of a group of near neighbours from this small Sussex village, all of whom were at least three drinks ahead of her, and it showed. When she was finally alone with Laura and Nicholas they stayed up late talking and drinking coffee, which had then proceeded to keep her awake until the early hours of this morning. Now, late on the Saturday night, she found herself seated next to a pleasant but boring young farmer at a dinner party for eight.

One glance at the head of the table showed her that Laura at least was happy, which was a relief. The last time they had met she felt certain that her friend was suffering from some form of post-natal depression although it had not been mentioned. However, tonight she looked her exquisite best. Her dress of turquoise printed silk with narrow shoulder straps and softly draped bodice accentuated the slight increase of weight that Edward's birth had caused, and it suited her. If I looked like that, thought Victoria ruefully, would I settle for life as a rich man's darling? How much easier than her life of long hours and continuous studying. Easier, but less fulfilling. Laura's achievements: good wife, capable mother, were now. Victoria's would come more slowly, but last a lifetime. She would not want to have her friend's life in fifteen years time. She hoped by then to have her own medical practice, run strictly according to her ideas of how a general practitioner should function, and that would keep her busy and satisfied for the rest of her days. She doubted if she would find the time to marry, and certainly she was unlikely to find a man willing to go along with her plans. At present it was a small regret, but she accepted that one day when she was too old to make any other choice she might feel more strongly.

After coffee they drifted into the living-room where the talk turned to government policies and industrial trends, a subject dear to Nicholas's heart and that of most of the men present. Laura, not even attempting to hide her boredom, yawned delicately.

'Tired?' asked Victoria.

'A little. We've nothing special on for tomorrow; I hope you don't mind. I thought we could go for a long walk and have a proper chat, if the weather stays dry.'

'Lovely! I've hardly seen Edward as yet, I'd like to take a few snaps of him before I leave.' Always, before this visit, any mention of her godson had induced a torrent of lavish praise from his devoted mother, and Victoria had made the remark on purpose to keep Laura occupied until the men had finished. This time no such response was forthcoming.

'If you like,' said Laura in an offhand tone. 'He's grown quite a lot, but then he'll be ten months old next week.'

'Yes, well all the more reason to get an up-to-date snap. Is he still as good as ever?'

'Good?' Laura looked puzzled.

'Yes, good! Ye gods, Laura, you were always on about him being too good. Never crying, all that sort of thing. What is it; does he howl these days?'

'No,' said Laura slowly, 'he's still . . .' she hesitated for a moment, 'good,' she concluded.

'Well, I must say I never hear him cry. Trust you to have a well-behaved child. Your life runs so smoothly I find it quite unnatural!'

Laura put a hand on her friend's arm.

'Vicky, don't say that, please.'

'Say what?'

'About it being unnatural.'

'Why Laura, I only meant . . .'

31

'Now then ladies, gossiping in corners is not encouraged tonight!' It was Victoria's jovial farmer, and with one quick puzzled look at Laura she allowed him to engage her in conversation on the merits of life in the country as opposed to existence in town.

When the evening finally broke up it was so late that Vicky was anxious to get to her room and had no time to talk to Laura alone again until the next day.

On Sunday morning, after a late start, Vicky repeated her request to take photographs of Edward.

'Sure!' Nicholas was obviously pleased. 'Take as many as you like. We used to take loads before the novelty wore off. Now Laura keeps forgetting to take the camera when we go out.'

'Come up with me if you like,' invited Laura. 'He's probably been up for hours already. Sandra says he exists on two or three hours' sleep a night.' I wish I could, thought Victoria, smothering a yawn. She had hoped to study tonight when she got back, but was far too tired.

Inside the spacious nursery there was absolute silence. It took a moment or two to realize that there was anyone there. Then Victoria noticed a slight movement in one corner, and realized that the baby was sitting with some bricks, patiently trying to build then up. His nurse was seated in a comfortable rocking chair, magazine in hand, watching with approval. As well she might, thought Victoria, who knew that most ten-month-old children lacked the concentration let alone the manual dexterity to perform such a task.

She waited for Laura to point out how clever the child was, and was ready to agree, but Laura merely said 'Here he is!' Her tone was that of a woman quite indifferent to the listener's reaction. How she had changed, reflected Victoria, and wondered why.

'Hello Edward,' She said clearly, and he turned his head towards her. Her first thought was, what a beautiful child! He possessed his mother's ash-blond hair and dark brown eyes, but his skin had a wonderful golden hue to it and he exuded health and intelligence. He watched her as she came towards him, and she was amused to see that he neither laughed nor cried at this approach of a stranger but seemed instead to be weighing her up, deciding whether or not he liked her. It was a trick of the light, she thought, that gave his eyes such an adult stare.

Sandra got to her feet and picked the boy up, handing him carefully to Victoria. She took him awkwardly. Her experience with babies was not great, and she had no intention of specializing as a paediatrician. The few babies that she did know showed an alarming tendency to cry the moment she took them, sensing her lack of ease. Edward appeared quite unworried. One of his tiny hands reached out and touched her face.

'Mind!' Laura's tone was sharp. 'His nails get sharp. He scratched me quite badly the other day.'

'His nails are short now, Madam,' interjected Sandra, and Victoria sensed that there had been trouble over the incident.

'Come on then, godson,' she said briskly, 'let's go and take some photographs for my album shall we?' He stared solemnly at her, his head slightly on one side as though he were listening intently to her words. It was a position that he adopted frequently, she noticed as she clicked away with her camera. Nicholas, inspired by her activity, went and fetched his own Nikon and took several shots of Vicky and Edward sitting on the rug before the real log fire.

'Makes a lovely picture,' he commented idly, and she noticed a fleeting look of alarm on Laura's face. Quickly she stood up.

'I always look dreadful in photos,' she said. 'Take some of Laura with him.'

It seemed to her that Laura was reluctant, but once she was seated as Nicholas wanted she relaxed, and as she watched Victoria was struck by the striking resemblance between mother and baby.

When Edward began to grizzle and Sandra came to take him away, she commented on this to Laura. 'He really is incredibly like you, Laura, don't you think?'

'Is he? I can't see it. He has my colouring, I suppose, but I was more of a chubby, babyish little thing at his age. He seems very grown up to me.'

'He is. You must be proud of him, Laura.'

'We've got roast beef for lunch,' responded Laura. 'Will that be all right?'

Despite a slightly damp February drizzle Laura still wanted to go on her walk. Nicholas declined, saying that he had plenty of work to do, and the two friends went alone. As they walked along damp paths, deserted today even by horses and riders, Victoria sensed that Laura wanted to ask her something but was unable to begin.

'Everything all right, Laura?' she asked at length, offering her an opening for any sort of confession or query.

'I suppose so. Well, actually I'm a bit worried.'

'What about?'

'I'm pregnant again.'

'Oh!' Victoria didn't know what else to say. She could hardly ask if it was intentional, or if Nicholas knew or minded.

'As you say, "oh"!'

'Well, you always planned on a large family, didn't you?'

'That,' said Laura sharply, 'was before I had Edward.'

'There's nothing wrong with Edward, is there? He

looks such a super child, but I know that looks can be misleading. You haven't discovered that he's ill in any way?'

'No, he's fine, according to some expert or other.'

'Which one?'

'Dr Castle.'

'You won't find anyone better,' said Victoria; 'he's quite incredible with children.'

'There you are then.'

'So, what's the problem?'

'I'm not a good mother.'

'Nonsense, look how he's thriving.'

'Vicky, listen to me please. I don't love him any more.'

'Who, Nicholas?'

'No, Edward. I can't love my own baby any more!'

There was such pain and anguish in her friend's voice that Victoria was shaken to the core. She tried to adopt a professional briskness. After all, it wasn't unheard of, and it would most certainly pass.

'Laura, listen to me. You worried so much about him those first few months that you wore yourself out emotionally. You've nothing left at present, but it will all come back. It's a temporary state of affairs; the less you worry the quicker it will go. On top of that you're pregnant again, which is bound to be tiring coming so quickly after Edward's birth.'

Laura listened carefully, and learnt one thing: Victoria did not understand. She made one final attempt at getting through to her.

'Have you noticed how he listens to people all the time? Well, I hate that. It makes me nervous.'

'Precisely!' Victoria was gaining in confidence. 'You are nervous, tense, and over-reacting. Of course he listens, he wants to learn to talk and how else is he supposed to do it?'

I give, up, thought Laura: I should have known better.

'Listen,' continued Vicky, 'how does Nicholas feel about another baby?'

'Delighted.'

'Which is just how you'll feel, once you're less tired. How far gone are you?'

'Two months.'

'Another six weeks and you'll see things quite differently. Why not have a chat with your GP?'

Anxious now to head her off the subject Laura pretended that such a mundane idea had never entered her head.

'I think I will!' she said with false enthusiasm. 'And thank you for your help.' They talked then of Nick's hopes for a daughter, and finally moved on to Victoria's life in London. They did not speak of Edward again.

At six o'clock, her suitcase packed, Victoria crept quietly into the small room that contained Edward's cot.

'Goodbye, little fellow,' she said gently. 'Be good, and stop upsetting Mummy now?'

He was sitting up, and as she spoke he took hold of the sides of the cot and pulled himself upright.

'There's a clever boy. You'll soon be walking I expect.'

Slowly he tilted his head on one side, listening attentively.

'What a clever godson,' crooned Victoria, laying her hand over his fingers where they curled round the bars.

'God!' she thought to herself, 'how pathetic I sound! I wonder why we don't talk properly to babies?'

As the thought crossed her mind Edward rattled his cot bars sharply, then gave a loud gurgle of laughter.

'You can laugh,' she said lightly. 'It's lucky you don't realize how foolish we women are over babies; you'd make our lives even more of a misery!'

'Da!' shouted Edward. 'Da! Da Da!'

The room flooded suddenly with light. 'Why aren't you asleep yet?' demanded Sandra as she hurried into the room, only to stop abruptly as she saw Victoria.

'I'm so sorry,' she apologized. 'I heard him shouting and came to lie him down again. Once he starts rattling those bars it's difficult to stop him.'

'I'm sorry; I only came in for a quick peep. He's very engaging.'

'I know,' agreed his nanny. 'Come on young man, sleepy time.'

Victoria turned away. Just as she reached the door she heard a quick intake of breath from the nurse.

'What's the matter?'

'He scratched me by mistake, that's all. His nails grow so fast it's unbelievable.'

'Goodnight then,' called Victoria. 'See you in the spring, I hope.'

In May Nicholas's father died of a coronary thrombosis, and the business passed directly to him. It entailed a lot more work both at the factories and with his father's estate. His mother, after nearly forty years of domination, found it impossible to come to terms with life on her own. Even a simple decision, such as which dress to wear, was beyond her and she drove her son to despair.

'Laura, I simply don't know what's to become of mother. When I called in today she hadn't eaten; she simply couldn't decide what she wanted to eat. Frankly I think she's virtually certifiable.'

37

Laura ran her hands soothingly over his broad back. 'There's plenty of room here; invite her to stay for a couple of months. I expect that she'll improve in time. After all, your father was pretty much of a tyrant; she's having to learn a whole new ball game, as they say.'

Nicholas looked at her gratefully. 'You're fantastic, Laura. I don't know what I've done to deserve you! Are you sure you can manage?'

'Quite sure.' She was quite sure. She would encourage her mother-in-law to help with Edward, who was quite a problem now that he was on his feet and into everything. Edward would help his grandmother, who in turn would be helping Laura. As usual things were working out well for Laura, who had a feeling that any day now Sandra was going to hand in her notice. But, with additional help, Sandra would probably stay. She seemed to be the type of nanny who loved babies, and the new one would keep her fully occupied.

The new baby. Every night, before she fell asleep, Laura would pray: 'Please God, don't let it be like Edward. Let it be a baby I can love!' If she couldn't love it then she would begin to believe, as others did, that the fault lay with her and not with her son. It was unthinkable, and she prayed earnestly for the new baby to vindicate her.

Nicholas's mother duly arrived, and her two months passed off so successfully that they became extended into three, then four. By the time September came round they had all ceased to speak of the older woman returning to her own home.

Three days before the new baby was due, on a warm September morning, Laura and her mother-in-law sat on the lawn watching Edward as he tried repeatedly to kick a beachball over the grass. Sometimes he missed, sometimes he fell over, but he never got angry and he never gave up. It had been a fine summer, and he was a deep golden brown, his hair bleached white by the sun.

'Is he like Nicholas as a baby?' asked Laura.

'Not at all. Nicholas didn't have Edward's perseverance and good humour. He was quite a difficult child, as I recall. Justin was far more like him.'

'It's a pity Justin lives abroad now. I'm sure Nick misses him.'

'Elizabeth was offered a wonderful opportunity when that American fell in love with her. It would have been selfish in the extreme for Nicholas to have tried to keep Justin over here.'

Laura shifted as the baby inside her kicked hard. Not long, she thought, and was filled with apprehension. Soon, very soon, she would know.

'Mother, don't you think Edward is a little, well, strange?'

'Strange, dear? How do you mean?'

'I don't know; he seems too self-contained, too adult.' As she spoke she looked for her son. He was standing by the ball, but his interest in it had gone. His head was on one side, and he was listening. What does he hear she wondered? It was almost as though he were waiting for something, and had been all his brief life. Waiting for it to arrive. Within her the child moved again. She felt a quick stab of pain in her back and all the muscles in her stomach tightened. Well, not long to wait baby, she thought, and rose awkwardly from her garden chair.

Edward ran towards her, a smile on his usually impassive face.

'Baby! Baby!' he shouted, his most recent addition to his vocabulary.

'Dear God,' thought Laura, as a fresh pain assailed her. 'Is this what he's been waiting for?'

On 22nd September Nicholas found himself pacing round the plush waiting room supplied for expectant fathers in this exclusive private nursing home only ten miles from his house in Sussex. His feelings were mixed. He wasn't worried about Laura, at least not about her bearing the child; after all to lose a woman in childbirth was virtually unheard of these days. What most concerned him was her mental state of health.

Looking back over their marriage so far he had to face the fact that in some respects he had been sorely disappointed. True Laura was attractive, a social asset, and an excellent companion in bed; but he had not bargained on such a strong streak of hysteria in her makeup. He would never use the word to anyone else, but to himself he accepted that there had been moments during Edward's first year when her behaviour could only be described as unbalanced.

He had spoken to Dr Anderson privately, and been assured that these things happened, and in most cases they passed off gradually. Laura's neurotic fretting hadn't passed off gradually; it had stopped abruptly, as though someone had pulled a switch. One moment: worry, tears, more worry. The next moment: nothing, not even normal casual concern. Now he feared it all happening again, and he wasn't sure that his patience would stand the strain, especially since he found living under the same roof as his mother something of a trial. The only advantage to that was that it pleased Laura.

This baby, about to be born, had been a complete accident. 'One of those that arrives clutching a pill in its fist and shouting "I fooled you!"' he had joked to a friend. However, it was sure to bring its love with it, and they had intended to have more children, simply not quite so quickly.

The nurses looked in on him more than was strictly

necessary to give progress reports on his wife. At thirty-nine he was still a most attractive man. The touch of grey at the sides of his dark hair merely added that touch of distinction previously missing from his regular good looks. He had always known that women found him attractive, and had made good use of this gift from the gods when he was younger. Since marrying Laura there had been no wandering, not even mentally, but once or twice when she had been at her most neurotic he had found himself thinking longingly of some warm-hearted brunette offering him solace.

This was his area of weakness, and he was quite determined that it was a phase that he had now put behind him, but every man had his breaking point. If this baby could only prove to be a noisy, attention-demanding little girl how grateful he would be. There would be nothing to trouble Laura then, and life would go on as he had always intended it to. He wanted a daughter for another reason. He already had two sons, and sons went off to boarding school and had to be strictly trained in order to go out into the world and be successful. He could spoil a girl, not too much, but just a little.

At that moment in his thoughts a nurse appeared again, smiling warmly at him. 'A lovely daughter, Mr Wells, 7 lbs 4 ozs. She's as pretty as a picture too! Would you like to come in now?' Thank the Lord for that, he thought as he followed her; the answer to my prayers.

Laura, propped up on three pillows and in a new nightdress with her hair tidied and caught back in a bow, looked ridiculously young. She was a trifle pale, but no more than was to be expected.

'Darling, well done! A girl as well! How was it?'

'All right; quicker than the last time. Look, she's over here.'

There she lay in her perspex crib, a tiny wrinkled scrap

41

of humanity. His first daughter. He felt a surge of love and protection that took him by surprise.

'Isn't she sweet, Nick? She looks like a Belinda too, don't you think?'

'She certainly does; we couldn't have chosen better!'

His eyes met Laura's across the small cot.

'She's isn't a bit like Edward, is she?' He could hear the note of anxiety in Laura's voice, but was able to answer firmly and truthfully, 'No! Not at all!' She seemed to sink back on her pillows. 'I'm so pleased,' she whispered, and he felt sorry once again for their small son.

That evening, Nicholas opened a bottle of good claret and toasted his daughter. Later on, remembering that there was a list somewhere of people he was supposed to ring he finally located it and then spent half an hour over the calls. When that was done he went up to the nursery and in to where Edward was being read nursery rhyme stories.

'Been a good boy then?'

'Yes.' Edward nodded. That was one thing that Nicholas found endearing, his son's lack of baby talk. No lisping or baby words from him; presumably Sandra had never encouraged it. Still, it was a bit unusual.

'Good boy! Well, we've got a surprise for you. Mummy is going to come home tomorrow and bring you a baby sister, isn't that nice?' He didn't expect any response; after all, at seventeen months the boy could hardly understand what a baby sister meant, let alone the effect upon his own life. He was somewhat startled therefore by the gleam of pleasure that shone in Edward's eyes.

'Baby!' he shouted. 'Yes! Baby here!'

'Well done, Edward, you're right, the baby is here. She'll come to see you tomorrow. Now off to bed with you and be a good boy. Morning will come all the quicker if you're asleep promptly.'

Sandra smiled at Nicholas. 'Congratulations, Sir. You and Madam must be very pleased.'

'Indeed we are. I hope it won't prove too much for you, the two I mean.'

He was sure she hesitated before replying, but her answer was reassuring enough. 'Oh no, Sir, I like babies.'

'Excellent. Time he was asleep I think.'

'Yes, Sir.'

Nicholas turned to kiss Edward, but the boy was holding on to the leg of the nursery chair gazing towards the nursery window, and he appeared to be listening to the birds outside.

That night, sleeping only fitfully despite her sleeping pill, Laura could hardly take her eyes off her new daughter. She felt a tender love for her that had never been there for Edward, not even at the beginning, before he became such a worry. Once, when she dozed off, she dreamt that Edward was holding the new baby in his arms and that when she approached them he ran off, taking the baby with him. Laura was crying, "She's mine, not yours", but the toddler took no notice and sped out of sight.

She awoke from the dream shaking and weak, and it troubled her so much that she refused to allow herself to sleep again. It was foolish, she knew that, but Edward's face in the dream had been demonic in its possessiveness. Not the face of a small child at all.

Her homecoming, and the first few weeks passed off very well. Edward would look at his sister, and utter a few words, but most of the time he was too busy playing outside to bother about her much and Laura began to relax. How foolish she had been over the past seven-

43

teen months. She must pull herself together now, and make amends.

By the time that Belinda was six months old Laura's life had settled into a very pleasant routine. Nicholas was extremely busy at work, and had to spend a lot of time in the London flat. Rather than be parted most of the week Laura would travel up with him each Monday, and then come home on the train on the Thursday morning, with Nicholas joining them all on the Friday night. Her mother-in-law and Sandra were well able to cope during her absences, and Nicholas needed her. An excellent cook and a daily help ensured the continual smooth running of the household, and left little for her to do when she was at home. Now and again she would ask Sandra how Edward had adjusted, and whether Belinda was good. The answers were perfectly satisfactory. Edward was fine, Belinda cried some of the time, but no more than was normal. Laura remembered Dr Castle and his refusal to define 'normal' for her; but it was a distant memory now, and did not trouble her.

On this particular Thursday morning she caught an earlier train than usual, and her taxi deposited her at her front door at 11.40 am instead of 12.40. The first thing that struck her as she walked into the house was the silence. They must all be out, she thought. She wandered into the kitchen, and there was Sandra peeling carrots and talking to cook.

'Hello!' said Laura brightly. 'You have got them well trained!' A carrot dropped from the nanny's hands.

'Why, Mrs Wells, you're early.'

'I caught an earlier train. Where's my mother-in-law?'

'In the living-room, Madam, reading.'

Slightly surprised Laura went to find her. Sure enough she was deeply immersed in one of her highly romantic novels, but she too jumped and looked strangely guilty when she saw Laura.

'Why, Laura, dear, you're early!'

'That's right. You all sound quite put out! Where are the children?'

'Upstairs dear. In the nursery.'

'Both of them? Alone? Is Edward sleeping too?'

'No, dear, he likes to play up there with the baby.'

'But, not alone surely? Why isn't Sandra watching them?'

Her mother-in-law licked her lips nervously. 'He doesn't like anyone else there.'

'Who doesn't?' Laura almost shouted.

'Why, Edward, of course.'

Laura gripped the strap of her handbag tightly. She must not allow herself to over-react. It was these two women who were behaving strangely, not her, but she must keep control.

'You mean to tell me that when I'm away Edward dictates who goes into the nursery and who does not?'

'Not all the time, Laura; it's just for a couple of hours in the morning, and only when you're away.'

'He isn't two years old yet,' said Laura slowly and precisely. 'He is not going to turn into some sort of tyrant just because I'm away so much. I shall speak to Nicholas about this tomorrow. Right now I'm going up there to see what he gets up to.'

'At least let him know you're here,' called her mother-in-law after her. 'He doesn't like surprises.'

Well, he's bloody well going to get one, thought

Laura grimly. She was quite wrong. Presumably disturbed by the briefly raised voices, Edward was standing in the nursery doorway, his arms spread across it.

'Go away!' he said gruffly. 'Mummy go!'

'No, my lad, Mummy stays,' said Laura firmly, and scooped him up in her arms as she walked over to Belinda's cot.

Belinda was sitting placidly on her quilt, sucking her plastic teething ring, and her wide blue eyes surveyed Laura peaceably. Laura looked quickly round the room. Nothing was out of place, not even a toy. There was no reason to be alarmed, no reason at all, yet her heart had started to pound in that old, almost forgotten way. She looked at Edward, stiff and sullen in her arms.

'What were you doing up here?'

He watched her face, as though searching it for a clue.

'Edward, what were you playing? Why wouldn't you let me in?'

'Baby!'

I'm wasting my time, she realized; he wasn't doing anything, just trying out his power over two doting women who should know better. There's no harm done, as long as it doesn't go on.

'Play nicely then,' she continued 'but nanny will be up now. Baby needs her nurse even if you're too big.'

She put him down on the ground and he ran straight over to the cot. He pressed his face up to the bars, and Belinda gurgled. Laura went over to the door.

Half-way down the stairs she realized that she hadn't given Edward his bar of chocolate that she always bought at the station, and she went back with it. In the doorway she halted. He was still standing by the cot, completely silent, his blond head jammed up as close as possible. Opposite him, teething ring abandoned, sat plump, beautiful Belinda. On her face was a look of intense concentration, and then, as Laura watched, the little girl tilted her head to one side and began to listen.

She never intended to, it was quite involuntary, but Laura gave a muffled cry and Edward's head spun round. For just one fleeting second his face bore on it the exact expression that she had seen in her dream, and then it was gone and his handsome impassive features watched her. Laura rushed over to the cot and picked Belinda up, almost crushing the child as she held her tight.

'There, there,' she crooned, aware that Belinda needed no soothing but regaining her own composure with the maternal action.

She heard Edward run from the room and her shoulders sagged with relief. Belinda, probably uncomfortable in such a strong embrace, began to howl and within minutes Sandra was there.

'Get her changed!' Laura had never sounded so sharp. 'Furthermore, in future please do not leave Edward playing up here unattended. Anything could happen. He's at an age where he's into everything, and you should be watching him.'

'Yes, Madam, but he does like . . .'

'I don't care what he likes, I'm his mother, and I'm telling you what I want.'

'Very good, Madam.'

Laura's head was beginning to throb and she wanted nothing more than to lie down. Once in her room she took off her shoes and rested on the top of the bed. She went over the scene in her mind, and knew that to any onlooker she would have appeared a complete fool, but she had done the right thing. She was in no doubt about that. She had to stop Edward from influencing Belinda.

For some reason he wanted the baby to himself, and she was convinced that she mustn't allow it. She didn't know why, or what it meant, but she knew that she was right. From now on she would be very vigilant.

When Nicholas arrived home on the Friday evening he found Laura prostrate with a bad headache, Edward in a sullen and unresponsive mood, and Belinda howling loudly. A fine homecoming for a business man, he thought, but there it was. After all, what was a headache compared with all Laura's previous troubles? It would be over by tomorrow, and he could be patient that long. In fact Laura was never to be the same again.

By the Sunday morning Laura was up and about as usual again, but she looked pale and heavy-eyed, and Nicholas thought that it might help if he took one of the children out for a couple of hours. He suggested this to Laura, who agreed gratefully and said that a good walk would probably benefit Edward as much as her.

'He needs to work off some of his energy and it is quite spring-like today for the end of March.'

At 11 am promptly Edward was brought down to his father, suitably dressed in a red quilted all-in-one top coat, with matching boots and gloves. He stood happily in the hallway, looking from his father to his nanny as they discussed how far he could go without needing to be carried.

'Up Cross Lane and back through the copse is just about right for him, Sir. I find that a useful little walk of an afternoon.'

'Sounds fine,' agreed Nicholas cheerfully, 'off we go then!'

'Baby?' Edward's face was anxious.

'Just us, old chap; Belinda's too little to want a walk like that.'

'Baby go in pram.'

'Not today; this is strictly men only.'

There was a short silence before Edward pulled off his woollen cap and threw it onto the floor.

'No!' His voice was firm. 'No walk.' Nicholas was surprised, Edward had always been so easy going.

'Come on, Edward, it's a lovely morning.'

Edward turned and stomped towards the stairs, muttering beneath his breath. Nicholas glanced at Sandra, there was no surprise on her face, she seemed rather to be interested as to how he was going to handle the situation.

'Edward, you are coming out with me if I have to drag you through the front door. Put your hat on at once.'

'Shan't!' His sturdy form proceeded to disappear upwards at great speed.

Right my lad, thought Nicholas, this is where you get your first real taste of paternal discipline. He took half a dozen swift paces, grabbed Edward round the waist and deposited him none too gently back in the middle of the hall.

'Put your hat on Edward, now!' He had expected another outright refusal, or a sullen pout; instead to his utter amazement the small boy began to rock backwards and forwards humming gently. Nicholas glanced at Sandra, her face had lost its usual healthy glow, and she met his eyes anxiously.

'Sir, I should be careful, he can. . . .'

She never finished her sentence. In one mad rush Edward had thrown himself at his father, and by some stroke of misfortune caught him entirely off balance. Nicholas fell to the ground, with Edward's arms still locked round his knees.

As he picked himself up slowly he waited for the howl of fright that any toddler would release after such an accident, but Edward was now standing some feet away and watching his father carefully. Nicholas stood upright, feeling slightly shaky, and moved to pick up the troublesome red hat. The humming began again, a gentle hypnotic sound. Nicholas halted in mid-action, glancing at the boy. He was rocking again, and his eyes were closed.

'Edward, stop that noise and come here at once!' The humming merely increased in volume, and irritated beyond measure Nicholas took a determined step forward ready to administer a hefty slap. Before he could reach him the sound stopped. The sudden silence lasted only a few seconds. This time Edward drew in one mighty breath and held it.

Nicholas watched in amazement as Edward turned first pink and then slowly a dark shade of blue. His lips lost their rosy hue, and panic stricken now Nicholas was convinced that the boy was about to kill himself. Sandra laid a restraining hand on his arm.

'It's best to leave him, Sir. Nature knows best in cases like this.'

After a few more agonizing seconds Edward's eyes rolled up into his head and he collapsed limply on to the Persian carpet. As soon as he lost consciousness he automatically began to breathe again, and his colour quickly returned.

Nicholas knelt down beside the boy, whose eyes opened almost immediately. He picked him up and held him gently.

'Now then, my boy, what was all that about?' He glanced at Sandra as he spoke.

'It's temper, Sir,' she said shortly. 'He does it quite a lot, but never when you're here. Until today, that is.'

'You should have told us.'

'It isn't unusual, Sir; he's at the age for temper tantrums.'

'We'll discuss it later,' he said curtly. 'What's the best thing to do now.'

'To go on your walk, Sir, if you still want to, that is.'

He didn't, realized Nicholas, but he knew that he must. Edward couldn't win this particular battle or they would be subjected to numerous repetitions whenever the child was crossed in any way.

'Fine,' he said heartily. 'Come on Edward, time for our walk.'

'Baby come?'

'No!' He had never shouted so loudly at either of the children before. For a few moments they stared at each other, this tiny boy and his all-powerful, adult father. Finally small hands picked up the red woollen hat and he toddled to the front door. Nicholas opened it and Edward held out his hand, throwing a beaming smile at his father as he did so.

Outside Nicholas drew a deep breath of relief. It hadn't been that difficult; it only required firmness. Now the child knew who the master was and would, according to all the books that he had read on child discipline, feel far more secure for his knowledge.

As they walked Nicholas pointed out things of interest to Edward. Some snowdrops beneath a tree, a horse cantering round a field, and he was pleased that it was easy to hold the boy's interest. He seemed anxious to learn.

They were half-way up Cross Lane when Nicholas felt a sharp stab of pain in his right ankle. He looked down, but could see no stone upon which he could have turned it. They walked slowly on, but the pain grew steadily worse until eventually he had to stop.

'Wait a minute, Edward. Daddy's got a sore foot.' Edward didn't appear to hear, and went trotting on up the lane.

51

'Edward,' shouted Nicholas, 'come back. Wait for me!' It was no use, he boy was quickly round the corner and out of sight.

This serves me bloody well right, thought Nicholas ruefully. I drag the poor child out against his will and then hurt myself and can't keep up. He wasn't really worried; Edward was bound to come back, unless he really lost his head but that didn't seem likely. He surveyed his ankle. To his surprise it was already badly swollen and beginning to discolour. He couldn't understand it at all, but the way it looked he wondered how he was going to get home.

After five minutes or so he was relieved to see a small figure in red trotting back towards him.

'Daddy? Daddy come walk?'

He tried to stand up. The pain was excruciating, but he had no choice.

'We'll have to go back Edward. I've hurt myself.'

'No! Edward go walk.'

Oh Christ, don't let's have all that again, thought Nicholas. He adopted his severest tone.

'We are going back home, now. Home to baby.' He added this as a sop, an encouragement to lure the child back.

'Baby!' Edward's voice was full of satisfaction.

'That's right; you got your own way in the end, we're going home to baby.'

It took nearly half an hour to cover the five-minute walk back to the house, but Edward stayed close to his father and seemed to realize that Nicholas had no breath left for conversation. It was one of the longest half hours that he ever wanted to endure, and when he finally made it through his front door he sat on the floor and sent Edward for Laura.

Late that afternoon, his leg bandaged and resting on

a footstool, Nicholas recounted the temper tantrum to Laura. She listened carefully.

'You didn't win,' she said at last. 'You had to come home.'

'That was hardly his doing; unfortunate I admit, but at least I made him start out. He needs firm handling.'

Laura hadn't told him about the scene when she had arrived home that week, and she had no intention of doing so now. Let him take more notice of their son for a time, then he might not be so quick to scoff at her.

'Your ankle looks really bad,' she said slowly. 'Haven't you any idea how you did it?'

'None at all, that's the odd part. If it doesn't go down by tomorrow I shall have to get Anderson to take a look at it.'

'You do that.'

'You don't sound as though you think much of Anderson.'

'He's all right, but I don't imagine he'll find anything wrong.'

She refused to elaborate on her statement, and Nicholas was too tired to pursue the matter.

Late that night, long after Laura had fallen asleep, Nicholas suddenly realized that he must have twisted his ankle when he fell in the hall. For some reason it hadn't hurt immediately; possibly it had gone numb at that time. He felt disproportionately relieved at finding an answer to the problem. With his mind clear at last he too began to drift off to sleep, lulled in the final stages by a gentle murmur that seemed to come from Laura as she slept.

At two in the morning Laura awoke abruptly. She sat up in bed, her heart racing and her stomach churning. She knew the symptoms only too well, but never before had she experienced them in the night. Slipping from the bed she put on her dressing gown and then tiptoed in bare feet along the landing to Edward's room. He was sitting up in bed, his eyes closed fast in sleep, and he was humming. She had never heard him make the noise before, but it was undoubtedly the same sound that he had made that morning in a temper. She wondered why he was making it now.

It was a melodious sound, and had a gentle rise and fall that almost turned it into a tune. She found that she was listening intently, waiting for it to change, but it remained constant. She must have stood there for ten or fifteen minutes, but he did not alter his upright position, and the humming was continuous.

Slowly she made her way to Belinda's room. She was disturbed, deeply disturbed, but she didn't know why. Belinda was standing in her cot, holding tightly on to the top rail and looking far more secure on her feet than she ever did when she pulled herself up in the day. Her eyes were wide open, but she gave no sign that she had seen her mother enter the room. Her plump little body was rocking slightly and all her concentration was being focused in one direction. Beyond all doubt, beyond any question, Belinda was listening.

Laura felt very cold, goose pimples ran down her arms and up the back of her neck. She herself listened, but there was nothing to hear; Edward's nocturnal humming did not carry this far. At least, not to Laura's ears.

'Belinda!' Her voice was a whisper. 'Belinda, lie down now. Go to sleep, darling.' There was no change; Belinda continued to stand, rock and listen. Laura closed her eyes. She concentrated as hard as she could.

'Belinda,' she said silently, 'stop listening. Go to sleep for Mummy.' She repeated it over and over, willing her daughter to obey.

The scream when it came was terrifying. It shattered

the stillness of the night as a stone shatters a sheet of plate glass. Then came another scream, and then another. Laura flew from the nursery and towards Edward's room, but Sandra was there before her. By the time Laura arrived he was already being comforted in his nanny's arms, sobbing pitifully.

'There, there, darling, it was only a nasty dream,' soothed Sandra, casting a worried glance towards Laura as she stood in the doorway. Laura nodded at her and turned away.

Back in the baby's room all was normal again. Belinda lay on her left side, thumb in mouth, sleeping soundly. The screams evidently hadn't disturbed her. With one last reassuring glance Laura walked back to Edward's room. Nicholas was there now, awoken himself by the noise.

'Where were you, Laura?'

'I got here just after Sandra, so I checked that Bee wasn't frightened.'

He accepted that. 'Poor chap must have had a terrible dream. He seems to be settling back all right though. I'll get back to bed. Work tomorrow.'

'I'll just settle him down.' Laura walked over to the bed with its protective bars round the head to prevent falls. 'Goodnight, Edward darling; sleep well now.' His blond hair was plastered to his head where he had been sweating, and his forehead was still damp to the touch. Just as she bent to kiss him he turned away and seemed to fall asleep immediately.

Laura walked slowly back to her own room. I won, she thought, I managed to interfere. She wondered how vigilant she needed to be as Edward grew older. Perhaps she should stay in Sussex more. Belinda needed her. She knew that she couldn't tell anyone else; they would think her mad, but for the next few years she intended to devote herself to protecting her daughter from her son. She had to. But she had to be careful; people wouldn't understand.

It was a cool April evening, and the sound of the Mayfair traffic carried clearly through the flat window which Nicholas had left open in order to clear his cigarette smoke. He was annoyed, and when he was annoyed he always smoked too much. He looked at himself in the mirror; he wasn't too sure that the green tie went with the brown-and-green shirt. Laura could have told him, but Laura wasn't there. This was the basis for his annoyance: her recent withdrawal from their London life.

For some peculiar reason she had decided that the children needed more of her time and attention, and now she only joined him for really important functions, of which tonight was not one. It was simply a social gathering at which people would, during the course of consuming expensive champagne and eating exquisite canapés, bid for items of clothing from assorted celebrities in order to raise money for the Heart Foundation.

Nicholas felt obliged to show his company's support for the Foundation. After all, his own father had been killed by a heart attack and his absence would be conspicuous. He disliked going alone; most of the people there would have partners, and there was no legitimate reason that he could offer for Laura's defection. All of his friends had nannies who were perfectly capable of taking care of their children for most of the time; as indeed he knew Sandra was.

He arrived late, and drank his first glass of champagne too quickly. The second he kept in his hand without actually sipping from it; the night was young and he found the drink had an alarming tendency to put him to sleep. He mingled with the crowd, finding many familiar faces, but few true friends. It wasn't so bad until the auction was over. Once that had finished everyone grouped into small circles, and he felt the lack of Laura keenly. One or two wives gave him more than friendly encouragement to join their particular groups, but that only made him the more anxious to remain alone.

He was startled to hear a familiar female voice hail him from half-way across the conference room.

'Nick? How nice to see you here!'

'Victoria! What a surprise!'

She smiled. He noticed that her thick dark hair had been stylishly cut since her visit to Sussex, and the short layered cut emphasized her fine eyes.

'I'm the one who should be surprised, Nicholas; after all I am a doctor, or nearly a doctor!'

He always forgot her profession. Unlike most career women it was not something that she discussed away from her hospital, and somehow it was difficult to associate a doctor with being a friend of Laura's. Laura conjured up an altogether more frivolous image.

'Of course. Are you here alone?'

'Not in theory, but my partner was in charge of sorting out the various "lots" and it seems to be taking up most of his time. No Laura?'

'No.' He realized that he sounded abrupt, and qualified it. 'She spends more time at home now; she feels that the children need her at present.'

Victoria didn't respond, nor did she probe, she merely took him by the arm and steered him into a quiet corner.

'Could you find me some food, Nicholas, I'm really famished. I'll keep your air space.' He was pleased to have something positive to do, and when he returned she was leaning against the wall and smoking.

'A filthy habit, not suited to one of my calling I know, but it's my only vice I assure you.'

'Don't apologise. I'm nearly forty a day now.'

She frowned: 'That really is too much.'

'I know, but somehow . . .,' he tailed off. He didn't want to sound disloyal.

They chatted about the Heart Foundation, and she commiserated with him about his father. Later on it seemed natural to leave together; she simply went away for a moment to tell her escort, and then collected her coat. He wondered where she lived, and if she had brought her car.

'We walked,' she said abruptly, 'so that's how I intend to get back as well.'

'There's no need to sound so aggressive,' soothed Nicholas, 'but I would like to walk with you. It will clear my head.'

'Fine.' She didn't protest falsely, nor ask him how far out of his way it was. She was as direct as he had always suspected, and it made the fact that he was escorting a single woman through London late at night seem less disloyal to Laura than if she had been more of a flirt. Less disloyal, and yet perhaps more dangerous. He found her direct approach strangely stimulating tonight.

'How is Laura?'

'She's fine.'

'I know her, Nicholas, she's my friend; you don't have to pretend with me.'

'Well, you know Laura. She's getting a bit obsessive over the children again.'

'Again?'

'You remember how she was with Edward.'

58

Yes, Victoria did remember, only too well. She wondered how bad Laura was this time.

'Is she still worried about Edward being good? Or is it both of them?'

'No!' He laughed a little. 'On the contrary, Edward throws some fine old rages these days. No, she just seems to think that unless she is there herself the children aren't safe.'

'You mean, that they'll hurt themselves?'

Nicholas stopped walking. He had asked himself this question so many times: what was Laura afraid of? He had asked her too, but her answer had perturbed him. He decided to tell Victoria what Laura had said. She was, after all, a doctor. She wouldn't laugh, or scoff; she might even be able to help.

'I asked her that, Victoria, and I'll tell you what she said; I remember it very well. She said: "As long as I'm here he can't interfere." I asked her what she meant of course, but she refused to clarify the statement.'

'I see.'

'Do you think she meant Edward when she said "he"?' He sounded anxious.

'Who else is there, Nicholas?'

'No one, but it doesn't make sense.'

Victoria touched him lightly on the arm. 'Do you think I could come down again? If you invited me, as a result of our meeting tonight, then I could see things first-hand. It might help. If there is anything wrong, then I could at least suggest who Laura should see.'

He had hoped that she might offer. 'I'd be eternally grateful, Victoria. Frankly I haven't known who to talk to about it. You don't think Laura's going off her head, do you?'

She could tell from the half-joking way in which he threw out the question that he was deeply worried but refusing to face it.

'Of course not,' she said automatically. 'Perhaps a touch

59

over-anxious, an anxiety state as we term it. People get it a lot these days, it's the pace of life they tell us!'

At the hospital gates she held out her hand to him and gave it a firm shake. He turned away, feeling much relieved.

'I'll get Laura to ring you,' he called.

'One thing, Nicholas.'

'Yes?'

'The children are all right, are they? Laura hasn't any need to worry?'

'Good God no! They're both absolutely super. Edward is turning into a very smart lad indeed, you'll get quite a surprise when you see him.'

'Lovely! Good night then.' Her heels clicked briskly away down the hospital path and Nicholas turned thankfully for home.

Alone in the double bed in the bedroom of their Sussex home Laura tossed and turned fitfully. She was finding it increasingly difficult to sleep these nights, waking every two or three hours and lying there for twenty minutes or so before dropping off again. Her dreams were horrible too, grotesque but without substance. She could never recall them. When she finally fell into a deeper sleep the house was silent. Far off a clock struck the hour. A beam in the roof creaked. Normal, country noises.

Gradually the peace was broken by a low, insistent humming. Sandra sat upright in her small room and switched on the bedside light. She was getting used to this and was at Edward's bedside in seconds, but to her surprise he was lying fast asleep, the corner of his sheet tucked into his mouth. She could still hear the humming noise, a trifle less melodious than usual, but not unpleasing.

Puzzled now she made her way back to the nursery

room. She opened the door. Belinda sat upright in her cot, her eyes closed, and as she hummed she swayed slowly to the rhythm. Sandra went over and gently put her down on her side. It was quite amazing, she thought, what small children could pick up. She had noticed that Belinda liked to copy anything that her big brother did, which was only to be expected, but this was most unusual. She wouldn't tell Madam about it, she decided, as she settled back to sleep. Madam didn't seem to like the baby trying to imitate her brother. What she didn't know couldn't upset her.

Finally they all slept.

Victoria was duly invited down to Sussex by Laura, and arrived two weeks after Edward's second birthday, bearing a suitable gift. It was a blue ball-shaped object with holes of assorted shapes and sizes into which the child had to try and fit the appropriate yellow pieces that came with the ball. It was for a two- to three-year-old, since she felt it better to give a gift that would stretch Edward a little and therefore hold his interest longer.

Laura was obviously very pleased to see her, and welcomed her warmly. Victoria was surprised by her friend's appearance. Her normal porcelain pallor had been replaced by a distinctly unhealthy off-white colour, and she had lost weight. In addition there were dark circles beneath her eyes, and a frenetic air about her that was disconcerting.

It was nearly 6 o'clock by the time that Victoria arrived, and another hour before dinner was over. Nicholas was not there. It was a Thursday, and Laura explained what Victoria already knew about their present domestic arrangement.

'Doesn't Nicholas mind?' She queried.

'I don't think so,' said Laura vaguely; 'he doesn't complain.'

'You must miss him.'

'Of course, but I'm needed here. The children were running wild.'

Victoria refrained from pointing out that Belinda couldn't walk yet, let alone run wild. She noticed too that Laura spoke as though both the children were troublesome, which was not quite how Nicholas had put the situation to her. She wondered which version was true.

After coffee she looked at her watch. 'Seven forty-five; too late to see my godson I assume?'

'Oh yes, he's always in bed by seven. He's on the go all the day; he needs his sleep.'

Victoria ventured a gentle probe. 'You don't look as though you're sleeping too well, Laura, not to my practiced eye!'

Laura didn't appear to mind the personal remark. 'No, I'm not. I don't know why but I'm getting a lot of bad dreams lately.'

'Since you stopped going up to London with Nick?'

'I suppose so.' She sounded reluctant to admit it, not wishing there to be a connection.

'Probably you can't get used to sleeping alone.'

A look of relief crossed Laura's features. 'I never thought of that. How silly of me! I'm sure you're right.'

If that hadn't been her own solution, thought Victoria, then what had? It had been connected with staying in Sussex, but not in the way Victoria had suggested. She wished that she had held her tongue and waited for Laura to give her own theory.

They didn't stay up late and by 10.30 Victoria was comfortably settled in the guest room. Driving always tired her, and she quickly fell asleep. It was very late when she awoke, but she had left her travelling clock in London and could not be certain of the time. She thought that it was about 3 am. At first she couldn't image why she had woken, but then she heard it. It was quiet to begin with, but it grew in intensity, a soft humming sound such as a mother might make as she soothed a fractious child to sleep.

Although in itself a soothing sound there was a quality about it that disturbed Victoria. She slipped out of bed and stood at her door listening. She wondered if it was Laura, if this was some nightmare from which she needed wakening. Eventually, justifying her curiosity on this somewhat flimsy ground, she opened the door and ventured out on to the landing. A night light burned overhead, and there was a similar bulb gleaming from what she remembered as Edward's old nursery. The sound seemed to come from there, and she went to look. Sure enough the little girl was standing up in her cot with her eyes closed and humming loudly, rocking herself from side to side at the same time. Victoria was slightly perturbed, she had seen similar actions in autistic children, but Belinda was asleep and probably it was merely comforting, similar to thumb sucking.

She tiptoed out of the room and stood listening again. There was a similar sound coming from the small room at the end of the landing, and with a furtive look round she followed the sound. The bedroom door was ajar, and she pushed on it gently. Edward was sitting bolt upright in bed, his arms stretched straight out in front of him, and he was emitting the same sound as his baby sister. He too rocked, but not as obviously, and his eyes were tightly closed.

Now she was disturbed. This had to be more than a coincidence. Laura's neurosis, whatever it was, was plainly beginning to affect her children. However normal they might appear in the daytime, they demonstrated their stress in their sleep. Having witnessed it she knew that she ought to take some action. Probably it would be best to tell Nicholas when the opportunity arose, and leave it in his hands.

Just as she got back to her own bedroom door she saw the nanny emerge sleepily from her room yawning as she walked.

'Did it wake you?' she asked Victoria.

'Yes. Do they do it a lot?'

'I'm afraid they do. It seems to be getting worse ever since. . . . Well, lately anyway.'

Victoria guessed what the woman had been about to say, ever since Laura had stayed at home, but she admired her for her loyalty. She smiled. 'Rather you than me!'

'Goodnight, Madam.'

When she finally fell asleep again she was wondering what Dr Castle would make of the situation. He was always interested in new ideas, and if she told him about her theory he might be appreciative. She rather hoped so. She found him an attractive man and admitted that a genuine reason to make an appointment to see him would give her more than professional pleasure. She managed a smile at her foolish romantic plottings, more worthy of Laura than herself, and then was lost in sleep.

In the morning, straight after breakfast, Sandra brought both the children down to the living-room. Mrs Wells senior was also there, a pleasant unassuming woman whom Victoria found easy company. She watched carefully as Laura kissed both the children, and noted how only Belinda received a hug. But then, Belinda was barely seven months old and had to be held in order to be placed on the floor. Edward, at the grand age of two, did not look to be a particularly kissable child.

He was nice looking, quite striking in fact. He was also big, in appearance more like a three year old. He showed no shyness of his Auntie Victoria, but walked cheerfully towards her as soon as his mother had kissed him.

'Hello!' Victoria tried to keep her voice adult, she despised baby talk.

'Hello!' He viewed her gravely.

'You've just had a birthday, I hear.'

'Birthday!'

'Did you have some nice presents?'

'Tricycle. I had a tricycle.' She had expected him to say "Edward had . . ." His use of the personal pronoun was interesting.

She picked up the package from behind her chair. 'Well, here's a present from me. I'm sorry it's a little late.'

Again he studied her carefully. Then he quickly took the parcel and retreated to the middle of the room to open it. Victoria glanced from beneath lowered lids at Laura. She was watching Edward carefully, and the expression on her face was almost one of dislike, although a better-mannered child it would have been hard to find. She also held Belinda firmly between her legs, so that it was impossible for her to crawl over the floor to join her brother. This of course could have been to protect Edward, but somehow Victoria doubted it. Not that Belinda seemed to mind. She had her back turned on her brother and was fiddling with her mother's shoes.

Edward managed the paper, but the box proved too tricky for his small fingers. Victoria went and helped

65

him. He tipped it on end, and watched as first the ball and then the small shapes fell out. She put out a hand to show him what to do, but he pushed her away impatiently.

'Now then!' the nanny chided him gently.

'Never mind!' Victoria could understand it. 'He'll be grateful for help once he's had a look and doesn't know what else to do with it.'

For about fifteen minutes the small boy sat engrossed, turning the ball this way and that, surveying it carefully from all angles. He had a lot of concentration for his age Victoria realized, and unusual determination. Both good, positive qualities. Then he picked up the shapes, feeling round them with both hands and holding them against the holes at random. She waited for the first shout when he failed to get the shape in, but it didn't come. He looked puzzled, put it down and picked up another one.

'Looks as though it's going to keep him quiet any way!' Laura didn't laugh in reply. To Victoria's surprise she was still staring at Edward, and the look of dislike was now unmistakable. Victoria glanced at Belinda. She had pulled out one end of the fashionable lace from the top of her mother's left shoe, and was holding it in her hand and looking as though she wanted to suck on it. Laura was oblivious, but she would realize soon enough when she stood up and her foot left her shoe behind.

Sandra, too, was watching Edward, but on her face was a look of good-natured pride. 'He's soon got the hang of it!' Victoria glanced back. Incredibly, by some lucky chance, Edward had managed to insert the star-shape through the right hole. As she watched he picked up another and inserted that, and then another and then another. Within a minute they were all done.

He looked at Victoria. 'All gone!' And then he smiled.
He had a wonderful smile, full of warmth and charm,
and her heart went out to him.

'Clever boy! Isn't that incredible, Laura? He really is
bright for his age.'

'Yes, I rather think he is.' She sounded as though
Victoria had confirmed a case of measles. Not alarmed,
but despondent.

'I wonder what his IQ is? You ought to take him to
an educational psychologist to have it checked.'

'No!' Laura's voice was loud, and alerted by her tone
Edward turned his face towards her. 'No! I don't want
anyone else seeing him. No one at all.'

'Fine, it was only a suggestion. Are we going to go
into town today? There's a few things I ought to get and
we could all have coffee while we're out.' She tried to
sound soothing, matter-of-fact.

'Yes, that would be nice.' Laura stood up. 'Would
you get their coats on please, Sandra?'

As the two women waited in the hallway Victoria
glanced down at Laura's feet. 'They're lovely shoes,
Laura; I like that lacing on the top.'

'Nicholas chose them for me; he thought they looked
elegant.'

'They do. I noticed that Belinda liked them too!' She
laughed.

'Did she? She's at the age when she likes almost anything, except her toys.'

'You ought to be careful though; I quite expected
you to fall. I suppose you're used to her habits?'

Laura looked puzzled. 'Why should I fall?'

'She left one end of one lace hanging down to the
floor. She'd got it unthreaded but couldn't get it back
through the holes.'

There was a short pause. Laura looked, if that were

possible, even more tense than she had done earlier. 'When? When do you mean?'

'Just now, when I gave Edward his present.'

'You must have been mistaken.'

Victoria was annoyed. 'I'm not a complete fool. I know what I saw. For God's sake Laura what's got into you?' There was another silence.

'Forget it!' Victoria moderated her voice. 'It doesn't matter, I'm sorry I shouted, Laura.'

Then the children were brought down and, despite protests from Edward, Laura settled herself in the back with the two children. By the time that she had parked the car in Crawley, Victoria was chiding herself for being so foolish. Laura was obviously far from well, it was unfair to pick a quarrel over such a trivial thing. Before she could apologize again Laura spoke.

'Vicky, I've just remembered, I had to tie my shoe up before we left the living-room. I wondered why at the time. I'm sorry.'

'Forget it, it really isn't important! Let's find a coffee house.'

When they were all ensconced round a table and the drinks were ordered Laura drew a small sigh of relief. How dangerous of her to make such a mistake. She was surprised that Victoria had been taken in by her palpable lie, but then people didn't understand, which allowed her to keep covering up. She understood. She understood more and more.

It wasn't until Sunday morning that Victoria had an opportunity to speak to Nicholas alone. Laura had gone out with her mother-in-law and Belinda to visit a friend only just out of hospital, and Edward was out for a walk with Sandra. Victoria had given packing as an excuse for not joining the walk, but had then thrown everything into the case in minutes. When she went into the dining-room she found Nicholas with the sherry decanter in his hand.

'I rather hoped that you might come and join me. Dry, or sweet?'

'Dry please.'

He handed her the glass, and they exchanged a brief glance.

'Well, what do you think? Was I wrong to be worried?'

Victoria took a deep breath. 'No, in fact I think that it was very fortunate that I came when I did.' Seeing his puzzled expression she told him everything about the happenings of her first night, and Laura's peculiar behaviour over her shoe lace. She also stressed that for most of the weekend Laura had appeared to be watching Edward, but in an aggressive rather than a protective manner.

'You think she's ill?'

'I think she's disturbed, Nicholas, and the children are being affected.'

'What should I do?'

'First of all, you must talk to her, try and persuade her to face the fact that she isn't well. Once you've overcome that hurdle it should be easy to get your doctor to refer her to the appropriate specialist.'

'What about the children?'

'They'll be fine, as long as their mother gets some help. I do think that Edward is exceptionally bright though. Would you mind if I mentioned that to Dr Castle, when I next see him?'

'Not at all.' Nicholas was scarcely concentrating; he was wondering how best to broach this difficult subject with his wife.

In fact Laura made it very easy for him. As soon as Victoria had left them, and about an hour before she and Nicholas usually had a drink, she went into the living-room and poured herself a large gin and tonic. Nicholas watched her closely; she looked annoyed and strung up.

'We shouldn't have asked her.' The statement was abrupt.

'Why ever not? She's your best friend.'

'She thinks I'm unbalanced. I can tell by the way she watches me. That's the result of studying to be a doctor. She thinks she knows everything.' The short sharp sentences were full of venom.

'I'm sure you're wrong,' said Nicholas diffidently. 'She may think that you over-react a little; but then she hasn't any children of her own, has she?'

'No. A fact that she conveniently forgets when criticizing me.'

'Did she?'

Laura hesitated. 'Not really, not to my face, but I could tell.' She doesn't sound like herself any more, reflected Nicholas, surprised at how much she had changed in so short a time and without him noticing.

'Did she speak to you?' The outright question took him by surprise.

'Why should she?' he queried.

'Because she thinks that I'm too unbalanced to listen, I imagine.'

'Laura, do *you* think you're quite well? Would you have talked about Victoria like this in the old days?'

The old days, thought Laura, the days before we had Edward. She could scarcely remember them now, those carefree days full of pleasure and anticipation.

She realized that Nicholas really wanted to discuss the situation, and was certain that her guess about Victoria having a quiet word had been right. Well, at least it gave her an opportunity to try, just one more time, to explain some of what was happening. Not all; he wouldn't understand it all any more than she did, but some. It was important though to keep calm, rational. She didn't want him to dismiss her as neurotic before she was even half-way through.

'Nicholas!' Her voice was low, but firm. 'I want to talk to you. Will you hear me right through, before you say anything at all?'

'Of course, my darling, anything that will help you.'

She knew by his tone, that she was probably too late. He was already behaving as though she was in need of treatment. She had to try this one time.

'When Edward was small, and I used to worry about him so much, it was because I thought he was backward. I can admit that now. I'd read about children who never cried and were later found to be brain damaged and it preyed on my mind. I was wrong. God, was I wrong! It was understandable, because he was my first child, but it's made this more difficult because from then on I got labelled as a worrying type of mother. The thing is, I was right to worry. My instinct was right, it was only the reason that was wrong. He isn't backward, he's forward. He's so far forward that it's quite beyond my comprehension. When he's quiet he's thinking. I don't know what about, but I'm quite sure if I did know I wouldn't like it. Normally, a bright child would be a blessing, I know that as well. The thing is, I'm not sure that it's simply a matter of IQ, brains or whatever. It's power. Edward has power.'

Nicholas never took his eyes from her face, and encouraged by this she continued. All her pent-up thoughts, all her conclusions so far came spilling out. It was a relief to talk.

71

'He isn't content with being bright and powerful. He's trying to influence Belinda. When she was born I was so happy, she was such a pretty, normal little girl; but she's changing. She always wants to be with Edward now, and if I separate them, take Belinda into another room for a rest or something in the day, then they start this ridiculous humming in order to keep in touch. When I take Belinda into town Sandra says that Edward will stand in a corner and hum continuously until our car draws into the drive. She never has to look out for us; she knows when we return because the humming stops. Don't you think that's eery? Well, I'm not going to let him swamp Belinda's personality with his peculiarities, and that's why I stay here. To watch over her. To try and help her keep her own identity. If he succeeds with her, who knows where he'll try next. I have to stop him. Do you understand any of this Nicholas? Tell me you do; the signs are there for you as well. I can't be the only one who sees!'

When she finished she was shaking with emotion, her determination to explain fully had drained her and she sat back exhausted and closed her eyes. He was her husband, her lover, the father of these children. He must have seen some of it; he simply hadn't understood as she had. Together they would be so much stronger.

He looked at her as she sat there, white and trembling; he remembered her as she had been not so long ago, elegant and beautiful. She is destroying herself with this madness he realized, and she must be helped. I've let it get out of hand, but now there is no excuse for me. I've heard the way her poor mind is working, and it's up to me to act. He lent forward, his voice low and kind.

'Laura, the one thing I know is that you truly believe all this. I don't doubt your sincerity or your good inten-

72

tions for one moment. What you have to face is that Edward is only two years old and Belinda seven months. It's natural for Edward to want to boss her, and it's natural for them to want to be together. That's why we had them close together, to be company for each other. I know Bee was a little premature, but we had planned on a second child within two years.

'I don't think you ever really recovered from that depression after Edward was born. You admit yourself that you worried about him being backward, and you've never picked up. I'm to blame for not spotting it sooner. I suppose I felt that you were neglecting me, and I reciprocated. I apologise, but I didn't realize how worried you truly were. Tomorrow morning we're going down to Dr Anderson and we'll tell him some of this. Not everything, he wouldn't understand, but a general picture. He'll fix you up with a specialist, and within a few months you'll look back on all this and be amazed that you could ever have had such thoughts about two such gorgeous children. What do you say?'

She wanted to say: you bloody, bloody fool; why don't you listen to me instead of Victoria? She didn't. She had tried and failed. That was it. She would never bother again. From now on she would have to continue fighting alone; it would have helped so much to have had an ally. Now she was going to have to face some know-all of a head-shrinker, but the sooner it was over the better. She could pretend to get better, it was easy to give people what they wanted. Life was only difficult when you persisted in giving them facts that they preferred not to face. So be it, she had learnt.

'All right, Nick, if you think we should.' She sounded quite placid he was relieved to note, just tired, as though she wanted it all to end.

He poured her another drink, and himself a large

73

Scotch. 'I wish you'd talked about this before, Laura. I had no idea you were in such a state. I feel ashamed that I could be so blind.'

'Can we drop the subject now, Nick? I'd really prefer it if we could.'

'Of course.'

It was difficult for him to sit there and make ordinary conversation after listening to her twisted logic concerning Edward, but he did his best. He wanted to tell her that Vicky had thought their son exceptionally bright, but somehow that didn't seem much help in the circumstances.

When they finally went up to bed the constraint between them was even more obvious. Laura slept perched on the very edge of her side of the bed, as though afraid even to touch him by accident. If he hadn't felt so sorry for her he would have been hurt by this further rejection. Surely she realized that he was the only person who could bring her out of all this? She would receive full support from him during any course of treatment that was found necessary.

Through May, June and July Laura struggled along with her psychiatrist, who specialized in post-natal depression. Despite her best efforts he refused to be convinced that she was cured, and letters passed frequently between this small, bespectacled man and Dr Anderson. On a routine visit to her GP for a renewal of the anti-anxiety pills that she threw down the toilet regularly four times a day, he suggested that she try a psychoanalyst.

'I have found,' he said, 'that they can get some truly spectacular results. They enable you to come to terms with yourself.'

'And my son?' She regretted the small joke immediately; it would show how far from well she was, to his distorted mind.

'Yes, he may even enable you to come to terms with your son, Mrs Wells.'

She shrugged and agreed. What did it matter? None of them understood. If she were a National Health patient and not private she would probably be in hospital by now, doped up to the eyeballs and Edward would be completely free. There were many compensations for being rich.

The psychoanalyst was ridiculously young, all bright-eyed and enthusiastic. He was tall and gangly with innocent blue eyes that reminded her of Belinda. He asked her all about her childhood, and her mother. She told him that her mother had been an actress, and often away from home.

Had she minded? Of course. Did she resent her mother now? Never thought about her. Was that true? Certainly, she had too much else to think about. Such as? Her son.

Time and again he caught her out in this way. It was impossible to fool him. At the end of every session there would be some small pointer to show that she was not progressing. He seemed amused at her determination to trick him.

'If you do fool me, Mrs Wells, then what have you gained? Life will be as difficult for you as before. It's in your own interest to get well. Your own and your husband's.'

Edward's third birthday came and went and still they tried to help her. She was unable to watch him as vigilantly as before, lest they notice and report unfavourably. She could tell that he was making full use of this golden opportunity. He had a satisfied look in his eyes, as well he might. Life was being good to him.

Then, one October day, the solution came to her. She must convince herself that everything was normal, no matter what the effort. Only then would she be able to convince the specialists. She must ignore any signs to the contrary, see only what other people saw. It must be possible. It had to be, or she would be too late. She began to put this into practice the very next day, and by Christmas time her analyst was very pleased with her. She resolutely concentrated on the positive sides of Edward, his aptitude for music, his physical co-ordination, and found herself relating his achievements with what was presumably normal maternal pride.

It was hard, especially when she knew that Edward was triumphant, but she would push even that thought out of her mind lest it betray her. By the following spring, one month before Edward had his fourth birthday, she was pronounced cured. Not in so many words of course, but she didn't have to visit the gangly young man any more, and was given fewer tablets to throw down the toilet. She bided her time. She continued with her double deception until she knew that everyone was convinced.

Nicholas took her on a second honeymoon to Corsica and they had a wonderful month in the sun. She was happy for him; she didn't want to make his life a misery. She still loved him, and was grateful that as far as she knew he had remained faithful to her during the difficult last years. He had supported her in every possible way, except that he had refused to believe her. Deep down she knew that she would always hold that against him, but she would never show it. There was so much that she could never show from now on.

Victoria knew that she was going to have to make a move soon. She was wasting time, and even worse she was deeply involved in what she knew to be an unproductive personal relationship. It was worse than unproductive, it was self-destructive. No one forced her to continue it, she was bitterly aware of that fact, but she was restrained from leaving by her own late-discovered streak of sensuality. He had disclosed that streak to her, and had encouraged it. She was probably the best mistress that he could wish for, given his circumstances. All this she knew; she lacked the power to make the final move today, but soon, soon.

She looked at her watch. She had only been back in the flat half an hour and already she was looking to see how long before he joined her. Another hour at least. She had to do something, find some way of filling in the time. She decided to ring Laura.

She felt guilty about Laura. She had neglected her shamefully over the past two years, at a time when she was probably badly needed. It was pure coincidence that her affair with Adam had coincided with Laura's breakdown, but a coincidence that she feared might have put a strain upon their friendship. She hoped not.

She did not recognize the voice that answered her, but guessed that it was Edward's. She had not seen him for over a year, but she knew that he would remember her.

'Edward? This is Auntie Vicky. Is your mother there?'

'I'll fetch her for you, Auntie.'

No hesitation, such a self-possessed four-year-old.

'Vicky? How nice to hear from you!' Laura sounded genuinely pleased. No note of recrimination in her voice. 'Quite a coincidence too. We have to bring Edward to town to see that consultant again, a follow-up to the visit when he was a baby. I wondered if we could meet up. You're still at that hospital, I take it?'

She tried to disguise the surprise in her voice. 'Yes, yes I am. We'll meet up then, and I'll take you both out to lunch. Is Nick coming too?'

'He isn't sure. Let me give you the date, and the time of the appointment and we can check the details later.'

The call had taken little more than ten minutes. She would be seeing Laura and Edward in two weeks. She had not been found lacking as a friend. She had escaped lightly. Not really though; she was losing her self-respect, and that was a very high price to pay for an affair. She took some case notes out of her briefcase and forced herself to read them slowly. She simply must look for a suitable partnership before long. It was becoming more and more obvious that Adam was not going to suggest marriage. At the beginning of their affair he had made his views on marriage very clear. It was not for him. She had hoped to change him, of course, but to no avail. She could not complain, but she felt sad. Their life together had been good.

Immersed in her notes the time flew and when she heard his key in the door she was amazed. He sank down on to the settee next to her.

'Christ, what a bloody foul day! Some mothers should be shot as soon as they've produced; save us poor consultants a lot of trouble!'

'You don't mean that, Adam!'

He opened the heavy-lidded grey eyes wide. 'I do, I swear it!'

'I'll fix you a drink.'

'Scotch, neat. How was your day?'

'The same as usual. I'm getting itchy feet, Adam.'

'You've been here too long. Time to move on. Pastures new and all that.'

How could he sound so unconcerned, she wondered? 'I intend to.'

'Excellent!'

There was silence. Calm, untroubled, on his part. Fraught with tension on hers.

'You won't miss me?' She despised herself for saying it, but was unable to refrain.

'Naturally I'll miss you. We will, I trust, meet up from time to time!'

He was mocking her now, as he frequently did. When she turned ultra-feminine on him he despised her. She was aware that basically he disliked women, not sexually but emotionally. She thought he was right to remain single. He would be an intolerant husband, demanding everything from his wife but giving nothing in return.

'You didn't tell me you were seeing my godson.' The abrupt change of subject should have disconcerted him, but there was no sign of this on his face.

'That's because I didn't know. Is it a follow-up or a fresh request?'

'Follow-up.'

'That's why then. Claire will have dealt with it.'

Claire was his secretary, in her late fifties and mannish. He was never sharp or sarcastic with Claire.

'Don't forget what I told you about him.'

'I'll form my own judgement, Dr Tyson, we can compare notes when I've seen him.'

'Of course, Dr Castle!'

After they had eaten he washed up while she laid the breakfast ready for morning. He was good like that. In the two years that they had lived together he had always done his share round the flat. As soon as they had both finished they went to bed. Often he had work to do, or a book to read, in which case Victoria kept herself busy too, but tonight he went straight to bed.

He was quickly out of his clothes, and then he lay on

the bed and watched her as she undressed. A pleasant ritual, played out so many times, but for how much longer, she wondered? She lay down next to him and he rolled over on to his stomach, resting the weight of his body on his forearms. She was on her back, looking up into his face. He gently outlined the curve of her jaw with his right hand.

'You're angry, Vicky. Why?'

She turned her face sharply away, but he tightened his grip on her jaw. 'Tell me why?'

'I'm being stupid, Adam; emotional and foolish, all the qualities you despise. I'll get over it, just let it pass.'

He was watching her closely, eyes narrowed in concentration. 'We've had two good years, Vicky, don't forget that. We've been good together.'

'But now it's over?'

'That's right. You're ready to move on, and so am I. I've been waiting for the right moment to tell you this, and tonight seems to be it. I'm off to the States in seven weeks' time for a six-month exchange. It's a great opportunity for me. I'm ten years younger than my American colleague, and lucky to have been chosen.'

'You deserve it.' She knew that he did, but it didn't lessen the pain.

He nuzzled the hollow in her neck with his evening stubble, and she felt the familiar tremor of anticipation go through her.

'You've only seen the good side of me, Vicky. It's been a great strain, but at least we'll part friends!' He was only half-joking; there was a dark side to him but it was under control. If he had wanted to marry then it would have been Victoria, but he preferred to remain single.

'You've seen every side of me.' She sounded regretful.

'How true!' He moved his mouth down her neck and fastened on to her left breast while his hands moved everywhere like relentless butterflies. She began to tremble beneath them. It was always stimulating for him to watch her come alive. He had taught her so much, but she had been a very quick pupil.

He was quicker than usual in entering her, but he sensed that she needed the closeness, the reassurance that it would give her. It was not a night for experiments that lasted until they were both exhausted. Tonight was for loving, or as near as he could come to it. He heard her loud cry of satisfaction and it gave him the final impetus that he needed to join her in her release.

Later he sat propped up in bed smoking while she slept beside him. It would be pleasant in a way to have a bed to himself again, and the complete privacy that he always craved. She would find someone else, someone warmer, more able to give her the love that he knew she needed in order to blossom fully. He was too cold, too occupied to be the one. He wondered what sort of a woman she would become.

She awoke late the next morning, her day off, and he had already gone. His side of the bed was cold. She remembered what he had said. In seven weeks he would be gone. It gave her the necessary motivation to get out and begin looking for the partnership that was to start her on the road to her goal: her own practice.

'Edward Wells, Dr Castle.'

He had already read his old notes and he was well prepared too by what Vicky had told him; nonetheless he was surprised. She had not been exaggerating.

Edward walked confidently into the large, clinical room. He looked all round before acknowledging the man behind the desk. Mrs Wells remained in the background, strangely remote as though reluctant to become involved. Not at all as he remembered her.

He indicated a chair near to him. 'Sit down, Edward. Now, how old are you?'

'Four.'

He looked and acted more like a five-year-old noted Adam, and wrote it down.

'What are you writing?' The boy sounded sharp, almost annoyed.

'Your age.'

'That's not a four, that's words.'

'I've written it down in words.'

Edward fell silent. Adam looked over to the mother. 'Any problems, Mrs Wells?'

'None at all.'

Not what he had heard. He was even more surprised. He had expected a catalogue of trivia.

'You have another child now?'

'Yes, a daughter. She's coming up to two.'

'A nice sister, Edward?'

'Very nice!' He sounded genuinely enthusiastic too; there was not a trace of jealousy.

Adam couldn't force Mrs Wells to talk. He could only go through the routine of heart, lungs, eyes and ears. The boy was exceptionally well developed physically. He would probably be a fine athlete, well co-ordinated, which made such a difference.

'Now, Edward, will you do a jigsaw for me?'

'No!'

'But surely you'd like to show me how well you can do it? It's all about trains. The nurse will show you.'

'No!'

He was used to children who didn't want to co-operate, who were shy or plain defiant. This was different. He couldn't define the difference, but it was there.

'What do you want to be when you grow up, Edward?'

'A man.' The look in the child's eyes was insolent. Adam knew that sounded ridiculous, but there was no other word for it. This boy was sending him up! He began to get annoyed, but knew that it wouldn't show, except perhaps to Vicky, if she were there.

'Do the jigsaw please, Edward.'

'I don't want to!'

The nurse came forward, jigsaw in hand. She was a pretty young girl, fond of children, especially the nice-looking ones like Edward.

'Here you are, darling; come and do it with me.'

Edward waited until she was right up to him and then his fist shot out and by unlucky chance he caught her full in the face. The jigsaw fell to the floor as she clapped a hand to her nose which Adam was horrified to see was bleeding.

The Clinic Sister, waiting unobtrusively in a far corner, stepped forward and led the girl away. Adam glanced at the boy's mother. She looked troubled, but unsurprised. He looked at the boy. Nothing, no expression on his face at all.

'That wasn't very nice, Edward.' A mild enough reproof God knows, but it brought forth a look of withering hatred from this obstructive child. He wondered why Vicky had never mentioned the vile temper. Or perhaps she had, and he hadn't been listening.

'You won't leave,' he said evenly, 'until the jigsaw is done.'

They stared at each other for a few seconds. Edward

got down stiffly from his chair and stood in front of the consultant. He was rigid with rage, but fighting for self-control. Adam had never seen such adult emotions from a child this young. After a brief struggle he mastered himself, walked over to the jigsaw and almost without looking pushed the pieces together.

'There's a good boy! You can sit down again now.'

Adam turned his attention to Mrs Wells. 'You said there were no problems?'

'That's right, Dr Castle.'

'Do you have many scenes like this?'

'Yes. Every day, whenever he's crossed. Far worse than this one quite often.'

You stupid woman, he thought. When there was nothing wrong you plagued me and now you refuse to admit what a little horror you've got on your hands. He kept the annoyance out of his voice, he even managed a pleasant curve of the mouth that he hoped would pass as a smile.

'Mrs Wells, do you really think the scene today was quite normal for a child of this age?'

Her brown eyes flashed, and for a moment she became animated.

'I'm not qualified to judge, Dr Castle, but I have been assured by every expert including you that my son is perfectly' and she stressed the word, 'normal in every way. Indeed, I have been undergoing treatment myself for doubting this.'

He looked down at the desk, scribbling random notes to give himself time. Was he over-reacting? Was it misfortune, not spite, that had caused the bloody nose? Could he be wrong, and everyone else right? He doubted it. He, however, was going away. This woman had to go on coping. What should he say to her?

The sound of his pen reverberated in the room. I

don't like this boy, he thought. I distrust him. He's big, and he's bright, but he isn't quite right. It was an instinct, that was all, and he kept it to himself.

'I'm sure that's correct, Mrs Wells, but he does need firm handling. Do you think you can manage that? He's going to be a big lad. I'm off to the States soon, but only for six months. I think I'll take another look at the boy when I return. All right?'

She nodded.

'Fine. I'll see you in six months, Edward. Be good for me.'

'Goodbye.'

'Goodbye, Edward.'

He watched the boy walk straight-backed to the door. As he left he cast one final look back. Some trick of the light made it appear that he was laughing. Adam sighed and closed the folder. He would talk it over with Vicky before she went at the weekend.

In the newly opened hamburger bar Edward and his mother waited for Victoria. Edward drew many admiring glances from middle-aged women, and now and again he would favour one with a beaming smile. He was enjoying himself looking at all the new sights. He liked London. Laura sipped at her coffee. Dr Castle had felt it too, she knew that. He had been uncomfortable about Edward this time. You've taken too long she told him silently; he's had two years of freedom now and he can't be stopped. You're too late.

Edward tapped her on the arm. 'Late!' he said regretfully. She felt her flesh prickle.

'Who is late?'

'Auntie Vicky.' He gave her a bland stare and buried his head in his milkshake.

A few minutes later Vicky rushed in. 'I'm sorry I'm so late, I had a last minute emergency. Have you ordered?'

'Only the drinks; Edward felt thirsty.'

Vicky turned her attention to her godson. 'Hi Edward! Did you have a nice time with Dr Castle?'

'Not very. May I have fish fingers please?'

'Of course.' She glanced at Laura, who shook her head warningly. Surprised that anything could have gone wrong Vicky sat down and wondered what else there was to talk about.

Laura looked fairly well. A trifle pale perhaps, but not as thin as she had been just after Belinda was born. Edward looked as bonny as ever. He still had that golden aura about him, a strange mixture of hair and skin tone that made him literally seem to glow with life. Intelligence shone from his large brown eyes, but his face was rapidly losing its baby chubbyness, giving him a prematurely adult look round the top of his face.

When Edward was finally involved in his fish fingers and chips she asked Laura again about the morning. Since Laura knew nothing of her friend's association with the consultant she would be perfectly frank, which was what Victoria wanted.

'It went badly I'm afraid. Edward threw a temper tantrum and refused to do a jigsaw for the doctor.'

There she goes, thought Victoria, making too much of everything again.

'They all play up,' she reassured her friend. 'Believe me nothing will have surprised Dr Castle.'

Laura shrugged. 'If you say so, but he didn't seem too pleased. We have to go back in six month's time.'

Vicky was pleased. Obviously Adam had seen the boy's ability for himself and wanted to keep it monitored. She looked forward to discussing it tonight. She would mention Laura's attitude as well.

Laura supported his anti-mother theory very well, the epitome of all he disliked. Poor Laura, she obviously wasn't as well as the doctors thought, but at least she was more in control.

'How's Nick?'

A slight pause. 'He's fine. He's very busy, that's why he couldn't come today. He wanted to, and he sent you his regards.'

'That was kind. Remember me to him as well.'

Their bill arrived, plonked down on the table with the usual impoliteness that marked casual labour these days, reflected Vicky. Edward had become bored now that his food was finished. He too watched the young waitress as she proceeded to lean against the counter and nibble the skin round her thumb nail.

Laura leant towards Vicky. 'You must come down and visit us again, now that I'm quite recovered.'

'I'd like that. As a matter of fact I hope to be near you permanently soon, but I should know more about that within a week or two.'

Laura smiled. 'How nice. Well, let's make it in month's time then. How about the first Saturday in September?'

Vicky checked her diary. 'Looks all right. Can I confirm by 'phone next week?'

'Of course, I thought we . . .'

The sentence was never finished. An ear-splitting scream rent the hamburger bar, and all eyes turned towards the casual young waitress. She was casual no longer. As she continued to scream she ran in frantic circles, clutching her arms to her body and plucking at her dress front. Vicky realized that the water boiling for coffee and tea had somehow drenched the girl, and was continuing to pour forth its steaming liquid from a pipe on the counter. She leapt to her feet and hurried towards the scene.

'I'm a doctor. Someone call an ambulance.'

There was little that she could do except try and keep the girl as calm as humanly possible, and the ambulance arrived swiftly. By the time that she had seen it speed away and walked back into the restaurant through the manager's office the room was nearly empty. A maintenance man was already working on the hot-water dispenser.

'Can't think how she turned it on,' he muttered as she passed. 'It's never happened before.'

'I should hope not!' Her tone was sharp. It was plainly negligence. The tap must have been opened when the girl leant on the counter, but even if they were successfully sued for lack of safety precautions the girl would have weeks of pain to endure. A very nasty accident.

Laura and Edward were still seated at their table, Laura paler than ever.

'How perfectly horrible! That poor girl. Will she be all right?'

'She'll live,' said Vicky shortly, 'But it must have been agony.' She glanced at Edward, the horror of it had passed him by and he was playing with a finger puppet.

'I really must be off, Laura. I'm sorry that we weren't able to talk more, but I'll see you when I come down. Give Auntie a kiss, Edward?' He turned his mouth up to hers, and she wanted to hold him tight, but refrained. She knew that he wouldn't like it.

'Girl cried.' His tone was solemn. She knew that there was no point in lying.

'She was burnt, Edward, by some hot water.'

'Rude!'

'What was rude?' His choice of word surprised her, he was usually so correct in his speech.

'Girl, she was a rude girl.'

'No just in pain. See you soon darling, 'bye now!'

She hurried along the crowded pavement, jostled on all sides by busy people. Something was nagging at her, something peculiar. Suddenly she stopped short. The waitress had been rude. Edward was right. She herself had thought the same thing. How very observant he was for such a young boy. She must remember to tell Adam.

In the restaurant Laura gathered up their belongings and helped Edward off his chair. She had an air of defeat about her now. The day had proved as difficult as she had feared, and if he had been in any way connected with the incident of the waitress then he was rapidly becoming uncontrollable. She looked at him as he stood patiently waiting, and for once her feelings were normal maternal ones. Did he know what he was doing, she wondered? If so, how frightening it must have been for him on the day he had first realized that he was different. Because he was different, in many ways. But she had trouble defining them all.

She took his hand. Outside she hailed a taxi. Once in the back she ventured a question.

'That girl, Edward, the one who got hurt in the restaurant, why did you say she was rude?'

'Because she was.' He sounded impatient at her stupidity.

'She wasn't. She didn't say a word to us, so how could she be rude?' His eyes flickered towards her, and then he gazed out of the window. The taxi drove slowly on. Laura waited. At last he turned back to her. 'She leant in front of Auntie's face and pushed against her arm. That's rude, nanny says so!'

There it was then, the perfect, logical answer. Perhaps it was true.

'Did it upset you, darling, hearing her cry?' She

hated herself for the false note of concern in her voice, but hoped that it deceived Edward.

'No, it didn't hurt me at all. Can I have cheese sandwiches for tea? May I?' The correction was automatic.

All children were egocentric, she knew that. His answer made sense, but most children would have cried at all the noise and commotion. Unless they'd caused it.

Neither of them spoke again until they reached home, Edward because he had nothing to say, Laura because she was busy thinking.

Adam didn't return to the flat until nearly 8 pm that evening. Vicky knew that he had his visa to attend to and was then meeting friends for a drink, but she was still impatient. She wanted to know why Laura hadn't wanted to discuss Edward's visit, and even more important why Edward hadn't liked it.

From the moment that Adam stepped through the door she knew that she should wait until another day to talk about it. His face was drawn with tiredness, his eyes deeply shadowed, stubble showing dark against his complexion. She knew, but she could not wait. Once he had drunk two cups of coffee and changed into casual clothes she began.

'Well, what did you think of Edward then?'

'Not quite what I'd expected.'

'You sound annoyed, as though I'd misled you. Don't you think he's bright?'

'Oh yes, he's bright.'

Adam buried his head in the evening paper. Vicky was aggrieved. Edward was someone special to her, and Adam knew it.

'Put that paper down for five minutes, Adam Castle. I want to know how the appointment went off.'

He sighed, and placed the paper by his side. 'You saw them after I did. What did his mother say?'

'The usual Laura line, about him throwing a temper and refusing to do a jigsaw. I've told you how she makes every normal childish act of assertion sound like a major catastrophe; it was a typical Laura-type reply. I don't suppose that you liked her any more this time?'

'As a matter of fact I did. I felt quite sorry for her. I'd feel sorry for any mother who had to raise an egotistical, overdeveloped four-year-old like your precious godson.'

'Adam! He's an intelligent little boy, you make him sound like a potential criminal!'

'He probably is, if he lives that long!'

'What on earth happened today?'

'Nothing special. I asked him to do a jigsaw; he refused. I asked him again, and he punched one of the trainee nurses on the nose causing a nasty nosebleed and a great deal of confusion. He also decided to send me up whenever possible.'

Vicky was shaken, not by what she was hearing but by Adam's over-reaction to it all. 'Send you up! Steady on, Adam, you're thirty years older than he is remember.'

'I admit that, which is probably the only reason that I finally triumphed and the jigsaw was completed. He's an aggressive, anti-social small boy to whom I must admit I took an unreasonable dislike. He is not, by any stretch of the imagination, the golden wonder of your recent tales!'

Vicky watched as Adam glared at her for a moment before resuming his reading of the paper. How stupid she had been. She knew that although he disliked being contradicted himself he took great delight in doing it to other people. His attitude tonight was typical of this. He knew that she liked Edward, and had hoped that Adam would find him as unusual as she did. As a result he had taken the opposite line. He wanted to show her that he was the expert, while she was merely a foolish beginner. She often wondered if his attitude hid a deep-seated inferiority complex, but she would never know. It was impossible to get close enough to him to find out.

She went into the kitchen and sat at the small break-fast table smoking a cigarette. Soon now they would be parting; foolish then to mind so much when he deliberately tried to hurt her. Their relationship had always been too one-sided; it was impossible for her to hurt him even if she wanted to. She should never have discussed Edward in the past. She had ruined Adam's reaction to him, and that was by far the most unfortunate outcome of today's meeting.

She was nearly asleep when Adam came to bed. He tapped her on the shoulder.

'Awake?'

'Sort of!'

'I'm sorry about your godson, but there's something about him that I just can't take to.'

'Forget it, Adam. It isn't important any more. Not to us anyway.'

Adam stared into the darkness. 'I know, but I wish I could put my finger on the cause. It isn't like me to react like this, now is it?'

She turned sleepily towards him. 'No, but I think I'm to blame. I tried to lead you my way, and you've gone the other way instead.'

He wished it was that, he really did. For some reason when he had looked at the boy as he stood there in defiant rage he had seen about him not the golden glow that Vicky was so proud of but a darkness. Adam believed strongly in the existence of the soul. Indefinable, but nevertheless there. The darkness that emanated from Edward was the darkness of the soul. Not something that he would ever tell anyone, but something to remember when he next saw the child. As he drifted off to sleep he wondered how it was that two intelligent people such as himself and Vicky could see one small boy in such differing lights. Was the boy different with each of them, or did they simply see the same thing and interpret it differently? Still pondering upon this he finally slept.

Now that she no longer had to pretend to herself that all was well with Edward she could have made the mistake of once again watching him too obviously, but she was wiser. She made sure that no one realized what she was doing. Since her illness she had become more cunning, more adept at lying and deceiving. She was perfectly well, she knew that, but other people might still doubt it; therefore she watched secretly and with care. It was her own private war.

Nicholas was pleased that she was better, but regretted how much she had changed. She was no longer open and trusting, asking constantly for his judgement on matters and grateful for his guidance. Now she was more restrained, and her self-confidence had increased. There was a part of her that he could not reach, and he resented it. It no longer appeared to be the fault of her relationship with the children, but something was wrong. He found himself more and more reluctant to make love to her, and while ostensibly he blamed this on pressure of work he knew that really he loved her less. Gradually their relationship disintegrated, but Nicholas tried to make sure that no one else would know this. He too became adept at a form of deception.

The children were as they had always been.

It was a Friday morning. By tea-time Vicky would be with them for the weekend, but there were eight wet hours to be filled before then, realized Laura, as she looked out at the pouring rain. From the nursery rooms came the sounds of boisterous play. Sandra had left recently, but the new girl Heather was a great success and less expensive as well. Neither of the children were babies any more, and so they had settled for a less qualified but cheerful girl recommended by one of the company director's wives.

She turned away from the window and looked round the living-room. It was immaculate as always. Nick's mother dusted and tidied every single day, worried lest the cleaning woman ever found any dust on her twice-weekly visits. Laura had ceased to remonstrate with her mother-in-law; it made her feel useful and certainly it was nice never to have to clean round herself.

She heard a sound in the doorway and turned to find Edward standing there.

'I thought you were playing upstairs with Heather and Belinda?' His face was set in a truculent expression.

'I'm bored!'

'Do you want to do some reading?'

'No!'

'Drawing?'

'No!'

'What then?'

'I want to go to school.'

They went through this at least twice a week, often more.

'Soon,' she promised, 'next term, when you're almost five. After Christmas you can go.'

He was down for a small prep school nearby, and both Laura and Edward would be pleased when the next three months had passed. He was ready for school, and if Laura had doubts about his ability to fit into a disciplined life they weren't shared by her son. She watched him as he tossed a small rubber ball from one hand to the other, lost in bored daydreams. As she walked by him to go up to Belinda she could hear him softly humming.

In the nursery Heather was putting away some toys while Belinda cuddled a doll. 'My baby' she told Laura proudly.

'Beautiful. What's her name?'

'Elaine.'

Laura was surprised. They didn't know any Elaines, and it was also one of her own favourite names. If she ever had another daughter she wanted to call it Elaine.

'That's a pretty name; where did you hear it?' A hesitation, her head slightly on one side. 'Telewision!'

For a moment Laura watched Belinda, whose large blue eyes were open and innocent as she nodded firmly. 'Yes, telewision.'

Laura turned away, refusing to think about the implications. 'Here, look at these nice wooden puzzles. Can you do them, Bee?'

By the age of two Edward had been bored by the small cut-out figures that fitted back into the spaces on the wooden board, but Belinda had yet to master them.

'Come on,' she encouraged her, 'Mummy will help you.' She tipped the pieces out on to the carpet, and watched as Belinda tried to put a large horse into the small space for a pig.

'No, look it's too big. Try over there.' Belinda promptly tried to put it into the space for the tractor, and when that failed she put it down, and stuck her thumb in her mouth.

She really isn't very quick at all, thought Laura, but strangely she didn't mind. It was a relief after Edward.

'Come on, let's try again.' Belinda shook her head. 'Look, watch Mummy do it.' She put the horse into his space, and then picked up the pig.

'Now, where does he go?' Belinda watched the board for a moment and then tilted her head to the left. Her eyes clouded over and she began to rock to and fro, humming gently as she did so. Laura felt cold.

'Stop it! Stop humming, Bee! Come on, we'll play with the dolls house if you don't want to do puzzles.'

Belinda rocked faster and faster. The humming grew in intensity; it sounded like a small swarm of bees. Frantically Laura glanced round for Heather, but Heather had left the room. She shook Belinda by the shoulders.

'Shut up, Belinda! Stop that noise!' She could have been invisible for all the notice her daughter took. Laura rushed to the top of the stairs. At the bottom, in the middle of the hall, stood Edward.

She looked down at him for a minute. He was only standing there. Standing motionless and silent. He looked up at her and smiled.

'Stop her!' Laura had forgotten Heather, forgotten to be careful, she knew only that she wanted silence in the house. Behind her the volume of the humming increased. It was now almost a keening cry. 'Edward, for God's sake stop it!' Still he smiled at her. She ran down towards him. She would make him stop it; she wasn't going to allow him to ruin her daughter. She hated him at that moment, and wanted to get hold of him and shake him like a terrier shakes a rat.

As she took hold of his shoulders, Heather called down the stairs.

'Is something the matter, Madam?'

'Tell him to stop her,' shrieked Laura, 'I can't stand the noise!'

'Mrs Wells, I can't hear any noise.'

Laura let her arms drop to her side. The grandfather clock in the hall ticked loudly, in the kitchen she could hear the gardener talking to the help. Apart from that there was no sound.

Slowly Edward backed away from his mother, keeping his eyes fixed on her face until he reached the kitchen door. Then he turned his back on her and belted through it, slamming it closed behind him.

Laura looked up to see the shocked faces of Heather and Belinda looking down at her. She forced herself to go up to them, but a smile was impossible for her.

'I'm sorry I shouted, but I can't stand Belinda humming like that.'

'They both do it, Madam, but it doesn't trouble me. Was Edward doing it too?'

'No.' Laura realized that in that case she had no obvious cause to rush down the stairs at him. 'No, but he was encouraging Bee.' It sounded very lame she knew. Heather was young and polite. She thought that perhaps Mrs Wells had a bad headache and didn't like to say so.

'Would you like me to make you a cup of tea, Madam?'

'Thank you, but I'm fine. I'll go back in the nursery with Bee.'

97

'Then I'll finish off Edward's bed.'

In the nursery Belinda was once again bright-eyed and cheerful.

'Mummy, look!' She sat down by the wooden puzzle.

'It's all right, darling, I think that's a little difficult just yet.'

'Look!' With speed and complete accuracy Belinda then proceeded to put all the pieces into their spaces. 'All gone!'

Silently Laura took the puzzle away and replaced it with a similar one that had nursery-rhyme characters instead of animals. She tipped them out.

'Try that one, darling.' Belinda picked up a small Little Miss Muffett and tried to fit her into a large Simple Simon, she also held Miss Muffett upside down.

'He hasn't told you how to do that one yet, has he?' Laura kept her voice matter-of-fact, but Belinda simply stared at her before puckering up her face and letting large tears flow down her rosy cheeks.

Laura got up and walked out of the nursery, calling to Heather to attend to Belinda as she went. She walked down into the kitchen. The two grown-ups were chatting to Edward, but fell silent as she entered. Edward placed himself between the two, who moved nearer to him as though in protection. Laura glanced briefly at them, removed her coat from the back of a chair and despite the rain walked out of the back door.

The rain was steady, but more of a fine drizzle now than a downpour. She needed to be away from the house, away from Edward. She wanted time and space to think clearly. At the end of the drive she hesitated, and then made for the footpath through the woods. She would certainly be alone there. If she walked round the village there would be people to be acknowledged, small-talk to make.

This was the very first time that Laura had attempted to put her thoughts into order, and it wasn't easy. She knew that Edward was different, and knew that he was influencing Belinda, but until now it had been an awareness, only vaguely definable, with few concrete facts. After four years of careful study it was time that she assembled her thoughts carefully, separating what she knew from what she guessed. One fact stood out above all else: Edward could communicate with Belinda without speech. He passed her messages, but whether by images or actual words Laura could not tell, and Belinda responded. He could also pick up thoughts from other people. He had done it to Laura. He would repeat what she was thinking, always altering the context when he realized what he had done, but it happened too frequently to be a coincidence. Apart from these abilities he generated in her a great sense of unease, which she realized might not be logical but which increased week by week.

Probably researchers in America studying the untapped potential of the human brain would be fascinated by him, but two things worried her apart from his mental powers. Firstly, he automatically tried to hide his gift. He had always known that he was different. It would have been more normal if he had expected everyone to be the same as himself and then shown signs of rage when they were not or when they failed to understand him. Secondly, he kept himself too isolated. He appeared interested only in his relationship with Belinda; his father, his nanny, they were of little account. There was no emotional balance in his life. Only he and his sister mattered. The pressure on Belinda as the years passed would be tremendous unless he could be diverted.

Out here, surrounded by damp trees and grass, she

could admit that as the months passed she was coming to dislike Edward more and more. He knew this too; she was quite certain of that. Strangely he didn't seem to mind, it was as though he quite expected it. She knew that outsiders would say she had programmed him to expect rejection. She had always been critical of him, always been anticipating trouble from him. The difference was that both she and Edward knew why. The others didn't matter, they would never understand.

In a few months he would be off to school. She knew why he was anxious to go: there would be more children there and doubtless some would be as susceptible to his peculiarity as Belinda. For a five-year-old this would be heady power indeed. She wondered if he ever looked ahead and thought about what he wanted from his life. He would always have a great advantage over other people if he continued to be able to pick up their every thought. It would enable him not only to learn, but to adapt his social behaviour accordingly, and do whatever was required of him.

The drizzle was becoming heavier now, and she began to feel cold. She knew that soon she must go back home, and face her staff. Her behaviour would be put down to 'bad nerves' again; she only hoped that no one decided to mention it to Nicholas. He was already becoming a polite stranger in their house. She found it impossible to remember how she had once felt for him; these days she only had enough energy for Edward. One day Nicholas would find someone else, a pretty, younger woman who would provide comforts that no longer interested Laura. Well, as long as he was discreet she didn't mind. It wasn't his fault that she had changed, he had been everything that she had wanted. One day, when he realized that she had been right all along, he would understand and they would become close again.

With her head down against the rain she walked back up the driveway. If there was one thing that comforted her, one thought that sustained her, it was that Belinda was normal. She could receive Edward's thoughts, but she couldn't transmit her own. She would be quite all right, if it weren't for Edward. They would be all right if it weren't for Edward. Laura suddenly stood still. It was the first time that she had realized this simple fact. If Edward weren't there then life would be normal for them all, for ever. But he was there. He would always be there. Unless . . . She shut her mind to the thought, but she was relieved to be seeing things more clearly at last. How much better she was now that her mind was no longer dulled by the drugs she had felt obliged to take from time to time. Feeling more cheerful she re-entered the house.

Laura and her mother-in-law ate alone, the children preferring fish fingers and chips in the nursery. She looked at the older woman. Ruth was well preserved for her age, and since her husband's death had slowly grown in self-confidence. She was cheerful, helpful and the children both liked her. She wished that she could talk to Ruth, ask her if she ever noticed things, but that was impossible. Nicholas would be told, and be convinced that she was becoming ill again.

'Vicky is coming tonight, did I tell you, Mother?'

'Yes, dear. Has she got a young man yet?' Without a man you were nothing in Ruth's eyes, even the wrong man was preferable to living alone.

'Not that I know of. She is too busy working I imagine.'

'Her patients won't keep her company at night.'

How amazing, thought Laura, that even a woman

101

like Ruth who had been completely dominated for all of her married life, felt that it was more important to marry than to be a good doctor. The whole world was mad. Sometimes she thought that she was the only sane person in it.

'Did you enjoy your walk, Laura?' Although she kept eating Ruth's eyes were sharp and alert.

'Not much, it was very wet. I was angry with Edward. I thought it best to walk it off.' There, that sounded normal enough surely.

'Heather said there was trouble. She couldn't quite explain what he had done though. Was he having a temper tantrum again?'

You know he wasn't, thought Laura, you're trying to trap me into a lie.

'No, Mother, it was more a case of dumb insolence. Now, I'd rather forget it if you don't mind.'

'As you like. You look a little tired, Laura. Did you sleep all right?'

'Fine, Mother, thank you.'

Ruth gave in, and the meal was finished in silence.

During the afternoon Belinda came downstairs and played with her dolls, but Edward remained upstairs and out of his mother's way. Heather stayed with him, and Laura could hear their chatter. After tea Belinda was put to bed, but Edward stayed up to see his aunt. His father arrived home first, and Laura tensed herself for some sign that Edward would complain about her to him. When Nicholas came into the dining-room for a drink he looked perfectly amiable, and so she assumed that Edward had wisely chosen to forget the matter. After all, what could he say?

'Be nice to see Vicky again,' commented Nicholas, 'she's getting very striking looking as she gets older. Have you noticed?'

'Not really. I suppose I've known her too long. I see what I expect to see, not what's there. The same as most people do.'

'Quite. I remember that I used to think her rather plain when I first met you. No one could say that about her now.'

Laura felt irritated. 'If you fancy her, why not come straight out and say so!'

'I don't fancy her, for God's sake, although if I did who could blame me. You're not much of a wife these days, are you? How long is it since there was anything between us? Two months? Three?'

'Here we go, back on the old treadmill. Marriage equals sex to you, doesn't it? How often and how well. There is more to life than that.'

'Yes, there certainly is. A normal home life. Nice, uncomplicated children. A wife who accompanies her husband to business functions and who asks after his work from time to time. The trouble is, I'm not getting any of that either!'

Laura felt her temper rising. 'Poor little boy, do you feel cheated then?'

'Too right I feel cheated. I married a beautiful, loving girl and I gain a haggard, neurotic and frigid wife. Who wouldn't feel cheated?'

'You bastard! What filthy things to say to me, and with such exquisite timing. Any minute now we've got a weekend guest arriving, and your haggard and neurotic wife has to smile in welcome and chat normally while you ogle this dynamic and incredibly striking single friend of ours.'

She was astounded at the depth of his ill feeling. He was right, which made it worse.

'If I'm suddenly such a failure you should think hard about yourself,' she flung at him. 'I'm your second wife remember! Number one failed to keep up to your demanding standards, and now number two is falling by the wayside. Could it be anything to do with you, I wonder?' Bitch, she thought, but it was the only way out.

He went very white, and his voice became quiet. 'If I'd known then what I know now,' he said slowly, 'I would never have divorced Elizabeth for you. I lost a reasonable if somewhat unintelligent wife and a perfect son when I married you. It was, upon reflection, the biggest mistake of my life.'

If he had shouted the words then she would have taken them for a spur-of-the-moment attempt to hurt her as much as she had hurt him. Spoken so softly they carried complete conviction. He had thought about this a lot, and now she knew how he really felt. We will never recover from this she realized. No matter what happens neither of us will forget the things we've said.

The sound of the doorbell was the signal for them to cease. Nicholas turned and walked out and up the stairs, leaving Laura to go and welcome Vicky. She took a deep breath and straightened her shoulders. Appearances must be kept up at all costs. She opened the door with a smile.

'Hello there. Nice to see you again!'

By the next day the rain had stopped, and Laura and Vicky went shopping together on the Saturday morning. Nicholas went off to play golf, and Heather stayed at home with the children. All in all a perfectly normal morning.

Over coffee in the small, old-world coffee shop that Laura usually frequented she took the opportunity to ask Vicky about the men in her life. She made it sound light-hearted, but after Nicholas's comments the night before she was genuinely curious. After all, they were both twenty-six and as yet Vicky had never mentioned a casual affair let alone a serious liaison.

'Actually I'm without a man at present.' Vicky tried to sound casual, but it still hurt. Adam had moved out of the flat only two days earlier, spending his last few days in England with his parents, and his absence still caused her pain.

'Anyone in mind?'

'Really Laura! You don't change. Marriage was all you ever talked about when we were at junior school. Is it as wonderful as you thought then? Or do you just want to see me suffer as well!'

'It's not quite as I thought,' said Laura slowly, 'but that isn't to say that I don't still approve of it in theory. I'm just having some trouble making it work out.'

'I'm sorry, I didn't mean to pry; it was only a joke, Laura!'

'That's all right, after all what are friends for if not to hear confidences. It isn't serious, don't worry, just a marital hiccup.' If only that were true, she thought to herself.

For some reason Vicky discovered that she didn't want to hear what was wrong between Laura and Nicholas. She didn't know why, but she simply preferred not to know. To divert her friend she plunged back into her own emotional life.

'At least you've got your man, Laura. Mine slipped softly away last week and won't be back. No rows, no third party, it just ran out of reasons to keep going. Perhaps that's what's wrong with live-in relationships; once the glitter wears off there's no reason to work for anything deeper or more lasting. It's off to start again, with a fresh face and all the emotional 'high' of a new affair.'

Laura studied her friend. 'You really cared for him?'

'Yes, I did. I cared too much, because I always knew that it was only temporary; he said so at the beginning, and yet I allowed it to rule my life. I've wasted time, Laura, so I should be grateful that he's gone and I can get on with my work. I suppose I am grateful, but it still hurts like hell.'

'What was he like?'

'He was young, intelligent and rather hard. An elusive sort of a man, a challenge to me in a way.'

'Good looking?'

'Not really. Unusual perhaps; not a man you'd forget easily.'

'A doctor?'

'He was connected with medicine.'

Vicky became evasive, she didn't want Laura to know it had been Edward's paediatrician.

'Oh well, some day . . .'

'Perhaps. I don't think like that though, Laura. Apart from this man there's never been anyone special for me, and there might not be again, but there's certainly plenty for me to do and now I intend to do it.'

'Good for you. I hope you do well.' Laura meant it, Vicky deserved to succeed.

They are both pleasantly relaxed when they arrived back at the house, and quite unprepared for the uproar that awaited them. Belinda was screaming her head off, Edward was hurling every toy that he could lay his hands on round the hall, and Heather was red in the face and desperately shouting for some sort of order.

'What on earth is going on?' demanded Laura. Vicky stood as unobtrusively as possible in the background.

All three suddenly stood silently, the two children

glancing at each other, Heather looking in a shame-faced manner at Laura.

'I'm so sorry, Mrs Wells, but they both got a little out of hand.'

'That appears to be an understatement. Precisely what has happened?'

Edward began to move slowly towards the kitchen.

'Stay where you are,' said Laura sharply.

'It began with Edward. He kept playing up after you'd gone to town, cheeking me and so on.' Heather paused.

'Go on,' said Laura.

'Well, I shut him in his bedroom, only for fifteen minutes, but he took no notice of anything I said so it seemed the best answer. Then I took Belinda downstairs with me and she was playing with her soft toys.' A nod of Heather's head indicated these same toys, now lying strewn around the hall floor. 'After a few minutes Belinda started crying, and saying that she didn't want to.'

'Want to what?'

'That's what I couldn't make, out Madam. I kept asking her, I thought she wanted a different game or something, but she just kept shaking her head and crying that she couldn't do it. Then she wanted Edward to be let out to play with her. I know it was wrong, but I gave in. She was really distressed and I know how well they play together. I went up to get him, and he was being perfectly well behaved. I could hear him sort of singing to himself in his room.'

'Singing, or humming?' interjected Laura.

'Well, I'm not sure, Madam. Anyway, I told him he could come out and join us in the living-room, and he tore past me and down the stairs in seconds. I heard Belinda start to scream and I ran down after him. I

107

found him like this. Throwing all her toys round the hall, and shouting at her that she was stupid and disobedient. I didn't have a chance to find out what had happened, what with Belinda crying and Edward being in such a rage. Then you came home. I'm very sorry. It's never happened before.'

'Never mind,' said Laura, 'I'm sure you did your best. I think it's time Edward was at school really. Both of you children are to come into the living-room with me while Heather goes upstairs and has a quiet rest.'

Heather retreated with obvious relief, and Victoria saw how Belinda kept glancing uncertainly at her brother as they followed their mother into the living-room.

'Right then, what was it all about? Edward, why were you throwing your sister's toys round the hall?' Edward's face was red with temper, his mouth a thin line.

'Because she wouldn't do as I said, because she's stupid, she's a great big baby, a silly fat pig, a . . .'

'That will do, thank you. What were you asking her to do?'

Silence.

'I repeat, what were you asking her to do?'

'Let me play with her.'

'I see. Belinda, why wouldn't you let him play with you?'

Belinda's face bore an expression of puzzlement and distress. 'Play, Edward play with me. Nanny let him out to play.'

'Then why wouldn't you let him?'

The big blue eyes swivelled in desperation towards Edward again, but he was staring stonily ahead and refused to meet her gaze. Belinda took refuge in noisy tears.

'I want my Grandma!'

Laura ignored her and caught hold of Edward by the arm. 'You're lying aren't you? You were asking her to do something while you were in your room and she refused. Hasn't that ever happened before? Did it annoy you to find you weren't all powerful? She does have a mind of her own you know, and she's getting old enough to realize it.' He glared at her; the intensity of his rage seemed to strike her in the face, and she jerked her head away from him without releasing her grip on his arm. 'I'm right, aren't I? Admit it!'

His eyes became darker and darker, they no longer looked brown they were almost jet black, the pupils were no longer visible. It was like looking to two black holes in a tiny face. He was rigid beneath her grip, trembling with rage, and she felt the first stirring of fear. Before she could analyse it she was struck by the most appalling pain in her right temple, it lanced through her head and behind her eye and it was like a red hot poker stabbing into her brain. She gave a startled cry and released Edward's arm.

Her small cry was drowned by the sudden outburst of sobbing that Edward's release engendered. He was howling and screaming that Mummy had hurt his arm. Dimly, through the pain, she was aware of Vicky coming into the room and leading both the children out. The pain continued to throb mercilessly, and she held her hands to her temples. She heard Vicky asking if she wanted any pills, and managed to ask for some pain killers. Then a glass was pushed into her hand and she swallowed down two Paracetamol, hoping against hope that they would work. She didn't think that it would be possible to live with such pain for very long.

It did not abate. She rocked to and fro in her agony, wanting to dash her head against the wall in an effort to blot out the terrible sensation. She could hear herself moaning, but was powerless to stop. It was beyond endurance, she would go mad. She lost all sense of place and time, there was only the pain engulfing her. Then, suddenly, it was gone. She sat immobile, her hands still to her temples as she waited for it to attack again, but it didn't. She cautiously sat more upright and opened her eyes. No pain. In her relief she felt like crying.

As she slowly became aware of things again she saw Vicky sitting opposite her, her face full of concern.

'Is it better now, Laura?'

'Yes,' she said nervously, 'it seems to have gone.'

'You never told me you suffered from migraine.'

'Migraine? I don't.'

'Well you do now. Believe me, I know a bad attack of migraine when I see one.'

'Vicky, it was unimaginable pain. I wanted to hit my head against the wall to try and knock the pain out.'

'I know; that's what sufferers often say. Probably the scene with the children brought it on, but you should see your doctor about it.'

It was wonderful, thought Laura, how the doctors could always come up with the wrong answers. Without them to help him Edward would find life much more difficult. She remembered his eyes as they bored into her head, and she automatically tensed. He had inflicted that pain upon her, without any compunction at all. His own mother. She shivered.

'You should go upstairs and lie down,' said Vicky kindly. 'Come on, I'll tell Nicholas when he gets back.'

Laura let herself be led to bed, and lay down gratefully in the darkened room. Peace at last. She was exhausted by shock and pain and quickly slept.

In Edward's bedroom he sat silently as his aunt and his nanny examined his bruised arm. The marks of his mother's fingers were etched plainly along the top of his forearm, the marks already beginning to discolour. Heather swabbed them with Witch Hazel and chatted cheerfully about what a brave boy he was. When she had finished he raised soft brown eyes to his aunt, their expression one of bewilderment tinged with fear. It tore at Vicky's heart to see him so, and she leant down and hugged him tightly. As she left him to rest she heard him humming gently in an effort to comfort himself.

All the way home Nicholas had been aware of how much he was looking forward to seeing Vicky. Every time that she stayed with them he became more and more aware of her as a woman; he should have felt guilty, he supposed, but he didn't. It wasn't as though anything was going to come of it, he was only looking and imagining. Apart from his own marital situation there was the fact that Vicky was quite indifferent to him except as her best friend's husband. He could tell that. So, she provided a comforting piece of daydreaming, and a pleasant companion for a few days. At least it meant that he was looking forward to the weekend.

Surprisingly there was no sign of Laura to greet him, something that she usually did when they had visitors, although at no other time. A blatant piece of propaganda to demonstrate their supposedly solid marriage. He hung up his coat, and was then engulfed by Belinda as she hugged his knees and demanded loves and kisses. He put her on his shoulders and went searching for the others.

He found Vicky and Edward playing snap in the living-room. Edward looked subdued, but it could have been concentration. He hated to lose at any game.

'Hello there! All right, Vicky?' She looked up and

smiled, and he was surprised to feel his stomach give a lurch. Surely he wasn't going to develop an adolescent-type crush on her after all these years? It was more likely the simple lack of normal female companionship that was telling on his nerves, he thought, but he must keep a watch on himself. His life was complicated enough at present.

'Fine thanks. Laura has a bad headache, so I suggested she had a lie down. I expect that she'll get up after the children are in bed.'

He frowned. 'I'm sorry you've had to look after these two. It isn't like Laura to get bad heads.' His tone indicated that she got everything else and bad heads on top was rather too much.

Vicky waited until Edward had won convincingly before she stood up.

'I wasn't sure what to do about a meal. Your mother said that there was a casserole prepared, but I had no idea of timing.'

'Don't worry, we can always rustle up some food later. Have the children had theirs?'

'Yes, we had jelly.' Belinda was still clutching him round the head, and he swung her to the ground.

'Fine. Well, off to Heather for your supper drinks and then auntie and I will put you to bed. How's that?'

'Yes, I want hot milk.'

'How about you, Edward? You haven't even said hello yet.'

Edward, busy putting the cards back in the box, glanced up.

'Hello!'

'Are you feeling all right?'

'Yes. My arm still hurts me.'

Nicholas frowned. 'Your arm? Did you have a fall?'

'No, Mummy pinched me.'

'Pinched you?' He could hardly believe it, but Edward looked serious enough.

'I'll explain later,' put in Vicky quickly. 'Off you go, Edward darling. We'll be up soon.' He gave her an impulsive cuddle before running after Belinda.

Nicholas watched him go. 'I've never seen him do that before. He isn't usually affectionate.'

'I'm a novelty, that's all.'

'What happened to his arm?'

Briefly, and playing it down as much as possible, Vicky told him of the children's tantrum and Laura's annoyance.

'I don't quite follow,' said Nicholas. 'Why did she grab Edward if it was Bee who wouldn't let him play?'

'I'm not sure, but as she had the beginning of this migraine attack she probably wasn't thinking too well and he was the one throwing the toys around.'

'I'll go and look in on her while the children have their drinks. Perhaps you and mother would like something stronger than hot milk while I'm gone?'

Vicky smiled. 'A good idea. Call me when the children are ready.'

In their bedroom Laura lay sound asleep, her right hand resting beneath her right cheek. She looked young and more vulnerable than she had for a long time. He coughed gently, and she stirred but then her breathing resumed its slow, even rhythm. Nicholas changed into a sweater and slacks as quietly as possible and went along to the nursery. Vicky was already there, reading one of the Mr Men books to Belinda. It made a pleasant domestic scene. Laura never played much of a part in their bedtime routine, preferring to leave it to Heather.

At 8 o'clock Laura was still sleeping, and so the three adults ate cold chicken and salad followed by fresh

113

fruit. The casserole was left for the following day. 'It will save Laura some work,' said Vicky.

'She isn't exactly over-burdened, you know. She does have plenty of help.'

Vicky flushed. 'I'm sorry, I didn't mean it that way. It's just that she did look very unwell this afternoon and I thought that she wouldn't feel up to doing much.'

Nicholas sighed. 'No, I'm sorry; I was being ridiculously touchy. It's just depressing to find that Laura isn't well again.'

'It's only migraine.'

'Is it?' Nicholas looked questioningly at Vicky. 'Is it? Or is it a symptom of another period of nerves and depression? Sometimes I wonder if she's ever going to recover completely.'

Vicky didn't answer. She wondered as much herself, and was deeply disturbed by the marks on Edward's arm. Laura certainly needed help again, but from whom? Doctors? Child care specialists? Impossible to tell from a few brief hours in the house.

After the 10 o'clock news Ruth went up to her room, leaving the other two alone together. Nicholas felt that Vicky must be aware of the tension in the air, caused by his own growing attraction for this calm, dependable woman. If she was she gave no sign of it. Her voice was as level and controlled as ever.

'Have you checked on Laura since dinner? She might be wanting something.'

He felt guilty. 'Of course, I'll go up now.'

Laura was awake, and had been for nearly an hour. She was quite content to remain in bed, trying to forget the intensity of the pain in her head. She felt quite well again, merely tired.

'I'm sorry you've been unwell,' said Nicholas stiffly. 'Vicky tells me it was a migraine attack.'

'That's her opinion, yes.'

'Do you have a better one?'

A brief smile crossed Laura's face. 'I'm not a doctor, am I. I only had the pain!'

'There's no need to be sarcastic. Vicky's done a marvellous job coping while you slept up here.'

'Yes, she's amazingly clever. Cooks, child minds, cures all ills and soothes harassed husbands; they should market her!'

Husband and wife glared at each other. Laura turned her head away first.

'Go back down, Nicholas, you've done your duty.'

'There's nothing you want then?'

'Nothing thank you.'

The door closed quietly behind him. We dislike each other now, she thought to herself, we can't even be tolerant any more. Strangely it didn't seem to matter at all. Far more important to her was the fact that she was now sure that Edward had the ability to cause physical pain when he was annoyed. Incredible pain, beyond imagination. Until today she had, despite his gifts and intelligence, felt superior to him because she was an adult. Now, after her experience downstairs, she felt afraid of him. She felt afraid, and he must know it. It would make things very difficult from now on.

The rest of Vicky's stay was not as enjoyable as usual for any of the adults. Nicholas, aware now of his rapidly growing affection for her, was unusually withdrawn and busied himself with the children and the garden. Laura, furious that her friend had witnessed a scene that to an outsider would not reflect particularly well upon her own behaviour, was stiff and awkward. She was anxious too lest Vicky think in terms of neurosis and breakdowns, so she spent most of the time being brisk and sensible, which was a tremendous effort and probably fooled no one.

Edward and Belinda too were different. It could have been that they were affected by the strained atmosphere, or it could have been the result of Laura's anger on the Friday, but whatever the cause they retreated into themselves. They spent most of the time when they were not with their father upstairs in the nursery playing games of make-believe. At night-time they were both restless, and Belinda began humming in her sleep again. This was a habit that had left her after her second birthday. It appeared that stress brought it back.

As a result everyone in the house was relieved after Sunday tea when Vicky made an earlier start back to London than usual.

'When I next see you I shall be taking up my partnership,' she reminded them as she left. 'Just think, I shall only be six miles away and you'll all be able to come and visit *me* for a change.'

'Lovely!' Laura's tone was cool.

'We look forward to it.' Nicholas meant it, meant it rather too much.

'Goodbye,' chorused the children.

The old Ford moved sedately down the drive and out of sight.

'I like Auntie!'

'I know you do, old chap; she's good fun isn't she?'

'She likes me!'

'And me!' Belinda didn't want to be left out.

'She likes you both, and so do we,' said Nicholas firmly. Laura turned and went back into the house. Belinda trotted after her. Edward's eyes met his father's, and they were old beyond their years.

'Mummy likes Bee best, Auntie likes me, and you like both of us.'

'Now just a minute, Edward.'

'But,' continued Edward remorselessly, 'you don't like Mummy.'

Before Nicholas could say another word Edward had run into the house, making loud siren noises as he went. Nicholas followed slowly. There were times when his son's perspicacity troubled him as much as it did Laura. If only she were more rational about things he would discuss it with her; as it was he had to keep his worries to himself. He did find it unnerving the way in which the boy could pick up people's emotions and then proceed to confront them with his own interpretation. It seemed unnatural for a child not yet of school age.

When he goes to school, Nicholas thought, and mixes more with others his own age he will automatically become more outgoing, more physical; he won't spend so much time analysing people to himself. School will be good for him. Briefly he hoped that the school was prepared for Edward.

That night, in her London flat, Vicky was surprised to receive a telephone call from Adam.

'I rang to say cheerio, and to see how you enjoyed your weekend of course.'

'That's kind of you, Adam. It was pleasant enough. At least, no, it wasn't really.' She then told him about it all. There was a long silence from his end.

'You don't care for Laura much any more, do you?'

She was surprised. 'What a funny thing to say. I fail to see its relevance, even if it's true.'

'Oh, it's relevant all right. You see, I can tell that you're blaming the entire business on Laura. You refuse to even consider that your godson might be rather a handful, to put it mildly.'

She was annoyed, and partly because she knew that she no longer did care for Laura very much.

'You approve of parents assaulting their children then do you?'

His laughter came clearly over the 'phone. 'A few bruises you said. Make up your mind!'

'You know where that sort of thing can lead; you've seen enough of it.'

'Vicky, why won't you even admit that Edward is very headstrong? What's so special about him? Tell me, I genuinely want to know.'

'Because he's perfect! He's the most beautiful, intelligent child I've ever seen in my life! I don't understand why you can't see it.'

Adam's voice lost its bantering note. 'I see. Look, as soon as I get back I'll take another look at him. Maybe you were right, and I didn't stay objective enough. Until then, will you keep me in touch with what goes on there. How he gets on at school and so forth. You've got my address in the States haven't you?'

'Yes. Why are you suddenly so interested?'

'I don't know, Vicky. You will do it for me though?'

'Of course. Adam, I miss you.'

'I miss you too. Surprising isn't it! Take care of yourself, Vicky, and good luck with all the measles and chickenpox. Cheers!'

'Cheers, Adam!' There was more that she wanted to say, but he disliked emotional displays and she knew that she was lucky he had called at all.

That night her dreams were confused. She was in a house, cooking for a man. She thought that it was Adam. She expected Adam to come in the front door at any moment. When a key turned in the lock and she ran to greet him he turned into Nicholas, and Nicholas was carrying Edward in his arms. In her dream she was overwhelmed by happiness at the sight of them both. It was as though secretly she had wanted it to be them all

118

the time. When she awoke she still felt happy, although the memory of the dream had faded, and she put it down to the fine weather and the call from Adam the previous night.

In the next three months Laura suffered three more debilitating attacks of headaches, and every one followed some clash of wills with Edward. Just before Christmas week she reluctantly went to Dr Anderson and recited her symptoms. She did not tell him when the attacks occurred, only how they felt.

'Any pattern? When you're off colour each month, or after eating cheese for example?'

'No. They're usually after an argument with the children.'

'Tension headaches,' he said as he scribbled on the pad. 'Any history of migraine in the family?'

'No.'

'Do you get visual disturbances?'

'Not really. It's as though I'm looking down a long dark tunnel when it begins, but after that nothing at all.'

'Try these, and come back again if they don't work. You take one three times a day for the next month. If they do work, ring up for a repeat prescription and come back after two months. Thank you.'

She took the tablets for ten days, but they made her so dozy, and there was a lot to do over the holiday period, that she then hid them away. After all, she knew what caused the pain, and knew too that no tablets could help her. She had only gone to the doctor to satisfy Nicholas.

On January 4 Edward proudly started school. Wearing the smart blue-and-grey uniform that he had coveted for the past year he left in the morning with his mother without a backward glance at Belinda who was standing in the middle of the hallway looking lost and tearful. Laura took him in to the cloakroom, and watched as he carefully changed into his indoor shoes and hung up his heavy coat. All around them small boys were either clinging to their mother's coats or knuckling their eyes to rub away the tears. Not Edward; standing tall he walked by Laura's side into his classroom and kissed her briefly on her cheek when she bent down to him.

'Be a good boy,' she whispered. 'I'll see you this afternoon.'

'I know that; goodbye Mummy.'

She walked away, the first mother to leave. She glanced back once, and saw that Edward was sitting quite still with his head on one side, listening to all the sounds around him.

Back home Belinda refused to be consoled. 'I want Edward. I want to go to school. I want milk and biscuits.'

'Heather, take her out for a walk or something; I'm getting tired of her whining.'

'Yes, Mrs Wells. Come along, Bee; let's go to the village for some sweets.'

Peace at last, thought Laura, and she sat down in her favourite easy chair in the living-room. It was absolute bliss to realize that Edward wasn't even in the house, and was incapable of causing any trouble until mid-afternoon. Feeling as though a heavy weight had been lifted from her shoulders she made herself a cup of coffee and telephoned her own mother.

Contact between them was rare. Since her marriage to Nicholas Laura had seen her mother twice, once when Edward was born, and once when Belinda was three weeks old. Presents always arrived on time for birthdays, and Christmas presents were lavish and popular, but no form of personal relationships had grown up even with the children. They didn't think of her as their grandmother, merely as a distant adult who dispensed gifts. Laura didn't mind very much. In fact, she would probably have resented it if her mother had decided to play the doting grandmother. After all, she hadn't troubled to play the devoted mother, and that still hurt Laura. However, she wanted to tell her mother that Edward was at school, if only to emphasize the passing of time to a woman who seemed from outward appearances to defy the years with great skill. 'Laura? What a surprise! Is there anything wrong?'

'Does there have to be if I telephone you?'

Her mother's laugh tinkled over the phone. 'Darling, how prickly you are still!'

'I only rang to let you know that Edward started school today.'

'Really! I can't believe it. It doesn't seem five years since he was born. Did he go off all right?'

'Fine thank you, Mother. He's been looking forward to it for ages.'

'I'll send him a pencil case or something. Would he like that, dear?'

'He'd love it I know, but that wasn't why I rang.'

'Of course not, darling. How are you keeping? Quite well now?'

'I'm fine, Mother, thank you.'

'Headaches better?'

A short pause. 'How did you know about them?' demanded Laura sharply.

'I saw Nicholas on the train one day; he told me.'

121

'How peculiar that he never told me about it. They're fine now anyway.'

'That's good. Try not to be so intense about things, Laura: you always were, even as a little girl. I must go now, darling. Love to everyone.'

Laura replaced the receiver. She was annoyed to think that Nicholas had spoken to her mother without telling her. He knew how she hated her mother to be involved in her life, and as far as she knew he had always respected her feelings until now. Now of course it was different. She and Nicholas no longer functioned as a pair, merely as two adults beneath the same roof, and she sometimes wondered how long even that would continue. Until Bee was at school perhaps? It appeared to her that Belinda was the only good thing that was going to come out of this marriage. One pretty, obedient daughter to love and cherish. Providing that Edward wasn't allowed to corrupt her.

For the first half of the spring term life was pleasant again for Laura. Edward was too busy adjusting to school life to cause any trouble at home, and Belinda quickly accepted the weeks and waited patiently for the weekends. Heather told Laura that the little girl was making better progress now that her brother was at school.

'She speaks much better, Mrs Wells, and she seems to be learning to read. She knows some of her letters as well. It's amazing the change in her.'

'How nice,' smiled Laura. She knew why. Edward was teaching her, but whether in the week or at weekends she did not know.

At the end of the first week of the second half of term Edward's class teacher asked Laura to make an appointment to see her when convenient. Anxious to find out what had happened Laura went along the very

122

next morning. Miss Fletcher was in her mid-thirties, smart and obviously a caring teacher. She was also observant.

'We were so pleased with Edward, right from the start, Mrs Wells. He settled in with no trouble, and he learns very quickly.'

'That's good.' Laura attempted a smile. 'What is the trouble then?'

'It's difficult to say exactly, but he seems to be an unsettling influence on the other children.'

'He's disruptive in class?'

'Not at all, Mrs Wells, he's very quiet. In fact, it's always the other boys who cause the trouble. No, the point is that every one of them says the same thing when sent to the head teacher; namely, that Edward told them to do it.'

Laura clenched her hands tightly in her lap. 'Have you ever seen him egging these boys on? Overheard him inciting them?' Her tone was as scornful as she could manage.

'No, I have to admit that I haven't. However, I fail to see why all of the children should tell the same lie at separate times and without the security of others to support their claim. I think that Edward is clever enough not to let me see him.'

'It's all pretty vague, isn't it? What do you want me to do?'

'Mrs Wells, Edward is a very bright boy and he may be bored. Because of this he's causing trouble for his own amusement. It doesn't affect his class performance, but it does affect the other boys. I'd like you to speak to him. Stress the importance of discipline at school. We're only asking for your support. He must understand that school is no place for these sort of games.'

'In other words, you can't keep him occupied but you want me to tell him to sit quietly when he's bored?'

'He does sit quietly.'

'Then precisely what do I say?'

'You're his mother, I leave that to you.'

'Miss Fletcher, do you truly believe that Edward is behind every piece of childish mischief that takes place in your classroom?'

'Not all, but most. One child told me that Edward made him get his brains mixed up, which showed that he knew what he was doing was wrong but couldn't resist Edward's personality. Believe me, this has become quite a difficult problem. If something isn't done we will have to think seriously about what to do with Edward.'

'I see. Well, nebulous as your complaint appears to be I will certainly speak to my son and to my husband. Perhaps you would be kind enough to let me know if matters improve?'

Miss Fletcher rose to her feet. 'I will indeed, Mrs Wells. The headmistress is also being kept informed.'

Outside, in the safety of her own car, Laura sat and lit a cigarette with trembling fingers. Getting a child's brains mixed up sounded a clear warning bell. Edward was playing around with his schoolfriends, seeing how many of them he could influence. Poor Miss Fletcher, if she only knew that she would never catch him talking. He had not need to talk. She wondered where she went from here. Should she face Edward squarely with it, as though his mental telepathy was an accepted fact between them? Perhaps that would be best.

When she took him home that afternoon they went straight into the living-room, instead of up to the nursery and Belinda.

'I saw Miss Fletcher today, Edward.'

He slipped his satchel off his back. 'I know, I saw her with you.'

'She told me that you were telling your friends to be naughty in class. Is it true?'

'No. If I did, she could put me in the corner for talking.'

'One of the children said you got his brains mixed up.'

Edward frowned. 'What does that mean?'

'What?'

'How could I mix his brains up. I'm not a doctor.'

'Don't change the subject, please. How you do it is not the most important issue. The fact is, if you don't stop they will ask us to take you away from your school. They can do that you know. We won't be given a choice. If you like the school and the children then you'd better stop playing games when you should be working.'

Edward stared at his mother. 'Do you understand, Edward?'

'Yes.'

'You'll be good?'

'Yes.'

'Fine. You can go up to Belinda now.'

God, how I hate him, she thought. So self-contained, so superior to the rest of us. 'Run along,' she added.

'Miss Fletcher doesn't like me.'

'She would, if you were good.'

'She wouldn't, I can tell.'

'Not everyone in life will like you, Edward; that's a fact we all have to face.'

Edward went red. 'I know that, I'm not a baby.'

'Fine, now will you please run along.'

'Won't Miss Fletcher ever like me?'

'Probably not.'

'Poor Miss Fletcher!' He ran out. A typically egotistical Edward remark, thought Laura to herself.

Nicholas had been away on business, and it was nearly

a week later before she had a chance to tell him about the conversation at the school.

'Sounds to me as though she's using Edward as a scapegoat,' remarked Nicholas.

'Well, I haven't heard any more, so perhaps Edward took note of my warning.'

That evening Nicholas took Edward on one side. 'How's school, old chap?'

'Great, Dad! I'm on my third reading book.'

'Miss Fletcher all right?'

'She's poorly; we've got a new teacher until she's better. She's called Mrs Ryan, and she's very nice.'

Finding the conversation of little significance Nicholas failed to relate it to Laura, who would have known at once the relevance of it.

Edward never mentioned Mrs Ryan to his mother, and it was only when school broke up at Easter that she saw the new teacher.

'Where's Miss Fletcher, Edward?'

'She's gone. We have Mrs Ryan now.'

'Gone; gone where?'

He shrugged. 'I don't know. She's poorly. Mrs Ryan is much nicer.'

Laura asked another mother.

'Haven't you heard? It's very sad. The poor woman has multiple sclerosis. She won't be able to teach again.'

White-faced, Laura hustled Edward into his blazer and out into the car. She could scarcely bear to look at her son. When she managed to speak her voice was high with anger. 'You did it, didn't you? You made Miss Fletcher poorly.'

For a long time Edward did not reply, and she glanced into her mirror. He was sitting in the middle of the back seat, a look of intense concentration upon his features. He moved forward, so that his breath tickled the back of her neck.

126

'Is your head all right, Mummy?' Such a tender enquiry, and as he spoke she felt the first stab of pain.

It remained manageable until they were safely back home. Once she was indoors it swiftly became the worst attack that she had ever endured. She was sick and ill in the bathroom, and lost her sight entirely. She sat on the edge of her bed and prayed for help. She knew that she could no longer manage alone. After a couple of hours the pain subsided. Edward and Belinda had gone out to some friends for tea, which had probably ensured her ultimate relief. On wobbling legs she reached the telephone and called Vicky, asking if it would be possible for her to go and see Dr Castle on her own. He was the only other person who had seemed to recognize that Edward was different, and she intended to tell him everything.

'I should think so. He's been abroad, but he ought to be back now.' Secretly Vicky felt guilty about not bothering to write to Adam. Under the circumstances, though, it would have been difficult, just as it was difficult to talk normally to Laura. Laura was too distraught to notice any nuance of hesitation in her friend's voice.

'What address?'

'Care of the hospital. Here, I'll read it out to you.'

Laura didn't bother to mention a weekend with them. She knew that Vicky was busy these days and besides her friend had changed since she had moved nearer to them.

Immediately after Laura had made the call she went downstairs and into the dining-room. There, despite the heavy lethargy that always followed the head pain, she sat down and wrote her letter. Not until it was safely stamped and sealed up did she give in to the overwhelming tiredness and go up to bed. She was fast asleep when Heather and the children came home, and

127

she remained so until the next moring. Nicholas was in town until the following day, and would not know that she had been unwell. She did not want him told, and felt quite certain that neither of the children would bother. As long as Heather kept quiet her secret was safe. Heather did, and by the weekend Laura felt much better, and her letter was on its way.

On the first Tuesday in May Laura found herself sitting nervously outside the paediatrician's clinic door, her fingers closely entwined. She felt sick, and the palms of her hands were moist. He was her only hope, and she was anxious to hold his attention, force him to believe her. It was the fear of failure that was causing her nerves.

Adam checked his notes and then asked the nurse to call Laura in. He had been perturbed by the letter she had sent him. Its abrupt tone hinted at someone under extreme stress, and yet Vicky had been quite offhand when he had called her to discuss Edward shortly after his return to England. As a result he hadn't hurried the next appointment for the boy, which he admitted now might have been a mistake.

'Well then, Mrs Wells,' he attempted to sound soothing and reassuring, 'what seems to be the trouble?'

She looked into the cool grey eyes. Nothing about him suggested tolerance. He was the last person that she would have chosen as an ally, yet she had no choice. She cleared her throat.

'It's going to sound very peculiar I'm afraid.'

'I won't interrupt. You tell me in your own time.'

'It began soon after he was born . . .'

Forty minutes later she finished speaking. Adam's

eyes had never left her taut, anxious face. He had noted every hesitation, had admired the way in which she had indicated that other people felt she was the one who was ill, offering him the same way out if he wished to take it. He didn't. Even allowing for some exaggeration he felt certain that Edward could, and did, have extraordinary powers. Whether this was achieved by sheer force of intelligence and personality, or whether he really could transfer his thoughts and read people's minds he didn't know. However it was achieved he wanted to help this woman who had struggled along alone for so long.

She was watching him anxiously now, waiting for his reply.

'I think you're right, Mrs Wells,' he said evenly, 'there would appear to be a problem. Now we must decide what we are going to do about it.'

It was only then, when she knew that at last she would have help, that she began to cry. Adam left her alone until the worst of the tension had drained from her.

'You must try and keep calm from now on. We don't want Edward picking up any strong emotions from you. When he comes to me it must be perfectly normal, no hint that we have seen each other in between. Do you think you can manage that?'

No, thought Laura, because I can't guard my mind day and night from him. 'I'll do my best,' she said aloud.

'Excellent. Two weeks from today then, at 11 am. In the meantime I'll look up one or two papers on ESP. That might be relevant in this case don't you think?'

Laura frowned. 'Extra sensory perception,' he explained.

'Yes, but I hadn't thought . . . I suppose it could be something like that.'

Adam stood up and escorted her to the door. 'I saw a lot of this type of research going on in the States; its the latest craze in Russia too I gather.'

'He isn't unique then?'

'We're all unique', he reminded her gently. 'Get plenty of rest and try not to worry too much.' Laura held out her hand.

'I'm very grateful to you, Dr Castle. You'll never know how lonely I felt until today.'

We're all lonely too, he wanted to tell her, but the moment passed.

After she had gone he sat thinking for a long time. There had been something about her that had aroused his compassion instead of his normal contempt for weeping women. He hoped that he really would be able to help her. She seemed to have been let down rather a lot by family and friends. He wondered why Vicky hadn't noticed that thing was going badly. It could only be because she was so busy in her new job. He hoped she was happy these days.

A couple of weeks later, after having read most of the available work on ESP and telepathy, Adam arranged to go and visit Vicky at her cottage in Horsham. He arrived late on a Friday night, bearing a bottle of good red wine and a bunch of flowers. He wanted her in a as co-operative a mood as possible, and remembered of old how much store she set by small tokens of affection. He was looking forward to seeing her again; they had always found plenty to talk about and should have a fund of new experiences to exchange. He also looked forward to sharing her bed. There had been a few women in the past eight months, but nothing regular and he always found casual sex far less satisfying than when hand in hand with a relationship of reasonable duration. He and Vicky had been comfortable together in and out of bed. There was no reason at all why the weekend should not prove thoroughly satisfying for them both.

His first thought when she opened the door to him was that she had changed considerably. Her face was thinner, she had lost the bounce that had characterized her. He smiled warmly.

'Here I am then, home from the seas!'

'You've been home some considerable time,' she commented sharply. 'I half-expected to hear from you sooner.'

'You could have called me.'

'I wasn't that desperate.'

Adam put his arm round her shoulders and kissed her on the top of her head. 'You don't sound too pleased to see me!'

'Of course I am. I'm always pleased to see an old friend.'

While Adam sat in the small living-room he wondered what was the matter with Vicky. She sounded aggressive, yet he could think of no reason for it. They had parted on good terms, and had spoken of continuing to see each other from time to time. He should have written, he supposed, but he had been extremely busy in the States and was a hopeless letter writer at the best of times. He shrugged to himself. Doubtless she was finding her new job hard work; she would settle down after a few hours and a couple of glasses of wine.

Certainly by the time they had eaten, and drunk the wine, she was softer; her voice had lost the strident note that had jarred him on arrival. Over the coffee he encouraged her to talk about her work. As he had suspected she was rushed off her feet, and finding it hard

131

to cope with the difficult patients of which every practice had its fair share. Despite that she assured Adam she was happy.

'I have time to see my patients as human beings, not just a number on the clinic sheet. It makes a pleasant change.'

'Well, if it's what you want then, fine. Personally I couldn't stand it.'

Vicky looked at him. 'How about you? Did you learn a lot in the States?'

'Quite a lot. I enjoyed the time, but I'm glad to be home again. American children are just as odious as I imagined, possibly more so!'

'How are your British ones since you got back?'

This gave him his opportunity to mention the true reason for his visit. 'I've been busy. I will be seeing your godson again soon.'

Vicky raised her eyebrows. 'Really? I thought he was fine these days?'

'It's routine, a final checkup now that he's at school. Is he settling in there all right, do you know?' He made the enquiry as casual as possible; he didn't intend to tell Vicky about his meeting with Laura.

Vicky stood up. 'More coffee?'

'Fine. Do you know?'

She turned back to him. 'Know? Know what?'

'About Edward, that's who I was speaking of, if you remember.'

She walked briskly to the kitchen. 'How would I know? I haven't heard anything to the contrary, but then I don't see that much of them these days.'

Adam was surprised. 'Really? I imagined that now you lived nearer . . .'

'I'm too busy,' she called from the kitchen, 'and I find Laura and her neurosis too much to cope with when I'm meant to be off-duty.'

Adam decided not to pursue the discussion. There was a peevish note in Vicky's voice that indicated it wasn't a popular subject. He must wait, and raise the matter again at a later time.

Shortly before midnight Vicky yawned, and Adam stretched lazily.

'I'm a bit tired too. Shall we turn in?'

A look of surprise crossed her features, but she agreed and together they went up the small staircase to the one bedroom at the top of the stairs. He washed and cleaned his teeth in the adjoining bathroom, and by the time he returned to the bedroom Vicky was ensconced in a high-necked Edwardian-style nightdress. He quickly got into bed, and watched her with interest.

She pottered around in front of the dressing-table for a time, brushing her hair and creaming her face. He reflected that she was certainly in no hurry to join him. At last, unable to think of anything else to do, she climbed into her side of the bed. He pulled her close to him and kissed her, gently at first but with growing passion. Whilst she did not draw away or attempt to stop him there was none of the enthusiasm or urgency that had once characterized their sex life together. When it was over and Adam lit his customary cigarette Vicky turned over on her side and prepared for sleep.

'I'm sorry,' he said slowly. 'You didn't seem to get much out of that.'

'I'm fine.' Her voice was brisk.

'You didn't seem fine.' Let it go, he urged himself, but was unable to stop. 'In fact it appeared to be something of a bore for you.'

Vicky sighed, and pulled the blankets up round her head. 'Not a bore, Adam, just not what I'd expected. It was pleasant though.'

'Pleasant! Christ, talk about damning with faint praise!'

'What do you want me to say? Wow, it was great! You were fantastic!'

'Just drop it will you? Obviously it was a mistake. One should never try to go back. I had just assumed that it would be as good as ever.'

'I've changed, Adam, I'm not the same any more. Now please, can we go to sleep?'

Saturday was an awkward day. Both of them were trying to ignore the previous night, and neither of them knew how to behave from now on. They went shopping, and in the afternoon saw a film in Crawley. After that they ate out, not arriving back at the cottage until after 9 pm. Over large brandies they discussed the film until every detail of it had been dissected and there was nothing left to say.

Finally Adam took the initiative. 'Look, shall I sleep on the settee tonight? Would that suit you better?'

'Would you mind, Adam? I know I should have explained when we arranged this visit, but at the time I wasn't sure how things were going to work out for me and I didn't want to put you off coming. I really am glad to see you; it's just that I'm involved with someone else.'

In a way he was relieved. It removed all blame from his shoulders. 'I rather guessed that. What does he think about me being here for the weekend?'

Vicky flushed, twisting the brandy glass round in her hands. 'There isn't a lot he can say; he's married.'

There was a long silence while Adam digested the remark. 'I see. Does he plan on getting a divorce, or are you just a little light entertainment?'

'You've no right to say that. You know nothing about it.'

Adam pulled a face. 'You're right of course. Call it wounded pride. Is it serious, Vicky, for both of you? You can hardly afford indiscretions in our profession.'

She sat forward on the edge of her chair. 'Adam, I need to talk to someone about it, would you mind if I talked to you?'

He did mind. He didn't want to hear about some sordid affair of the heart, but he could tell that she needed to unburden herself. He considered it the price of the weekend and for any information that he might finally manage to extract about Edward. He composed his features into a smile. 'Go ahead then, I'm listening.'

Vicky took a deep breath. 'First of all, you know the man. It's Laura's husband, Nicholas.' She paused, expecting a comment, but resumed when none came. 'He's terribly unhappy at home. They haven't lived as husband and wife for over a year and she's so neurotic that she makes the entire family's life a misery. He wants to leave her, but he doesn't know how he can. He doesn't consider that she's fit to bring the children up alone, but he doubts that she'd hand them over without a fuss.'

'A fair assumption,' commented Adam drily. 'Not many women want to lose their husband and children in one fell swoop, especially if they're in bad health themselves.'

Vicky frowned. 'There's nothing physically wrong with Laura. She's determined to turn herself into a complete mental case, that's all.'

'You don't think that she may have genuine problems?'

Vicky gave a short laugh. 'Such as what? A son who is too bright? A husband with too much money? Not enough to keep her busy?'

'My word, Vicky, I never realized what a little cat you could be!'

She stopped short. 'I'm sorry, I suppose that didn't

sound very nice, but she drives me mad. She's always moaning on about Edward, and he's the sort of boy I'd be proud to have as son.'

'You sound as though you hope to have him one day. Is that your idea? An instant family? If so, you're being totally illogical; no judge would allow it.'

'He would if she was found insane.'

In the silence only the gentle ticking of the grandfather clock in the corner of the room could be heard. Adam studied Victoria carefully, his grey eyes as cold as splinters of ice.

'What a thoroughly unpleasant person you're turning into,' he said at last. 'Perhaps you could certify her yourself, with Nicholas's support of course. I would say that Edward needs a broken home like I need a hole in the head. Have you considered that aspect of the affair?'

Apparently impervious to his distaste Vicky became animated. 'You don't understand. Edward would like to live with me. He told me so. He hates his mother; she's persecuted him ever since he was born. You know that.'

'I know no such thing,' retorted Adam sharply. 'She's worried about him yes, but it's a caring concern. However misguided you may think her she has his best interests at heart. Her fault, if indeed it is a fault, is that she cares too much.'

Vicky drained the brandy from her glass and refilled it without thought.

'I've never known you to champion a mother before. Why all this concern for a woman you once ran down so scathingly?'

'Because I'm beginning to think that she has a genuine problem; that's why I'm seeing Edward again.'

It was a mistake to tell her, he knew that as soon as

136

the words were out, but it was too late to call them back. He only hoped that she didn't pass the information on to her lover, and relied on her professional discretion. For some reason he was most anxious that Edward should not consider his next appointment anything but routine. He didn't want the boy to be on his guard during the visit.

'You're wrong,' stated Vicky firmly,' completely wrong. Still, you'll discover that for yourself soon enough. I expect that you're being influenced by Laura's pretty face and shy manner. Although you're the last man that I'd have expected to fall victim to her insipid charms.'

'Love,' said Adam sharply, 'has not improved your disposition. Did you always resent Laura so much I wonder? Is that why you're determined to show her that an intelligent career woman can snatch a husband and two children from under the nose of a beautiful, not-so-bright housewife? If so it does you no credit at all.'

Vicky was yawning with all the wine and brandy. 'I don't want the children,' she said sleepily. 'I only want Edward.'

'Laura should be grateful for small mercies then.'

Vicky chuckled. 'I never realized that beneath your surface liberalism you were such a stuffy prig!'

'You're drunk,' said Adam. 'You'd better go to bed and sleep it off.'

He watched as she made her way slowly up the stairs, and found that he felt profoundly sorry for her. She was involved in a situation that was entirely foreign to her nature, and he suspected that she was really more interested in Edward than she was in Nicholas. He wondered what it was that enabled this small boy to wield such influence over the adults in his life. It made him interested in what kind of person Edward would eventually become.

On the Sunday morning after coffee and toast Adam left. There was nothing more for them to say to each other, and Vicky was obviously regretting her confidences of the night before. He had no intention of keeping in touch any more. Nevertheless he felt a pang of sadness. She had been a bright, forceful young woman, and he could see nothing but disappointment ahead for her. However, she was a grown woman and had chosen her own path. He kissed her lightly on both cheeks.

'Good luck, Vicky! If you're ever in town give me a ring.'

'I will. Good luck to you.'

They both knew it was the end. They were unlikely to meet up again.

Laura sat in the long clinical corridor outside Adam Castle's room and hoped against hope that he could help her. This was her final attempt at convincing another person of her beliefs, but she felt that she stood a reasonable chance. He had listened to her before and had given no sign of scorn or disbelief. If he had only kept an open mind she would be satisfied. She watched Edward as he sat reading a book, his legs swinging idly from the chair. She wondered how he felt himself about being different, and if he ever wished for other children who were like him. She would never know; he confided in no one, and who could blame him?

There were times like this, times when he wasn't being difficult or hurtful, when she could actually pity him. He seemed so small for such exceptional power, and had no rules to guide him over its use. All children needed rules, but none existed for this strange world in which her son was trapped. In one sense he was himself a victim of his gift. Already he had lost much of a normal childhood, and whatever he achieved in later life he would remain as isolated as he was today. If only he were more placid, less self-centred, how much easier it would be. She sighed, there was no use in thinking that way. He was a forceful and ambitious boy; the very last type of child who should have been granted special mental powers, and it was up to her to protect other people from him. If no one else understood then that was all the more reason for her to be vigilant. She knew that the responsibility was hers.

At the sound of her sigh Edward glanced up.

'I'm bored, Is it our turn yet?'

Laura checked her watch; they were already half an hour late. 'Soon, Edward. Dr Castle's a very busy man; we're lucky to be able to see him at all.'

'Why? I'm not ill; Daddy said I wasn't ill.'

'It's just routine.'

'What does routine mean?'

Her patience snapped. 'You know perfectly well why we're going to see him, don't you?'

Edward glanced at her. 'Yes, I do.'

'Good, then please don't go on about it in front of your father.'

He bent his head back to his book. 'It's because you're nuts!' Laura heard his mutter, and she tensed, but refused to be drawn. He knew the truth, she was positive of that, and there was no point in causing a scene here. People would only endorse Edward's comment if she started shouting at him; they never realized how much he could annoy. No one understood yet, but when they did they would wish that they had listened to her from the beginning.

139

'Mrs Wells and Edward please.' The young nurse's voice broke into her thoughts, and she held out her hand to Edward. He ignored her and marched ahead into the doctor's room. Adam was standing by the window and leant forward over his desk to shake Edward's hand.

'Hello there! You're a big boy now. Let me see, how old are you?'

'I'm five.'

'Five! Goodness me, it doesn't seem possible.'

'Why?'

Adam looked surprised. 'I beg your pardon?'

'Why is it impossible?'

Laura sat down. Edward could keep this sort of conversation going for a long time when he was in a difficult mood. Adam was quickly aware of that fact. He sat down too and gave Edward a considering look. 'It is possible, of course, and I wasn't saying that you couldn't be five; I was expressing surprise at the speed with which the time had passed.'

Edward considered for a moment. 'What does expressing mean?'

'Edward!' Laura's tone was sharp. 'Please stop arguing.'

'I'm not, I just want to know . . .'

'Be quiet, Edward!' With a sullen set to his mouth she watched him climb on to the spare chair and then sit scowling at the paediatrician. The atmosphere in the room was distinctly chilly and she didn't imagine that there was any chance of co-operation from Edward from now on.

Adam fiddled with his pen and silently cursed himself. He had got off on the wrong foot and completely antagonized the child before he began. From the look on the small face opposite him there was no chance of a reconciliation. He would just have to approach the rest of the consultation man-to-man, and hope for the best. He drew out some books of elementary IQ tests from his top drawer. They were for six- to seven-year-olds and should keep Edward occupied for a reasonable time.

'Edward, I want you to look at this picture, and then when you've had a good look at it you can tell me how many things you can see that are wrong. Do you understand?'

'Yes.'

'Fine, here you are then.'

He pushed the book across the desk, and then sat while Edward studied it carefully.

While the boy worked Adam noted down one or two obvious physical facts. He was well above average height for five years old, and sturdily built. His approach to adults and his manner of speech was also well in advance, but this could be mimicry rather than an indication of intelligence. The tests would show if that was the case. What struck him most forcibly was the child's complete lack of desire to please. There was an air of beligerency about him that was surprising, and could surely not win him many friends at school.

After five minutes Adam took the book back. 'Now, Edward, there are twelve things wrong there. Let's see how many you found.'

Edward stared at him, his face impassive.

'Off you go then, take your time.'

'I don't want to, it's babyish. I want to go back to school. Daddy says I'm not ill. I want to go home.'

Adam allowed himself to smile. 'Fine, off you go home. You couldn't do the puzzle, I take it?'

'I could, but I'm not telling you.'

Laura stood up and came over to the desk. 'Don't be difficult, Edward. If you can do it then tell the doctor.'

The hatred that distorted the boy's face at his mother's interruption shook Adam. For a moment it looked positively malevolent. Perhaps he really can't do it, thought Adam, and he doesn't want to be shown up. Instantly Edward turned his gaze upon Adam, and this time the hatred was directed at this second interfering adult. He was flushing with temper, and raised his voice in anger.

'I can do it! I can! I can!'

A small shiver ran up Adam's spine. 'I never said you couldn't,' he remarked casually. Edward glared at him, uncertain for a second as to what he should say. Swiftly the uncertainty faded.

'Mummy said!' Adam glanced at Laura, unable to remember exactly what she had said.

'I said if he could do it then to tell you,' she put in, sensing his confusion. In Adam's view that was too mild a remark to occasion such a temper, but the boy had been clever, and he couldn't prove that his own opinion had been picked up. He couldn't prove it, but he was 99 per cent certain.

'Right then; you tell me the errors.'

Edward did, all twelve of them, plus an extra one because a cow's shadow was the wrong side for the position of the sun. Adam jotted down this additional error on the check list of answers and then put it away.

'Fine. Take off your shirt would you please, Edward?'

As the boy struggled with his top button Adam tried to picture this forceful and difficult boy in Vicky's small cottage along with his father and possibly his young sister. It conjured up an incongruous picture. He listened carefully through his stethoscope, finding, as he had anticipated, that Edward was in top physical condition. He checked ears, eyes and throat before signalling for the child to dress again.

'That's excellent,' he remarked to Laura. 'I've seen enough for today I think.'

'Thank you, doctor.' Laura was as circumspect as Adam. She had no intention of asking questions now. She felt that she could rely on this man to contact her in time, and in some way she also felt that Edward had betrayed himself. She didn't know when, but it was nice to know that he could make mistakes. She automatically straightened her son's tousled blond hair when he came to stand by her again. Adam stood up, holding out his hand to say goodbye. Edward had a puzzled look in his eyes.

'Do you know my Auntie Vicky?' he asked.

Adam remembered his fleeting vision of Vicky in the cottage.

'I don't know,' he said. 'Do you think I might?'

'Yes.'

'Why is that, Edward?'

'Because she's a doctor, and she works here.'

Adam smiled. 'So do a lot of other doctors you know, but you might be right.'

Edward looked at him with contempt. 'I'll ask my Auntie; she'll tell me.'

'You do that. Now then, if I need to see you again will you be happy to come along?'

'Daddy says that I needn't come again.'

Laura looked uncertain. 'It's a little awkward I'm afraid. My husband seems to think that our journeys are a waste of time. It's some new idea that he's got into his head, but . . .'

Blast and damn Vicky, thought Adam. She'd put her oar in already, so desperate was she to protect the boy from professional probing.

He attempted an easy assurance. 'Please don't worry. I've really seen all that I need to.'

143

Laura looked anxious, but he found himself unable even to think about contacting her lest the thought was picked up by Edward. He hoped that she had faith in him, and wouldn't worry needlessly until his letter arrived. He shook her hand firmly, and allowed himself a smile and a jocular remark as he walked mother and son to the door.

'You can go back to school now, Edward, if there's anything there that you think is worth learning!'

Edward did not even trouble to reply. He simply turned and bestowed upon Adam the most wonderful smile, a truly angelic expression of pleasure. Flattered, Adam held the door open, feeling fresh pleasure when the boy turned back once and waved at him, still smiling happily. Back at his desk he picked up the pen and began to jot down his thoughts. One moment he was thinking about the boy and the next he was watching a series of images as they flashed before his eyes. He was sitting in his Triumph Stag and driving along a winding road that was completely unfamiliar to him. He was whistling, apparently happy. Suddenly, out of a concealed drive appeared an enormous removal van, travelling at an incredibly fast speed and heading straight for his car. He felt the initial impact, and watched in horrible fascination as the windscreen moved towards his face, then there was a terrible pain and finally total darkness.

'Dr Castle! Dr Castle!' He jerked in his seat, wrenching his mind from the awful scene with great difficulty. He was gripping his pen with almost superhuman strength and there was sweat on his forehead. He attempted a normal tone of voice, but failed miserably.

'Yes?' It came out as a strangled croak, and he saw the nurse's look of surprise.

'Are you all right, Dr Castle?'

'A bit of a headache, that's all. Did you want me?'

'Not really. I came to remind you that you're seeing that Macfarlane girl at 1.30 as an emergency.'

He licked his dry lips. 'Of course, thank you. I'll take an early lunch I think.'

Left alone he took slow deep breaths and tried to banish the nightmare vision from his thoughts. It wasn't just the horror of the crash, it was the realization that someone else could tamper with his mind. He understood Edward's happy smile now. It had been in anticipation of the discomfort that lay ahead for the unsuspecting Adam. He walked slowly to the canteen, and spent his lunch-time wondering just what else the boy was capable of doing, and how it might be possible to prove it. He could not find a satisfactory answer to either question, but found instead that like Laura he was beginning to be afraid of the handsome small boy.

By the Friday of the week of the hospital visit Laura was feeling more cheerful than for a long time. Although she had not yet received either a telephone call or a letter from Adam Castle she felt certain in her mind that at last she had some support, and intelligent support at that. A top paediatrician should be able to think of ways in which Edward could at least be channelled into better social behaviour and more normal family relationships. For the first time since her son was born she began to envisage a future where he might blend into the background and possibly make a reasonable success of his life. Whatever happened to him she was no longer alone in her efforts to control him, and it was a wonderful feeling. Her state of mild euphoria was short lived, but for once that was not Edward's fault.

Nicholas was usually home by six on a Friday evening, giving himself a couple of hours to play with the children and generally make up for all the time that he spent away from them the rest of the week. Edward and Belinda were sitting in the bow window of the front room waiting by 5.45 pm, and at 6.30 they were both irritable and uncomfortable.

'Where's Daddy?' demanded Belinda in aggrieved tones. 'I want my Daddy.'

'He's late,' complained Edward. 'He's never late on Fridays.'

'I want my sweets!'

'I want him to look at my train.'

Laura sighed. 'Moaning isn't going to help; if he's missed his train then he'll be at least another hour. You might as well watch television both of you.'

This was a great treat for Belinda, whose viewing was normally restricted to an hour of children's television from 4 o'clock each afternoon. They both scrambled into the television room and were blessedly silent for the next hour. By 7.30 Belinda was over-excited and tried, a bad combination for any four-year-old. Thoroughly annoyed herself now Laura played cards with the children, but by 8 o'clock Belinda was too tired to concentrate and cried every time that Edward won. Heather came and took her up for a bath, leaving Laura and Edward to continue with the cards. At 8.30, just as Laura was beginning to worry, she heard Nicholas's key in the door. She tried to push down her rising irritability. It would be unfair to spoil his homecoming for Edward, and she assumed that there must be a good reason for the delay.

Nicholas was smiling cheerfully, trying to ignore the lateness of the hour. 'Hello there Edward! Beating your mother at cards?'

Edward stared at his father. 'You're late!' he said rudely. 'Bee's gone to bed, and I'm exhausted!'

'Late? Am I really? Sorry about that. I had a lift home tonight and gave the trains a miss.'

Laura could tell from the expression of concentration on Edward's face that he was trying to pick up some sort of a clue from his father. If he did there was no immediate result. He walked over to Nicholas and lifted his face for a kiss. Nicholas swung him up into the air, tickling him as he did so. Laura envied him his spontaneous gestures of affection with the boy. Her knowledge of Edward caused every emotion to freeze at birth lest it be stored away by her son and then used in future battles. The result, she knew, was that she appeared a cold and stilted mother. Another mark of her so-called neurotic state.

'Am I forgiven?' laughed Nicholas.

'A kiss, a kiss,' shouted Edward.

Nicholas held him close, blowing kisses into the creases below his chin and round the nape of his neck. Edward shrieked with laughter. Laura watched the tableau of normal five-year-old son romping with his father and admired Edward's skill. He was a consummate little actor. Whatever his real feelings he had decided to be what Nicholas most wanted for the evening, and he was doing it very well. If she didn't know better, thought Laura, then she might find the scene endearing. But she did know, and she found it chilling.

Eventually Edward tired of the romping and asked his father to put him to bed. Laura remained where she was, merely kissing her son on the cheek as he went up the stairs with Nicholas. His expression was cool and neutral when he received the kiss, and she realized that he probably knew he had failed to fool her.

It was nearly 9 o'clock when Nicholas finally came down after seeing to Edward and changing into casual clothes. The smiles had gone from his face now there were no children requiring a cheerful demeanour. He looked tired and pale, and he poured himself an unusually large scotch before sitting down in the armchair opposite Laura.

'Do you want to eat?' she enquired politely. 'I saved some pilaff for you if you do.'

'No thank you. I ate in town actually, with a friend. When I've had this I'll go up to bed. I'm rather tired to tell you the truth.'

They sat in silence while he drank quickly from the cut glass tumbler that was one of a set they had received as a wedding present. He didn't kiss her when he went up. They hadn't kissed for a long time now, and would both have felt awkward if a kiss had been attempted.

By the time that Laura had checked the locks and tidied the ashtrays away Nicholas was asleep in his single bed. They had decided upon single beds a couple of months earlier, concealing the final severance of their relationship behind polite phrases about disturbed nights and different hours. They had both been very civilized about the disintegration of their life together, as though they were determined not to sever the last few threads of politeness that enabled them to continue to live in the same house.

The Saturday started off as usual. Laura had her breakfast on a tray in bed while Nicholas coped with the children in the breakfast room. Later on they all went into the village and bought one or two oddments to justify the trip. Back home they had a cold lunch, and then they usually went for a walk or to the cinema if there was a children's film showing. This particular Saturday neither of the adults mentioned either a film or a walk, and there was a supressed tension around the lunch table that Laura found most unsettling. As soon as they had finished eating Nicholas told the children that their grandmother was taking them in to Crawley for the afternoon, and gave them a £5 note each to spend.

Laura was even more surprised than the children. Her mother-in-law was in failing health these days; she spent most of her time in her own room choosing to eat and watch television alone. The exact nature of her malaise had not been determined, but to herself Laura had thought it was some kind of heart condition. Seeing her come into the living-room looking spruce and as active as ever she realized that the older woman had probably merely been retreating from the increasingly uncongenial atmosphere in the house. She was another casualty of Laura's obsession with her son. Today, delighted by an opportunity of taking her grandchildren out and thoroughly spoiling them, she looked more cheerful than for many months.

After they had gone, driven in by Nicholas but planning to return on a bus as part of the treat, Laura wandered aimlessly round the house touching familiar objects as she passed them. It was plain that Nicholas must want to talk to her alone and at length, and she wasn't certain that she wanted to listen. If he would only wait, wait until she had word from Adam Castle, then together they could tell him how Laura had been right all along and that there was something different about Edward. Once he realized this he would be anxious to make up for the years of scorn and impatience that he had inflicted upon Laura. In time she felt sure that they would come back together again, as soon as Nicholas was made to face the truth. They had gone on so long like this that she couldn't believe he was going to do something destructive at such a vital stage. Couldn't believe it, and yet feared that he was.

She had composed herself by the time he returned. He found her sitting in her usual chair, coffee cup in hand and glancing through a magazine. He was strengthened in his resolve by her obvious lack of interest in his motives for this afternoon alone for them. If she had appeared worried, distressed even, then he might have hesitated for he was not by nature an unkind man. The sight of her remote and cool, involved in a situation only if it concerned Edward, spurred him on. He had a right to a life where he counted for something; he had to take this opportunity because another one might never come and he would spend the rest of his life regretting his weakness.

Laura looked up. 'I imagine there was a reason for despatching the children into town? Bribing them with money to keep them quiet about your repeated lack of attention that has now extended to the previously family-orientated weekends?'

'Yes, there was a reason. Could you put that magazine down, please?'

She placed it carefully on the coffee table beside her. 'Is that better? You now have my full attention!'

'Laura, I want a divorce.'

Ridiculously her mind took refuge in the past. She could recall as though it were yesterday his proposal: 'Laura, I want to marry you.' How excited she had been, how proud that he had been willing to discard a wife and lose a son in order to possess her, Laura Kenley. Now it was her turn to be discarded. It was her fault, she knew that. Years of neglect, ignoring him when he made it plain that they were drifting apart. But she had been so busy; Edward had consumed her emotionally and physically. She raised her eyes to find Nicholas regarding her anxiously.

'I couldn't help it,' she said to him. 'Edward demanded too much of me.'

Nicholas sighed aloud. 'I absolutely refuse to resurrect all that nonsense. I accept that you were ill a lot, and that you had depression and anxiety and God only knows what else, but you're running out of excuses now, Laura. He's a well-adjusted schoolboy, bright and popular. There's nothing wrong with him, Laura, and there never has been. You hide behind him, he's the excuse for all your inadequacies. Well, I'm sorry for you naturally, but I've tried as hard as I can, and there is nothing left for us, nothing at all. I've met someone else, and I hope in time to re-marry. Meanwhile I shall move out of this house and into a flat on my own, then in two years we can get a civilized divorce. It's the best way; it will cause less embarrassment and suffering all round.'

'Bright and popular?' Laura was incredulous. 'Bright yes, I'll give you that, but popular? He hadn't any friends at school, haven't you realized that? When did he ever get invited to a party? When did he ask to bring a friend home to tea? The other children can't stand him.'

Nicholas jumped to his feet, his face red with anger. 'For Christ's sake, I tell you that I'm leaving you for another woman and all you can do is start ranting on about our son again. You're bloody insane, woman; you ought to be locked up! Think about us for a moment, think about yourself if I don't interest you any more. I absolutely refuse to turn this into another discussion about Edward. I'm sick and tired of hearing you go on about him! Don't you care that our marriage is over? Doesn't it mean anything to you?'

Laura was very white, and her hands twisted together in her lap. 'There's no need to shout at me. Of course I care, but you refuse to face the fact that it's Edward's fault. I have to talk about him because he's the reason that we've finished up like this.'

'He isn't,' shouted Nicholas. 'You're the reason. You,

Laura Wells, are the sole reason for this unholy mess. I don't say that you can help it entirely, I appreciate that mental illness is just as bad as physical illness, but you simply refuse to face the fact that you are unbalanced. I need a normal wife!'

He would never understand, realized Laura, and there was really no point in trying to tell him. She changed her line of talk, trying to react in the way he wanted. Her personal pain was of no interest to him, he simply wanted her to behave in a manner that enabled him to reassure himself that he was free of guilt in choosing to leave her. He needed to have a chance to be reasonable and generous, and she was depriving him of it. The least she could do was oblige him on this point, since she appeared to have failed him in every other way.

'Who is she then?'

'It doesn't matter.' Nicholas sounded suitably relieved that she was behaving as a deserted wife should.

'It matters to me. Is she young? Does she satisfy you in bed?'

'She's irrelevant, Laura. If you and I had been getting on well I would never have got involved with her. She isn't the cause of this, she's the result.'

'Is she young?' repeated Laura. For some reason it would be harder to bear if she were young and full of illusions as she had once been.

'Not particularly; about your age.'

'Does she work with you?'

'No! Now let's stop talking about her. I want your word that you will help me to break this to the children in as calm a manner as possible. I don't want them used as a weapon between us, or to upset them more than can be helped.'

Laura looked cynical. 'You're the one who's deserting them. If you don't want to hurt them then you'd better stay here.'

'That's typical, just what I'd have expected. I'm going to get the blame, despite the fact that it was your behaviour that drove me out.'

'I'm not going to say that to the children; it was a remark between ourselves. I'm as anxious as you are not to disturb them unduly.'

'Excellent. I'll tell them of course; I realize that's my duty. I want you to back me up naturally, and we must remain civilized. After all, we both knew it would come to this one day, didn't we?'

'I suppose so.'

'I'll be generous, that goes without saying. You can all stay on here, unless you feel you can't cope with the children alone, and money will be no problem. I want life to go on as normally as possible for everyone.'

'That's very thoughtful of you.'

Unable to decide whether or not Laura was being sarcastic Nicholas lapsed into silence. Eventually, finding that Laura did not intend to prolong the discussion further he removed himself to his study until he heard the children returning. When he saw their happy faces in the hall he wondered how on earth he was going to find the courage to tell them, and immediately put it off until the following day.

After Sunday breakfast he took the children upstairs to their playroom, feeling that it was best to break the news in their own territory. Laura followed slowly behind him, her face a blank mask. Before the toys could be brought out he cleared his throat.

'There is something that I want to tell you both, something important if you would both stop and listen for a moment.' Two pairs of eyes swivelled towards him, Belinda's wide and trusting, Edward's dark and shuttered. 'We have decided, Mummy and I, that the time has come for us to live in separate houses. You will both stay here with Mummy and I shall visit you every weekend, and take you out somewhere nice, like the park or the cinema.'

'We go to the cinema now,' said Edward rudely.

'All the more reason to keep going, because really and truly things aren't going to change very much for you two children. It's just that Mummy and I don't get on terribly well any more, and although we will still be friends we don't particularly want to spend all our time with each other.'

'Is that all?' Belinda, having found that nothing drastic was going to happen to her, lost interest. Nicholas felt that he had handled it very well to extract such lack of reaction from her.

'Yes, that's all.'

'You mean, you're getting a divorce?'

'After a time we will, but not straight away. Do some of your friends have parents who are divorced?'

Edward stared at him. 'How should I know?' He sounded angry and confused; he knew that life would not be the same and he resented his father inflicting this upon him.

'Look, old chap, I'm truly sorry about this, but it isn't nice when Mummy and I quarrel is it? Won't it be better for you to have us both happy and cheerful again?'

'I've never heard you quarrel, and Mummy's never cheerful. I want to come and live with you.'

Laura bent down and helped Belinda with her dolls. Let Nicholas cope with it; he had been so sure that he could explain. She wasn't hurt by Edward's rejection; in fact she had expected it. It provided him with a golden chance to escape her watchful gaze.

154

'Well, you can't do that, Edward, because I shall be out at work all day and there won't be anyone to look after you. Here you've got Mummy and Heather and Belinda to keep you company.'

'If you can live with Auntie Vicky then I want to as well.'

Laura straightened up and caught sight of Nicholas's astounded and embarrassed face. Her heart began to pound loudly in her ears and she found it difficult to get her breath. Surely it couldn't be Vicky? Nicholas would never do such a thing to her. Her one friend, a visitor to their home ever since they married, it was just impossible.

'Who said anything about Auntie Vicky?' asked Nicholas at last.

'I did!'

'But why? I'm not going to live with Auntie Vicky. What an extraordinary idea, I can't imagine where you got it from.'

Edward went scarlet in the face. 'Liar! You're a rotten liar! I know you're going to live with her, and I want to come as well. She likes me. She likes me better than you!'

Nicholas crossed the playroom floor picked Edward up and shook him hard. 'Don't you ever speak to me like that again, do you understand? Save that sort of language for your school friends. Now go to your room until you've pulled yourself together. Now, at once!'

At the door Edward turned back to his father. 'Do you promise me? Do you swear that you'll never go and live with Auntie Vicky?'

Nicholas was unable to reply. How could he swear a deliberate falsehood to his own child? He tried desperately to think of an evasive reply, but the words could not be found.

'I promise you that at first I will be living on my own, is that sufficient for you?'

'Cheat!'

'Get to your room,' roared Nicholas, his temper inflamed by his own moral cowardice. The door slammed, leaving Nicholas, Laura, and Belinda standing in silence. Laura took Belinda's hand; it trembled in her own. 'Come along, darling, let's go out for a walk together. Edward will soon feel better and then he can play with you.' She walked past Nicholas without even a glance.

Alone and confused Nicholas wandered over to the window and looked out across the expanse of lawn and shrubs that had developed so nicely in the years they had been in the house. He would be sorry to leave the place, but what was a home compared to companionship? He knew that his rambling thoughts were merely attempts to ignore the recent scene. He just could not understand how Edward had known about Victoria. They had always been so careful. As far as he knew they had never been seen together. As soon as their affair really blossomed she had stopped coming to the house lest it proved impossible to conceal their feelings for each other. Yet somehow, somewhere, they had slipped up. They must have done. He refused at this late stage to accept that there could be any other explanation.

It took Nicholas several weeks to find himself a flat that was within reasonable distance of the children and also near enough to the station to allow him to commute each day. He no longer wanted to spend nights in the London apartment, his evenings could now be devoted to Vicky. It was something of a shock to discover that Vicky kept the most erratic hours. He had always realized that doctors had to go out on night

156

calls, but he wasn't prepared for the seemingly endless number of emergencies which meant that sometimes she was busy day and night for the best part of a week. Fortunately there was always paper work from the office that he could do, and it was also pleasant to be able to play his classical music loudly during the evenings. He did miss the children, but his Saturday visits were pleasant and neither Edward nor Belinda showed any sign of being disturbed by the change in the family situation. All in all he congratulated himself on how smoothly he had managed the entire affair.

Laura, who was with the children day and night, would have told a different story if he had asked her. It was true that both the children behaved well on their Saturday outing, but since it was the day that they had both looked forward to for the whole week that was scarcely surprising. She had to cope with the broken nights, the temper tantrums from Belinda when she wanted a toy mended and had to wait until the Saturday, and the sullen moods from Edward that proved impossible to break.

His class teacher spoke to her one afternoon and Laura expected to hear that Edward's work was suffering too. She was amazed to learn that, on the contrary, he was pulling further ahead of his contemporaries.

'He is learning with an almost ferocious intensity,' commented Mrs Ryan, 'and I'm afraid that the other children are inevitably holding him back. I have a duty to them all, you understand, and it is impossible to give Edward the constant stimulation that he now needs.'

'I see,' said Laura. 'Is there anything that I can do to help?'

'If you could come along and see the headmistress one morning then she has a proposal to put to you. Bring your husband too if you can.'

Laura glanced over her shoulder, and was relieved to find that the other mothers had gone. 'I'm afraid that won't be possible. My husband and I are no longer living together.'

'Oh dear, I'm so sorry. Well, in that case of course you can come alone.'

'I'll telephone and arrange a time,' said Laura, anxious to take Edward home before he began to wonder what was delaying her.

She called the school the very next day and found herself in the headmistress's room by lunch time. Mrs Griffiths was a middle-aged woman with a sensible face and a deceptively quiet way of speaking.

'We feel, Mrs Wells,' she said after the polite preliminaries, 'that Edward does need to be extended more. I would like to move him up a class after Christmas. I realize that he will only be five and three-quarters, but in every aspect he seems far older and should have no trouble in settling in well. How would you feel about that?'

'If you think that is the best thing for him, then please go ahead. Do you think that leaving his friends will trouble him?'

Mrs Griffiths busied herself with some papers. 'I don't think that he has any particularly close friends in his class, Mrs Wells, and here again the staff feel that he may make friends more easily amongst the older boys.'

Laura bit her lower lip. The older woman was too polite to tell her that Edward was not popular, but the fact was that her instinct had been right and he was unable to mix with his contemporaries. Personally she doubted if he would fare any better with bigger boys, but she had no intention of telling Mrs Griffiths this.

'Well then, that would definitely seem the best solution,' she said at last. 'Will I tell Edward, or will you?'

'You may tell him first, if you like, and then we will mention it to him just before they break up at Christmas, as confirmation.'

'Fine, and thank you very much for the trouble that you're taking over him.'

'Not at all, Mrs Wells. It would be a tragedy to allow him to slip backwards through boredom; he's such a bright little boy and that must obviously be encouraged.'

Driving home Laura realized that at no time had the headmistress made any comment about Edward's social behaviour or mentioned his personality. The entire discussion had been polite but cool. She thought that Mrs Griffiths too had private reservations about him, and she was glad that at least one other adult was not fooled by short displays of surface charm that appeared to work well on Mrs Ryan at the moment.

When she told Edward he was offhand about it all.

'I hope I don't have to watch "You and Me" any more,' he said; 'that is very babyish!'

'You won't,' said Laura briskly, 'but you will have to work hard.'

'I know that! Can I have an Action Man for Christmas? And a tank for him to drive?'

'I don't know. Run up to the nursery. Heather has got your tea ready.'

He ran off, and never mentioned the matter again during the rest of the term.

Christmas itself proved something of a trial for Laura. It was strange sitting down to Christmas lunch with only Ruth and the children, and stranger still when Nicholas collected his son and daughter for Boxing Day, leaving the two women alone in the house. She watched the three of them laughing as they made their way to the car, and she wondered how often Nicholas was seeing Vicky. He had never mentioned her friend, but after Edward had brought her name up during the scene in the nursery she had been convinced that it was indeed Victoria who was the cause of the final break-up. She had been amused by Nicholas's puzzlement and anger when Edward blurted out the name. She knew that he would never for one moment admit that Edward could have picked the name from his mind, and she wondered how he managed to rationalize it to himself.

When the car had gone she poured herself a glass of wine and curled up with a book. She didn't really read it; instead she thought about Vicky. She had not contacted her since Nicholas left. There was no point in embarrassing them both. There had been a Christmas card for her and the children, but she had not reciprocated. That should let Vicky know that Laura was aware of what was happening. Sometimes, alone in bed at night, she would try and picture Vicky and Nicholas together but she found it a masochistic pastime that achieved nothing.

Edward had been a little easier of late. There had been no obvious incidents to remind her of his mental powers, and she thought that he was now old enough to be more careful as to how he used them. Neither had she quarrelled with him so much, since she felt obliged to make allowances for the absence of his father. As a result she had been spared the blinding headaches, and her health had improved. She had heard from Adam Castle twice. Once after the last visit, when he wrote and told her that one or two small incidents had led him to consider that her theory was certainly viable although far from proven, and again via a Christmas card containing a few scrawled lines of enquiry as to how things were going. She decided to answer that when Edward was back at school.

The day passed very slowly. She and Ruth ate cold

turkey for lunch and then the older woman watched television. Laura went for a short walk before coming home and tidying up the nursery where presents were littering the floor and all available surfaces. Heather had gone to her own family for a week, and Laura quite enjoyed pottering round the children's rooms undisturbed. After that she too watched television, and then from 6 o'clock onwards found herself sitting in the bay window of the lounge watching for the children to come home.

They arrived shortly after 7 pm, and Belinda tumbled from the back of the car chattering and laughing loudly. Laura saw how Edward came out slowly, his mouth turned down and his face pinched. She saw too how Nicholas tried to jolly him as they approached the front door, but Edward drew away and scowled. She invited Nicholas into the hall, and offered him a sherry which he politely refused.

'I must get back,' he explained. 'There's some heavy snow on the way.'

Edward, who was pulling off his heavy coat, made a rude noise and ran upstairs banging his feet on every step. Laura looked at Nicholas enquiringly.

'He's a bit out of temper,' he apologized. 'I don't know why but he's been pretty difficult all day. Bee was fine though.'

'Edward has found it difficult to adjust,' said Laura. 'He misses having you around.'

Nicholas flushed. 'Yes, yes I realize that. Still, there was no need for him to spoil the whole day. I sometimes wonder if you encourage him in this sort of thing as a way of getting back at me. Hoping to cause me more guilt perhaps?'

She looked at his angry yet hurt expression and held back the biting reply that he deserved.

'No, Nicholas, I don't; and please don't try and put the blame on me. I'll see if I can find out what the problem is before he sees you next Saturday if you like.'

'I'm sorry, that was bloody of me. It's just that I found myself quite unable to talk to him today, and somehow being Christmas and everything it was all a bit too much. I'm sorry, Laura.'

'You'd better be off, before this snow arrives.'

He lingered awkwardly for a moment, not liking to shake hands yet knowing that a kiss was out of the question. She smiled brightly and held the door open.

'Kiss Daddy, Belinda!' Belinda obliged, and Nicholas went out into the cold night. Laura closed the door and then leant her back against it, the tears pricking at her eyelids. At least he had someone else to go to, another adult to comfort him. This Christmas had brought her solitude home to her in full force, and if she was now expected to help Nicholas as well then it would become impossible. It was as much as she could do to keep herself together as it was. With a determined bracing of her shoulders she started to ask all the right questions of Belinda, leaving Edward until later in the evening.

By 8 o'clock Belinda was in bed and asleep, and Laura went along to Edward's bedroom and knocked on the door. He didn't reply, so she gently pushed the door open. He was sitting on the end of his bed shoulders hunched, building some space Lego with an air of intense concentration. Laura sat down next to him.

'Is anything wrong, Edward? Daddy said that you were quiet all day.'

'I'm hungry. May I have some supper?'

She decided to wait a little longer before pressing him. 'Of course. Let's go down to the kitchen. I've put Belinda to bed.'

'I know.'

Once he was settled on a kitchen chair with a mug of hot milk and two mincepies Laura tried again. 'Edward, didn't you enjoy your day with Daddy?'

He flicked his eyes up from his plate. 'No, it was horrid!'

'Why? Belinda said that you had a lovely lunch and a present each off Daddy's Christmas tree. You went for a walk too didn't you?'

'Yes, yes, yes!'

'Then what was wrong? Daddy was most upset to think that you hadn't enjoyed yourself.'

Edward gulped all of his milk down and wiped his mouth with the back of his hand. 'Good, serves him right!'

'It doesn't. Daddy hasn't done anything wrong. Why he's even promised us a puppy after Christmas, hasn't he?'

She watched as Edward picked up a mincepie and absentmindedly crumbled it to pieces in his fingers. He was staring into space, apparently trying to assemble his thoughts.

'Daddy wasn't thinking about us at all today,' he said at last. 'All he was thinking about was Auntie Vicky.' Laura sat quite still, her heart beginning to hammer against her ribs. Whenever he did something like this she was unable to remain calm, unable to accept it, yet she was determined not to break his train of thought. She wanted to know what Nicholas had been thinking.

'Do you know?' His voice was high with indignation by now. 'Do you know, Mummy, that every time he thought about her she had NO CLOTHES ON!'

For a terrible moment Laura thought that she was going to break into hysterical laughter. If poor Nicholas knew that his every thought could be seen by Edward then he would probably be too scared ever to see the boy again. A vision of the sturdy Vicky stark naked rose before her, and she wished that Vicky too could know that she had been seen by a five-year-old boy. What a shock for both of them! And it served them right, she thought; they should have listened to her.

The crash of broken crockery brought her attention back to the kitchen.

'Stop it!' screamed Edward. 'I don't want to see her! Stop it, Mummy!'

At once she realized his confusion, his pain and his sense of rejection. She pulled him towards her, and held his struggling body tightly.

'Edward I'm sorry. Please darling don't cry. I know it was horrid for you, and I'm so sorry. Daddy didn't mean it. He didn't know that you could tell what he was thinking. He doesn't understand.'

At once he was still. Slowly, but calmly, he removed himself from her grasp. Putting a few feet between them he met her gaze squarely.

'I can't.'

'Edward, you've just told me that you can.'

'I was fibbing. I made it up. I wanted to be rude! It was just a rude story!'

'Edward you don't have to lie to me, I know what you can do. I've always known.'

His dark eyes searched hers, and she met them calmly, hoping that now they could talk about this openly together.

'Daddy's right,' he said rudely. 'You're stupid! You believe any old lie that I tell you! I was cross today because I didn't get my Action Man tank, that was why.'

'But Edward . . .'

'You're barmy, you're barmy. They'll put you in the

164

Army!' He chanted the rhyme defiantly, glaring at her from the opposite side of the table.

'Go to bed at once,' she said quietly. 'Get yourself washed and into your pyjamas this minute.' Edward pranced around the table, the epitome of any over-excited five-year-old on Boxing Day. It was, Laura reflected dispassionately, an excellent performance.

'Ha ha ha, hee hee hee! You've got a face like a chimpanzee!' He shrieked with laughter and poked out his tongue. Rage rose in her and she felt herself begin to shake. It was at times like this that she felt closest to doing him a physical injury.

'Get to bed!'

Either he had sensed her fury or he had tired of the game. Whatever the reason it ended abruptly. He turned away and ran to the kitchen door, slamming it behind him as he went.

Laura sat with her head in her hands. She had been so near to breaking through to him. It was the closest that she had ever come to a genuine conversation with him, and yet he had refused to allow her to penetrate his defence. Despite the hurt and bewilderment of the day he preferred to struggle on alone. She doubted if he would ever slip up again. From now on he would guard his secrets closely.

Feeling a complete failure she slowly climbed the stairs. Edward was in bed, breathing steadily and apparently fast asleep. She locked up the house and was in bed by 10 o'clock herself. There was nothing to stay up for and she felt exhausted by the happenings of the evening. Unable to sleep she cast around in her mind for someone to confide in, and then finally resolved to tell Adam about it when she replied to his Christmas card. Comforted by this she finally fell asleep.

At midnight, warm in the double bed of Victoria's cottage Nicholas lay in her arms. He held her close to him. Even now, thoroughly sated by their love-making, he enjoyed the feel of her naked body pressed close to his.

'I've been looking forward to this all day,' he whispered. 'I couldn't get you out of my mind.' She smiled, and stretched in a sensual fashion.

'I hope the children couldn't tell!'

'Of course not. I was the perfect attentive father.' His hand strayed to her breast and cupped the erect nipple.

'You have the most fantastic body, as no doubt all the men tell you!'

'Naturally!' Slowly they began to make love again, and Nicholas tried to note every action in order to be able to recall it at the times when they were apart.

On 4 January Edward went back to school and moved up a class. Miss King, his new teacher, was young and enthusiastic. She found in Edward the almost perfect pupil. He listened intently and learnt quickly. He never talked in class, and he didn't get involved in the giggling groups who disrupted the classroom from time to time. She reported to the headmistress that he had settled in marvellously.

Out in the playground it was a different story. The children found Edward strange. It wasn't that they minded him being good at reading, writing, and sums; but they did mind that he wouldn't join in their games. At playtime he would stand on his own, or perhaps watch a game of tag from a distance. One of the class, a tall but rather slow boy who was nearly seven, was the school bully. He had a reputation for being spiteful, but in order to appease him and avoid his punches and kicks, most of the children would pay lip service and pretend friendship. Not Edward. He made it plain that he thought Douglas a fool, and openly smirked in class when Douglas made some particularly foolish mistake.

Eventually Douglas turned his attention to this new boy. He would run up to Edward and push him in the small of the back, then run off before being seen. When this failed to achieve any result he started to crash into him head on, then fall on top and manage to poke an elbow into Edward's ribs as he got up. To the supervisor walking round it looked like normal rough and tumble, but both Edward and Douglas knew better. As the weeks passed Douglas grew bolder. Now he began to have one or two hangers-on with him when he attacked. Eventually Edward was going home with bruised arms and legs, then one day a swollen nose and reddened eye.

To the teacher Edward said that he had tripped and hit the wall, and although doubtful she felt that if Edward wasn't complaining then he was probably partly to blame. At home Laura was less easily satisfied. After extensive questioning she managed to extract at least some of the story. She wondered what she ought to say, and decided to mention it to Nicholas on his next visit. In the meantime she told Edward to try and stay out of his way, but if that proved impossible then to hit Douglas back.

'He's bigger than me, and he's got lots of friends,' he complained.

'Well you must learn to stand on your own feet, Edward. The more he gets away with it the worse he'll become.'

Edward shrugged. 'All right then, I'll just have to teach him a lesson!'

'That's right, you do that.' She was amused by the school-boy bravado.

The next day she was standing as usual outside the

167

school gates, holding Belinda by the hand and hoping that Edward's class wouldn't be late because the driving sleet was most uncomfortable and her feet felt numb despite the fleecy lined boots. Normally he was one of the first of his class to appear, but today there was no sign of him. She saw a bunch of his classmates tumbling out of the doors and surging to the gates where they split up to find their parents. One boy, bigger than the rest and with a heavy face, stood uncertainly looking around him, apparently unable to find anyone that he knew. Laura looked towards the school, and saw Edward appear at last. He stood in the doorway, his gaze fixed in her direction and she raised her hand to show him she was waiting. She was vaguely aware that the big boy was still standing uncertainly in the middle of the pavement. She waved again to Edward, but he refused to move.

Out of the corner of her eye she suddenly saw a flash of movement. She heard someone scream, and turned quickly to see what had happened. There was a squeal of brakes, and then a dull thud. Instinctively she pulled Belinda in to her, hiding her head in her coat. There were further shouts, and the lollipop lady ran out into the road. As the mothers parted Laura caught a quick glimpse of a boy lying twisted in the road, his cap several feet away, and blood pouring from his head.

Her body prickled with shock and horror, and she searched frantically for Edward. Other mothers too were trying to find their sons, no one certain who it was lying in the road. Laura saw that Edward was now strolling towards her, and her first emotion was intense relief. As Edward arrived she quickly took his arm and hurried him towards the car, keeping herself between both children and the scene in the road. There were plenty of people helping the injured boy, and she could hear the sound of the ambulance in the distance. In the car she sat shivering for a few minutes, unable to leave anyway because the boy's body was still blocking the road. Belinda was jumping up and down on the back seat.

'What is it, Mummy? What happened?'

'There's been an accident, darling. One of the boys got knocked down.'

'Is he hurt, Mummy? Is he dead?'

'Of course he isn't dead.' She wasn't sure of that, but she had no intention of letting Belinda know. 'He ran straight out into the road instead of waiting for the lolli-pop lady, which was silly.'

Laura craned her neck, and saw the stretcher being put into the ambulance. It looked to her as though the blanket was drawn up over the child's face, and her teeth chattered. It had been so sudden. She wondered who the boy was, and why he had been in such a hurry.

She drove home extra carefully, the automatic reaction of a driver who has witnessed an accident. Inside the house she made herself a cup of tea with plenty of sugar. Edward had made no comment on the incident, and she thought that it was fortunate he had been so late out for once and had missed it all. Doubtless he would hear about it at school the next day, but he had been spared the worst. She tried to guard her thoughts when he was near, and he remained quite untroubled.

As she tucked him up that night he wrapped his arms tightly round her neck. 'You were very clever, Mummy, weren't you?'

'Really Edward? What did I do?' Her face was buried in his neck, and she was unable to see his face. It was pleasant though to get such a display of affection from him.

'You told me to teach him a lesson, and I did!'

'Douglas, do you mean?'

'Yes, Douglas. I certainly taught him a lesson!'

169

She heard the triumph in his voice, the satisfaction of a boy who felt himself truly vindicated, and her mouth went dry. She released herself from his grip and stood looking down on him. He smiled up at her, but his eyes gleamed with unholy pleasure as he saw the realization dawn in her brain. She saw again the big boy standing on the pavement, and then the flash of colour as he charged out into the on-coming traffic. She pictured the body, and the slow thick stream of blood from the head. Her chest felt tight, her breathing constricted. She would not ask him. She did not dare, but she knew. She forced herself to speak.

'Goodnight, Edward; sleep well.'

'Goodnight, Mummy, and thank you!'

Somehow she stumbled down the stairs and into the dining-room where she poured herself an enormous brandy. She was still there, half-drunk and crying gently when her mother-in-law looked in to say goodnight. She didn't care. She wasn't even bothered if Nicholas was told. It was the worst moment of her life so far. All that she craved was a brief spell of oblivion, and eventually the alcohol obliged her and she slept in her chair.

Neither Laura nor Edward ever spoke of Douglas again. Laura sent some money to school when the parents and staff collected for a wreath, and she attended the small service at the local church, but to her son she made no comment at all. It was as though Douglas had never existed. As the weeks passed she noticed that Edward always came out of school either ahead of or behind the rest of his classmates, and if by chance another child was near him to begin with he would quickly move away and try to join other boys. When she asked Edward if the bullying had stopped he smiled and nodded, and she knew that the children were now too afraid of her son to trouble him any more.

At the end of February Mrs Griffiths asked to see Laura again. This time she was not so full of praise for Edward.

'He seems to be unwilling to mix, Mrs Wells; he won't take part in any team activity and refuses to play with other boys at playtime. School isn't only for the purpose of academic achievement; it should also teach young children how to socialize, and relate to their contemporaries. In this respect we are failing completely with your son.'

'I'm aware of the fact that he doesn't mix well,' said Laura. 'I do try to encourage him, but he is very obstinate. What would you suggest?'

'I have nothing to suggest,' said the headmistress frostily. 'I merely wanted to acquaint you with the facts. It is always possible that your domestic circumstances have contributed to Edward's difficulty. In any case we feel that Edward would benefit from attending child guidance clinic for a while.'

By the time that she left Laura had reluctantly agreed to this request. To obstruct the staff would have caused ill feeling, and although she knew perfectly well that child guidance would be as helpess as the teachers she failed to see how it could make matters worse. That evening she sat down and wrote to Adam Castle; she did not tell him about Douglas, but described the scene on Boxing Day in full and told him that the school had recommended child guidance. Once the letter was posted she waited anxiously each day, hoping for a reply.

Two weeks passed and none came. Laura began to

wonder if Adam had lost interest and her old sense of depression started to return.

One Friday night, after everyone else was in bed, she was startled to hear the doorbell. At first she did not recognize the young man who stood in the porch wearing a dark green parka and brown slacks. It was only when he spoke that she realized with incredulous delight that it was Adam.

'I can't believe it! I had almost given you up,' she said as she hung his anorak in the cupboard.

'Well, it was a trifle awkward to be honest. I'll explain in a moment. I had to come down this way, and I took a chance on catching you up. I hope you don't mind?'

'Of course not, I'm delighted!' She truly was; a visit in person was far beyond her wildest expectations.

She made a jug of coffee and then took him into the living-room. He settled down comfortably into Nicholas's old chair, and she thought how much younger he seemed in his casual clothes. He was looking at her critically, but his voice was kind.

'You look pale; how are you feeling?'

'I have been a bit down,' she admitted, 'but I feel much better for seeing you.'

He cleared his throat. 'The thing is, Laura – I may call you Laura?' She nodded. 'Good, well the thing is that I had a letter from your husband some time back informing me that he no longer wished Edward to continue as my patient. Naturally I had to respect his wishes. After I received your last letter I couldn't think what to do for the best, and then it came to me. I would call in as your friend, nothing to do with Edward. If we happen to talk about your son, what could be more natural? Any advice that I give would be on that basis, and free of charge! Completely foolproof, I think. Would you agree?'

Laura smiled. 'Nicholas could scarcely object, especi-

172

ally since he is involved with a doctor himself.' She suddenly realized how her remark might sound, and blushed. 'I don't mean that you and I . . . I was only saying . . .' Adam laughed.

'Don't worry, I quite understand what you meant!'

He watched as Laura stood up to refill their coffee cups. She had a quiet dignity that he found attractive, and it was refreshing to find a woman who blushed these days. Until recently all of his women had been forceful career women, full of energy and vitality. Laura was the complete opposite and he speculated as to what she would be like in bed. Probably not very good, but it might be pleasant to teach a woman something rather than hope desperately that you matched up to her previous lovers. When she sat down and crossed her legs he noticed that she had an excellent figure, but failed to display it to its best advantage. That was understandable. With all her problems, parading herself for a man's approval was probably the last thing on her mind.

Thinking of minds turned his own in the direction of Edward again.

'How is Edward?' he asked. Laura sighed, and settled back in her chair.

'Much the same as I told you.'

'I wonder if the child guidance is perhaps a good idea? After all, why hasn't he got any friends at school? Surely he wants some?'

' 'There's a very good reason for that, Adam, but I didn't want to put it in a letter. It's a horrible thing to have to discuss, and I've told no one so far.'

'Tell me,' encouraged Adam. 'That's why I'm here.' Laura did.

He made an excellent listener. He kept his eyes on her face, and made no comment at all while she was

173

speaking. Only the intensity of his gaze told her how keenly he was taking it all in. When she had finished she was trembling, but it was bliss to share the burden at last. 'So that's it,' she concluded. 'In the circumstances who can blame the children?'

'Does anyone know what made the boy run out blindly into the road like that? Was he crossing to meet his mother?'

'No. According to general gossip his mother was standing about ten yards away from the gates, in her usual place. She saw Douglas standing on the pavement, and couldn't understand why he looked so confused.'

'So how has it been explained?'

'They've put it down as "one of those things". A moment's inattention by a young boy. There was no real explanation.'

'And you think that the children know what happened?'

Laura hesitated. 'Not really, but I think they sense that Edward was involved. Children are good at picking up feelings, and they probably quickly grasped the fact that he didn't care. When Douglas was killed Edward looked positively triumphant, almost as though he felt vindicated.'

Adam nodded. 'He probably did. You have to remember that he isn't six yet. If someone bullies a child then that child automatically wishes for some terrible revenge; that's quite natural. It is only tragic if Edward can make this a reality and turn his fantasy into fact. The original thought is perfectly normal for his age.'

'I don't believe that normal children wish to see their contemporaries run over and killed like that. I refuse to accept it.'

174

'Perhaps not exactly, but they often wish for their enemies to die, because whilst they fail to grasp the finality of death they know that it is the one thing we all dread. Parents teach them this. If you eat those berries you'll die! If you put a plastic bag over your head you'll suffocate! Don't run across the road, you'll be killed! You know how it goes.'

'You seem to be trying to justify all this,' said Laura. 'Surely you don't approve?'

'I want to put it into perspective,' said Adam patiently. 'If you're right about this telepathy, call it what you will, then that is what needs watching. What you mustn't do is to start thinking of Edward as some sort of evil monster. He's a normal intelligent five-year-old who can't control his ability and is probably secretly frightened to death at some of the things that happens to him. It can't be very nice to know that your father is lusting after a woman when he's pretending to have a nice time playing with you, now can it?'

Laura began to feel annoyed. 'You don't know him, Adam. I can assure you that most of the time he isn't at all perturbed by his powers; he enjoys them. Furthermore he isn't normal, he certainly isn't like Belinda. He simply intends to get his own way in everything, and remove every obstacle by any method necessary.'

'So, I assure you, do a lot of other children. The only difference is that there is no way they can achieve their ambitions and so they never become known.'

Laura shook her head. 'You're quite wrong. I know that Edward is evil.'

'Well for your own sake I suggest that you refrain from telling anyone else of your beliefs. You'll only end up in trouble.'

He knew that she was upset, but he had to tell her for her own good. Her letter to him had been quite hysterical. He could understand this, and knew that he too found something unattractive about Edward, but she had to stick to facts if she was ever to convince other people of her beliefs. Generalities about good and evil were outmoded, and with her mental background would only lead to further visits to her analyst. He believed that there were dark areas in everyone, certainly he had them, and what you called them depended upon your religious beliefs. He stood up.

'Look, we mustn't talk any more, it's hellishly late and you're exhausted.'

Laura tried to hide her disappointment. She thought that he too had decided she was unbalanced, and he was now extracating himself from the problem.

'Of course,' she said politely. 'I'll show you out.'

He caught hold of her elbow. 'Don't look like that. I intend to come back, if I'm invited!'

'Of course you're invited. Any time that you like.'

'I wondered if I could take you out one evening. That way we could talk without any fear of Edward picking up our conversation. Besides, it would do you good to get away from the house. How long is it since you were taken out?'

She ignored his query. 'That would be nice. My mother-in-law can always baby-sit for me. She lives here you know.'

'Excellent. I'll pick you up a week today. How would 7.30 suit you?'

'That should be all right. Where are we going?'

'A meal and a chat; nothing too grand. I look forward to it, Laura.'

After he had gone she felt ridiculously elated. She knew that he was doing it all to prove that they were friends, and prevent anyone from realizing that he was actually treating Edward, but she was still excited. It would be nice to dress up and go out again. For the first time in months she fell asleep without thinking about Edward, and slept well all night.

The next week dragged slowly by. She tried hard never to think about Adam in front of Edward, but once or twice her mind would begin to stray before she realized it. As a result Edward started to play her up, probably confused by the broken images that he was intercepting. Ruth was delighted to think that Laura was going out for a change, and remarked upon how much better she looked when she had something to look forward to. It was true; even Edward was no longer a worry to be born alone.

When the evening finally arrived Laura was devastated by an attack of schoolgirl nerves. She couldn't decide what to wear, and she felt sick and hungry at the same time. The strain of not picturing Adam in her mind added to her state of stress, and when he rang the doorbell and she finally walked out of the house her sense of relief was overwhelming.

She liked the dark green Triumph Stag, and liked the way he drove it, fast but with quiet confidence. They drove for most of the way in comparative silence, broken only by Adam's remarks about his past week. All of his brief anecdotes were light and amusing. They arrived at a thatched and dark-beamed restaurant within half an hour, and as she drank her dry sherry she found to her surprise that she was completely relaxed.

Adam admired the simple understated blue wool dress that accentuated her good figure. He preferred women who dressed in simple styles; frills and trimmings were not to his liking. He was also pleased that she had relaxed. When he had collected her she had been strung as tightly as a piece of wire. Over the meal he tried to draw her out about herself, refusing to dis-

177

cuss Edward until later in the evening. She was very reticent about most things, and touched only briefly on her childhood and her gifted but busy mother.

'I wanted so much to be a good mother myself, to make up for her, I suppose,' she said wistfully. 'It never worked out like that of course.'

Adam began to wonder if that was the reason. She had wanted to be perfect, and hid her failure behind imagined faults in her son. He checked that line of thought quickly. He had seen Edward for himself; he knew that there was something strange about the boy. At least, he thought that he did.

After coffee they returned to the bar, and as Laura drank more so she softened, became far more warm and feminine. Adam wondered why Nicholas hadn't encouraged this side of her. Looking at her now it was hard to imagine any man rejecting her for the brisk, no-nonsense Victoria, who was capable of reducing a man to nothing if he annoyed her. As they walked out to the car park Adam put an arm casually round Laura's waist to guide her in the right direction. She moved abruptly away from him, almost stumbling in her haste to get free. Driving back she had become tense again, and it showed in the higher pitch of her voice.

On the outskirts of the village Adam drew the car into a layby.

'Laura, is something wrong? I didn't mean to offend you back there.'

'No, there's nothing wrong. It's just that I didn't expect . . .'

'What?'

'I imagined we came out to discuss Edward!' He felt a brief flare of anger and thought, as Nicholas had before him, how annoying it was to have the boy's name dragged into every conversation. He tried to keep his annoyance hidden. The last thing that he wanted to do was antagonize her.

'We have to establish ourselves as genuine friends,' he said in a semi-joking fashion. 'If we don't, your husband, as well as your son, is likely to smell a rat. I can't risk that professionally.'

'I'm sorry,' said Laura in a small voice. 'I hadn't thought of that.'

'Do you ever think of yourself as a person these days, or only as Edward's mother?'

At first he thought that she was not going to answer him. When she did there was pain in her voice.

'Of course I do, but it's dangerous. I don't want to have any thoughts that are unsuitable for Edward. I'd be too embarrassed. I spend my life guarding my emotions now. Surely you understand? I thought you did.'

'I do, up to a point, but I think you're taking it to extremes. I don't imagine for one moment that he's perpetually tuned in to you. I expect that 98 per cent of the time he's far too busy to intrude on your private thoughts.'

'I don't know.' She sounded very doubtful.

Sod it, thought Adam, I'm not being put off by all this rubbish! He moved nearer to Laura and took her in his arms. At first she merely accepted his kiss, but slowly she began to respond. He found the change from remote and cool blonde to passionate companion stimulating, and his instincts told him to press her further. Reason prevented him. He wanted to see her many more times, and the wrong move now could alienate her completely. He put her carefully from him, making sure that she knew how he felt in order that there should be no fear of rejection in her mind. He knew she badly needed a boost to her self-confidence, and he was more than willing to supply it.

179

At her front door Laura hesitated for a moment, but decided not to ask him in. Her face felt hot and she knew that her clothing was dishevelled. Next time, if there was a next time, she would ask him in. With a cheerful wave he accelerated away, leaving her to fumble with the front door key. Mother-in-law was still up, looking martyred at the lateness of the hour.

'Still up, Mother? You shouldn't have bothered.'

'I don't like to go to bed in case the doorbell goes.'

'Hardly likely at two in the morning. Still, it's up to you.'

The two women looked at each other for a moment. 'Goodnight then,' said Laura brightly, and watched as the older woman made her way up to bed.

She went into the kitchen and made herself more coffee. She could still remember the exact texture of Adam's lips on her own, and feel the strength of his arms around her. She was amazed at her obsession with what was, after all, only an ordinary kiss between two mature adults. She assumed that it was because she had been a stranger to physical contact for so long. It must be like alcohol, she thought with a smile, far more potent when you were unaccustomed to it. It had been nice though, a pleasant change. Next time she would make sure that they began to talk about Edward, but just this once it had been nice.

Through February and March Adam continued to take her out once a week. They did talk about Edward, but Laura felt that the more she saw of Adam the less he believed her. His own contact with Edward was minimal, the occasional glimpse in the hallway or a few minutes in the kitchen while the boy finished his supper. Every time Edward behaved impeccably, and she would see the look of doubt in Adam's eyes as he studied the boy.

She was right in thinking that Adam was no longer as convinced as he had once been. As the weeks went by he began to rationalize his own experiences with Edward. The only strange incident was the frightening images that he had seen when the boy had left him at his last visit. This, he finally decided, had been an extension of an old nightmare involving cars and flying glass that had started after a road accident when he was at medical school. He had probably been tired that day and had started to drift off in his chair. Everything else was a result of listening to Laura and then twisting facts to suit her theory. This was, he decided, exactly what she was doing too, but he could understand why.

She had never had much confidence, and lack of maternal affection had undoubtedly left its mark on her. She couldn't bear to fail in the maternal role herself, and made excuses for every imagined error that she committed. He rather thought that Nicholas, too, had failed to be as supportive as Laura needed, and her fears had grown until they took her over entirely. Normally, faced with such a woman, he would have been consumed with intolerance and anxious to be rid of her. Amazingly he found Laura attractive despite her faults. He was certain that given a sufficient amount of uncritical affection and support she would see for herself what she had done. Until then he appeared to go along with all she said, and made one or two intelligent remarks to stress his participation. Gradually Edward occupied less and less of his thoughts. His attention was now turned to getting Laura into his bed.

In April Edward was six. Unable to think of one boy who might come to his home for tea he suggested instead that Laura asked Adam over and they had a party.

'It would be like a proper family,' he said, his eyes

wide and innocent. 'That would be nice Mummy, wouldn't it?'

She felt a tremor of trepidation, but dismissed it. Adam accepted with pleasure, and arrived at 5.30 bearing a large Fisher Price fire engine. The four of them ate sandwiches and sausages on sticks, while the children had jelly and trifle as well. Finally Edward blew out the candles as the others sang "Happy Birthday".

After tea they all played with Edward's new games, and it was past 7 before Belinda was taken up to bed. Edward stayed downstairs, playing contentedly with the fire engine. Adam caught Laura's glance of pleasure as she watched him sitting in the armchair, and he thought that before long she should be more than willing to become his mistress. It was a long time since he had wanted a woman so much, and even longer since he had been forced to play a waiting game, but it was probably providing additional stimulation. He tried to picture her lost in passion, it was an erotic thought.

At 8 Edward went up for his bath, and Adam joined Laura when she went to tuck him in. Edward was lying on his back, the front of his hair slightly damp from the bathwater, and he watched the two adults intently as they approached his bed. He was unusual, admitted Adam to himself; not many children had such piercing eyes. It was almost unnerving, and he could understand why it troubled Laura. He thought of Laura in his bed again, once she became fulfilled as a woman she would find less and less time to fret over Edward. It would do the boy good to be left alone more. His mother ran around after him far too much for his own good, and he took advantage of it.

Laura stood back. 'Do you want to kiss Adam goodnight, Edward?'

Adam took half a step forward.

'No thank you,' said a cool little voice. 'He can shake my hand if he likes.'

He could do with a clip round the ear now and again thought Adam as he extended his hand. Edward's eyes glittered in the subdued light from the landing.

'Goodnight, Edward, pleasant dreams.'

Edward closed his eyes and did not answer. When I'm more established here things will change, Adam reflected; otherwise that boy is going to grow into an unbearable adolescent. As Laura checked on Belinda Adam heard a faint sigh from Edward's room, followed by silence.

Laura came out and smiled. 'There, they're both in bed and we can have a quiet evening together. That fire engine was a wonderful idea.'

'I'm glad he liked it. Laura, does he ever get smacked?'

She looked surprised. 'Well no, not really. I used to smack him, but then I got those terrible heads.'

Adam groaned to himself, but his face remained a polite mask. 'Of course, I forgot.'

'Why do you ask?'

He was about to extol the virtues of a quick clip when the pain struck him. It pierced through his left temple and there was an explosion of light before his eyes. He gripped the banister rail, wondering what on earth was happening to him and terrified lest he fall down the stairs. The pain struck again, lancing his skull and causing him to groan aloud. He felt the sweat break out on his forehead and upper lip and sank down on the top stair. He was dimly aware of Laura hovering over him, but he could not hear her. All that he was aware of was the pain.

He could not tell how long he sat there. At one time

he blacked out from pain, but as he started to come round it attacked again with renewed frenzy. Then, just as he felt certain that he was going to die, it went. It was as though a switch had been thrown. Everything came back into focus and there was not even a dull headache left behind. He felt fine. Impossible to believe that the pain had existed; but it had, and he knew it. He looked up into Laura's white and frightened face. Frightened yes, but understanding. He grasped her hand and pulled her down next to him.

'I've been such a fool,' he whispered, 'such a bloody fool!' She wondered what he meant.

'Don't worry, Adam, once it's gone it's gone. Let's get downstairs.'

As he sipped hot tea from a brown earthenware mug he wondered how he could explain to her. Fortunately she seemed to require no explanation.

'I suppose that you were thinking something that displeased Edward,' she said in conversational tones. 'You were talking about corporal punishment weren't you?'

'How can you be so matter-of-fact?' Adam was incredulous. 'How can you possibly live with this sort of thing?'

'I've had a lot of practice; six years to be exact!'

'But I had no idea. I thought that . . .' He tailed off, unwilling to admit to her that she had failed to convince him.

'Don't worry; I expect that you thought I exaggerated, didn't you?' He nodded. 'I don't blame you. After all, what sane person would believe it?'

The full horror was only just beginning to penetrate Adam's brain.

'But, how can anyone ever discipline him? What chance is there of bringing him up properly?'

'None,' said Laura flatly. 'I don't think that bothers him. He only wants to be looked after physically until he's old enough to do it for himself. After that he'll probably walk out of our lives for ever. Like a cuckoo!'

They sat in the kitchen for a long time, and now it was Adam's turn to be enveloped in the kind of despair Laura felt more frequently. She was strengthened by the fact that at last Edward had turned upon someone else; she was no longer alone. She took Adam's hand and held it tightly.

'Together we might be able to do something, Adam. He may have just made his biggest mistake.'

The way he felt at the moment Adam simply wanted to get the hell out of Edward's life for ever, but his feelings for Laura kept him where he was. He understood too her reluctance for physical involvement. It would be quite impossible for him ever to think of Laura in a sexual way when Edward was in the same house. In the early hours of the morning he drove slowly home, knowing that his life would never be the same again.

After Adam had left Laura found that her spirits were higher than she could remember for years. Naturally she felt sorry for Adam, but his experience was one that had become familiar to her and her concern was lessened by the realization that now, at last, Edward had over-reached himself and set her free from the burden of carrying on alone. She could tell that Adam had been completely shattered, pain and shock had combined to reduce him to a shell of his normal self. Once he had recovered then he would be a tower of strength, she was certain of that; together they would prove a powerful combination as they attempted to cope with Edward.

At breakfast the next morning both the children were subdued, partly due to their late night, but also she suspected because they were aware that a mistake had been made. She did not doubt that Edward would have told Belinda, and the little girl was heavy-eyed and silent. Once Edward was at school Laura tried to cheer Belinda up by taking her out for a milkshake and doughnut. Today even that tried and tested formula failed to work, Belinda's responses were muted, and she looked near to tears most of the time. Eventually Laura gave up. She took the child back home and handed her over to Heather. No one, not even a trouble Belinda, was going to spoil her good mood.

She waited for a telephone call from Adam, but by lunchtime he had not contacted her. Unwilling to put pressure on him she tried to be patient, but when the phone rang just as she was leaving to collect Edward her heart raced and she dashed to answer it.

'Hello!'

'Laura, is that you?' She recognized Nicholas's voice, and disappointment filled her.

'Nicholas?'

'Yes. Laura, could I come over tonight? I need to talk to you privately, when the children are in bed.'

'Is it urgent?' She had hoped for a chance to see Adam again.

'Actually it is.'

'All right then, about 8? I must go now, school ends soon.'

'Of course. I'll be round at 8. Goodbye, Laura.'

Edward turned out to be in such a difficult mood that the task of keeping the peace until bedtime fully occupied Laura, and she scarcely spared Nicholas a thought. She would have worried about Adam, but knew that with Edward around this was a luxury she

186

could not afford. If she had heard nothing at the end of the day then she would ring after Nicholas left.

Her husband arrived promptly, and as she took him into the dining-room the telephone shrilled out. Flustered she left Nicholas in the middle of the room and hurried back to the hall.

'Laura? It's Adam. How are things?'

'Why good evening,' she kept her tone neutral, 'how nice to hear from you, Sarah.'

'Sarah? Who the hell have you got there?'

'Fine thank you. Nicholas is here tonight otherwise I'd love to.'

'I'll call again about 10. I thought we ought to try and get away for a weekend to discuss everything; any chance?'

'Lovely; I'll see what I can do. Thanks for calling.'

She knew by Nicholas's guilty look that he had been eavesdropping. It had occurred to her lately that he was anxious for her to get herself a man friend and thus assure him that everything had worked out for the best. She refused to give him that much satisfaction, and was determined to keep Adam a secret for as long as possible.

'Well then, Nicholas? What can I do for you?'

Nicholas looked at Laura in surprise. She was far more decisive tonight, and had lost the air of defeat that had settled on her features over the past few years. In fact, he admitted to himself, she looked an attractive woman again. Illogically he found that he was annoyed that she was proving capable of coping on her own. Why hadn't she been like this when they were together? If only she had made the effort they would still be living in this house, and he wouldn't be in the mess he was.

'Laura, I don't quite know how to put this, and I

don't want you upsetting yourself when I tell you . . .'

'Tell me what?' She wasn't really interested, but tried to concentrate.

'Laura, I want a divorce.'

'Really? So soon? I understood that this was to be "civilized". A separation, and then a gentle untying of the marital knot. Do you mean that you want me to start proceedings against you?'

Nicholas frowned. 'I suppose so; I mean I can scarcely divorce you, can I?'

'Why Nicholas?'

'Because you haven't done anything wrong!' His aggrieved voice made her smile.

'I didn't mean that! I meant, why a divorce?'

'Oh. Well, you see . . . It isn't that I'm in a hurry for my own sake . . .' She was tired of hearing him talk around the point, and she wanted him out of the house as soon as possible. She tried to help him.

'Vicky wants you to divorce me, is that it?'

He turned red. 'You know about Vicky?'

'Yes.'

'Well, I can't imagine how, but that's a great relief because in a way it is because of her. She's pregnant.'

Her first thought was that Nicholas didn't sound very pleased. Obviously it was a mistake, and it would cause a hiccup in Vicky's career as well as pitching Nicholas back into the world of nappies and feeds.

'How careless!' It was all that she could think of to say.

Nicholas remained silent. It was careless, and damned annoying. It had caused Vicky to turn into a terrible shrew in her fury, and when he remembered the effect of children on his previous marriages he found his courage deserting him. However, it was an established fact and he must now do the right thing for them all. His days of romance in the cottage had been blissful but brief. This was the real world again.

Laura was trying to think quickly, and at first it appeared to her that this could be a benefit. Free, she would be able to see more of Adam, and she could play on Nicholas's sense of guilt and manage some time away from the children. She looked thoughtful, keeping Nicholas in suspense.

'Well, I don't know . . . I don't particularly want to be divorced. What advantages would it give me? At least while I'm your wife I retain my legal rights. There's the question of the house, insurance, pension rights.'

'You're a mercenary bitch, aren't you?'

'I'm being practical, which is more than you've been, if I may say so.'

'Look, Laura, you won't finish up worse off; you have my word on it.'

'Well, I don't know. I think it's best to wait. Suppose this affair doesn't work out?'

He was becoming annoyed, which was her intention. 'I shan't come back here even if it doesn't,' he said angrily. 'I couldn't live with you again ever.'

'Thank you, Nicholas! I'd like a little time to think this over.'

'Of course. How long?'

'Well, really I'd like to be on my own for a couple of days. I suppose you couldn't come here for the weekend and look after things while I go off and try to work things out?'

He looked doubtful, thinking of Vicky's reaction. 'I could, but where would you go?'

'To a quiet hotel somewhere. I can't possibly think clearly with Edward and Bee under my feet all the time. If you find it too much trouble then I don't know when I will be able to give you your answer.'

'I give in,' said Nicholas at last. 'Your piece of blackmail is effective. Do you want to leave Friday evening?'

'I'll let you know. Now, I expect that you're in a hurry to be off.'

Nicholas left. At least he had something to tell Vicky, even if it wasn't quite what she wanted to hear.

When Adam called back he was jubilant at her news. 'Thank God for that! The way I feel at the moment I wouldn't even dare think about food in case Edward poisoned it!'

'Friday then? I'll drive to Rottingdean and meet you in the bar of the White Horse.'

'Excellent! Take care until then, Laura.'

It was wonderful to have someone who was concerned about her again, and she felt no guilt at using Nicholas. After all, if he had only listened to her then they would still be happily married. He had been so swift to condemn her as unstable, and she would never truly forgive him for that.

Despite this she did feel vaguely sorry for him when she left the children in his care. He looked uneasy, as though the thought of forty-eight hours alone with them was something of an ordeal. The children were cheerful enough, although she could tell from Edward's refusal to kiss her goodbye that she had not managed to keep everything from him. She ruffled Belinda's dark curls, and realized that she was turning into a beautiful little girl. It was a good thing, since all her personality was slowly being submerged. She was simply a pale shadow behind her brother. Edward caught her eyes and smiled, so she put the thought away.

' 'Bye then. Have a nice weekend.'

'Drive carefully,' instructed Nicholas, terrified that she might have an accident and leave him stranded for weeks. She sounded the horn loudly as she swung away from the house. She was free for two whole days.

Edward ran up the stairs and pressed his face to the front bedroom window. He was consumed by rage, suddenly aware that she was going somewhere nice and he was too late to stop her. He tried to direct his rage at the rapidly disappearing car, but it was out of his range and he could only watch in impotent fury. He flung his temper at Belinda, and she winced as she caught the full force of it. Poor Edward, she thought, he was often angry. Her pity annoyed Edward even more. Slowly he resigned himself to the fact that there was nothing more he could do for now, but when his mother came home she would be sorry. She would be very sorry indeed.

Adam was drinking his second whisky when she arrived, walking slowly through the bar and causing men's eyes to turn and follow her. The white angora dress clung to her body, and the slim gold belt emphasized her narrow waist. He realized that when she was younger she must have been a real beauty. Running his fingers through his thatch of hair he got off the bar stool. This was the only difficult part, telling her what he had arranged. He was certain it was what she wanted, but a lot depended on how he put it. Women were unpredictable over such matters.

He smiled and took her hand. 'You look fantastic! Good journey?'

'Not bad. I took a couple of wrong turnings but nothing disastrous.'

'Have you eaten. I didn't book a table, but we can eat if you want to.'

'It's all right; I'm not hungry.' She wasn't, her stomach was tight with nerves.

'A drink then? Gin? Sherry?'

'I'll join you in a whisky, Adam, please.'

He watched her out of the corners of his eyes. She was nervous, but not too bad. They had plenty of time. He made a conscious effort to exercise his charm. He had plenty of charm, but it wasn't something that he exerted automatically. Every smile, every gesture, necessitated careful thought. It never failed to surprise him when it worked, the lack of spontaneity could not be as apparent as he thought. He sometimes regretted the need to pretend, but his naturally severe expression and the coldness of his eyes had in the past frightened women off. Laura needed an obvious display of warmth and attention if she was to unwind tonight.

She sipped her whisky slowly, noticing for the first time how detached Adam's grey eyes were when he was caught off guard, and noticing too the harsh set to his mouth when it was in repose. She knew that this weekend wasn't only to talk about Edward, it was their opportunity to become lovers. She knew, and yet nothing had been said. At home, when she had dared to think about it, she had been full of anticipation. It had been a long time since she had slept with a man, and she found Adam exciting and attractive. Now that they were finally free to make love all that she wanted to do was climb into a single bed and sleep.

'Laura?'

She jumped. 'I'm sorry?'

'I said, shall we go up? The room's lovely. I put my case there about an hour ago.'

'I am quite tired actually, so perhaps we might as well.' Not an enthusiastic response, she knew, but Adam's expression of attentive concern did not falter.

They climbed two flights of stairs without a word, and Laura followed Adam into the double room. He had been correct when he had said it was lovely. A vast

192

double bed dominated the room, with built-in ward-robes and a vanity suite. A door led off to a shower room, and there was a telephone, television and radio console. Green velvet curtains covered the windows, and a matching bedspread was turned down displaying crisp white pillows. She stood by the bed, her overnight case in her hand. Adam was whistling quietly as he took off his shoes and sat in the only armchair.

'Like it?' he enquired.

I can't do this, thought Laura in panic. I simply cannot climb into that double bed and make love with the wild abandon that he will expect. I'm too old to enjoy this, and I'm too inexperienced to satisfy him. A faithful married life wasn't good preparation for an illicit weekend in a hotel, and her courage drained away the longer that she stood there. Adam looked up at her, his eyes narrowed.

'Is there anything wrong?'

'No, of course not. It's a lovely room.'

He stood up and walked round to her, placing an arm over her shoulders.

'Don't look like that, Laura. I want you to enjoy your weekend.'

She tried to pull herself together. 'Of course I will; it's just that I'm not used to this sort of thing.'

That, thought Adam, was painfully obvious. Her terror-struck appearance bore no resemblance to that of an experienced woman away for a weekend with a lover. He had little patience with the games that women played, but this time he knew that however annoying it was Laura's doubts were genuine. He could blow the whole thing if he sounded irritable or impatient. He knew too that had he spent five years bringing up Edward his nerves would be frayed. He forced down a small flare of annoyance and smiled at Laura.

'I'm sorry if you didn't want a double room, and I know that I should have asked you first. If you like, you can stay here and I'll take a single room. After all, we can still discuss Edward over the weekend, which was one reason for coming away. What do you say?'

She wished that he hadn't asked her. If she did't take up his offer, then she could hardly continue to be coy. If only she could explain that she did want him, but not like this. She wanted an impetuous coming together, not a clinical coupling in a hotel bedroom. She gave herself a mental shake. Adam had been kind to her, and she had known what to expect, her last-minute nerves were unfair to him. She needed Adam, and suddenly terrified that she might lose him through her stupidity she put down her case and took off her light jacket.

'A double room is exactly what I wanted. I'm sorry, I was just being silly. Have you been to this hotel before?'

He had watched the play of emotions on her face, and guessed that she had made her decision for the wrong reasons. It didn't matter. In the end it would all work out the same. It was a pity that she was so terrified of losing him, but if their relationship had to be one-sided it was better that he held the balance of power. Her attempt at light conversation was unfortunate to say the least.

'No,' he said with a boyish smile, 'I don't take all my women to the same hotel. I might get a bad reputation.'

Laura coloured. 'I didn't mean that!'

'No; I haven't been here before. A colleague recommended it. Shall I shower first?' Laura didn't want Adam in bed watching when she came out of the shower.

'No, I will if you don't mind.'

'Suits me.'

She took her nightdress into the shower room with her. It was a new pink nylon one, with thin shoulder straps and a skirt that had lace round the hem. It was, she decided as she put it on, perfectly horrible. She felt like a badly decorated cake. Self-consciously she walked back into the bedroom, but Adam was putting clothes into drawers and scarcely glanced at her. She climbed into the bed, and picked up the newspaper he had left on the table. He was gone no time, and wandered back toweling his hair as though they had been married for years.

Obviously he never wore pyjamas, or not when on an assignation, she thought nervously. He got into bed beside her and looked thoughtfully at her.

'Feeling better?'

'Yes, much thank you.'

His right hand came over and traced the line of her jaw. She began to tremble as he drew her towards him. What surprised her was how patient he was. She had always been slow to become aroused, a frequent cause for complaint from Nicholas, even in their early days. She had expected Adam to do things in his own time, but he waited for her. Gradually, as she unwound beneath his expert and thoughtful caresses, she found that she was responding enthusiastically. She had one moment of panic when he moved on top of her, but was soothed by his whispered words of endearment. After that she gave herself up entirely to his expertise, and heard her own cry of release with genuine amazement. She had not expected it to be so good the first time.

Adam felt completely exhausted when it was over. He had never had to work so hard, because it had never mattered as much before. At least he had got it right, and next time she should be more at ease and take a more active part. Her gratitude touched him; women weren't usually grateful, just highly indignant if you failed them. As he drifted off to sleep a terrible thought struck him, and he rolled round to whisper in Laura's ear. You were fixed up were you?' Laura too was nearly asleep, and imagined that he was enquiring as to whether she was satisfied. 'Of course,' she mumbled, surprised that he didn't know. Relieved he fell asleep.

In the morning things were much better. Laura felt quite at ease with Adam, despite the surprise of waking up with a man next to her again. He found her increased confidence encouraging, and wanted to make love to her again. This time Laura tried to find out what Adam liked, and surprised herself by her actions.

'We must get dressed woman, or the day will be over,' laughed Adam. 'I hope I last the course!'

'I shall have to look out for a replacement, in case you don't,' retorted Laura. She got out of bed and searched for her nightdress.

'I shouldn't bother,' said Adam, 'it's hideous!'

'I know. I can't think why I bought it.' She began to dress, selecting blue slacks and a white polo-necked jersey.

'You're on the pill, are you?' asked Adam, as he pulled on his denims. Laura, struggling to get her head through the jersey opening, was grateful that he couldn't see her face. Suddenly she knew what he had asked her last night. He mustn't be told; it would ruin their weekend and cause ill feeling when everything was going so well. She would get a prescription as soon as she returned home and trust to luck for the next day. 'Yes,' she managed as she emerged from her dressing. 'I've never had any trouble on it.'

Adam had lost interest; he had only wanted confirmation of her sleepy response last night. They were both feeling very happy as they went down to breakfast.

Later in the morning they strolled along the beach, and Laura told him about Nicholas and his request for a divorce.

'That's how I managed to get a weekend away. He thinks that I'm going to make my decision while I'm here.'

'And are you?'

Laura shrugged. 'There's no decision to make. He can have his divorce as soon as he likes. Now that he's gone I suppose that it won't make any difference to me whether we're legally tied or not. In fact, in some ways it would be nice to be free. At the moment I'm neither fish nor fowl!'

'How will Edward react do you think?'

'I've no idea. He probably won't be too keen on Vicky having a baby. He likes his Auntie and enjoys her undivided attention.'

'That's her problem, not yours.'

They strolled on in silence. Laura knew that Adam might well feel under pressure once she became single again, and she hastened to put his mind at rest.

'I don't think that I would ever marry again,' she said quietly. 'Edward rather precludes that state of affairs.'

'Time might alter things; I shouldn't make a decision just yet. Why in five years you might meet your soulmate and live happily ever after!' They both laughed. Adam had made it clear that he wasn't her soulmate, and if Laura was secretly disappointed that he had been so quick to point it out she disguised it well.

They had lunch in a small pub, and then drove out of town and along the coast road. It was a warm day for the end of April, and Adam parked the car in a shady spot before they set off for a walk. Once they were well away from civilization, surrounded only by rolling hills and the occasional dog, Adam felt free to mention Edward.

'I've been thinking about the other night, Laura, when I annoyed Edward. I can't think of any way in which he can be stopped. After all – I know it's a terrifying thought – but he has the advantage of knowing in advance what we're going to say or do. It's got me completely baffled. One thing is plain; he must be talked to. Told how wrong it is to hurt people in the way he does. He can't be controlled, but he can be guided. That's all that's left.'

Laura sat down on a small hillock and put her arms round her knees.

'He pretends that he doesn't know what I'm talking about. He blocks me out. There's no point in talking to him.'

'Then let me try. He might take it better from a man.'

'You know that isn't true. He doesn't like being told what to do.'

Adam began to get impatient. 'He's only six years old! He'll have to listen!'

'He isn't six; he isn't any age. Can't you understand that? You will persist in talking as though he's a normal child, but he isn't. He knows that it's wrong to hurt people, but he doesn't care. Our rules don't apply to him. I don't think he can understand why we insist upon codes of conduct. For Edward, the end justifies the means, and it always will. Believe me, I've watched him long enough to know that I'm right.'

'Then what do you suggest that we do?'

Laura looked up into his grey eyes, and remembered how they had looked last night. She recalled the feel of his body pressed close to hers, and the sensations that he had aroused in her. She didn't want to sit here discussing Edward, she wanted to enjoy the weekend to the full; there might never be another opportunity for them to be alone together. 'I don't want to talk about Edward any more,' she said firmly. 'He's already spoilt too many things. I want us to have a good time.'

Adam's eyes left hers and gazed off into the distance. 'You don't really know me, Laura. Please don't expect too much of me. I'm a very selfish person, and far too old to change now.' Although he laughed lightly Laura knew that he intended her to be warned. She understood him better than he thought, and she liked him as he was.

'Don't worry, I don't want more than you're able to give. I understand that you're a busy, independent man who likes women, but only in their place! Now, I think this is the place. Don't you?'

'Shameless hussy!' She had managed to turn the serious moment away, and had reminded him too that for her there were few opportunities for sexual release. She deserved this weekend.

They went back to the hotel where he made love to her again. After, while she slept, he found himself regretting that he wasn't able to offer her a permanent relationship. He liked her more than any other woman he had met. Liked her even more than he had liked Vicky, which was surprising. Despite that, as soon as he had imagined that she might be hoping for marriage then he had begun to panic. He knew that he would never change.

They had dinner in the dining-room, and then some drinks in the bar. By 9 o'clock Adam wanted to go up to bed again, and knew from the glances that Laura threw at him that her desire matched his. This time he encouraged her towards more sophisticated preliminaries, and found her an enthusiastic pupil. It was after midnight when they eventually lay quietly, Adam with his head on Laura's breast while she slept. He was happy and relaxed, his thoughts wandering idly. One moment he was recalling Laura's face at moments of ecstasy and the next he was faced with an image of Edward's hate-congested features. The eyes gleamed blackly from the pale face, the lips were drawn back from the small baby teeth in a snarl of primitive fury. Adam sat bolt upright, feeling his heart racing.

The room was silent. Laura slept quietly on, her expression peaceful. He waited, certain that the vision would return. His body tensed, remembering the pain that Edward could inflict.

After a few minutes he began to relax. He could no longer picture Edward's face, and his pulse rate slowed again. He decided that it was his own guilty conscience that had caused the vision, and chided himself for fearing a child who was safely in bed and miles away. Laura stirred, and Adam stretched his body full length beside her. Despite himself he was still tense, waiting for something else to happen. As he drifted off to sleep he thought that he saw Edward's face once more, but it could easily have been a dream.

Edward sat crouched on the end of his bed. He had never been so angry, or felt so helpless. It was the worst weekend of his life, and he wanted to hit out at everyone round him. From the moment his mother had left he had discovered that his father was thinking only of Auntie Vicky. Even when he was smiling and playing with Edward and Belinda there was Auntie Vicky hovering in the background. As usual in his father's thoughts she had very few clothes on. Not that this disturbed Edward; he was used to it by now. What annoyed him was that his father could be so two-faced. He would tell Belinda how nice it was to be with her for a weekend while cursing in his mind because Vicky was alone and he couldn't see her.

As Saturday drew to a close Edward had worked out just who was to blame for his misery. It was Dr Castle. His mother had gone away to see him, Edward knew that, and she had been happy and excited. If Dr Castle hadn't asked his mother to go away then his father could have stayed with Auntie Vicky and everything would have been the same as normal. He didn't blame his mother too much, she was easily led, and her thoughts were always a scrambled mess. Not, it was Dr Castle who was responsible. Tonight, as he looked out at the dark sky, he held an image of the man in his brain and then focussed all of his hatred and resentment on it. He tried harder than ever before, almost forgetting to breathe as he concentrated. He couldn't tell if he succeeded or not, but he continued to try until he was worn out and reluctantly fell asleep.

'Sunday,' whispered Adam in Laura's ear. She opened her eyes.

'Is it morning already? I feel too tired to get up.'

'We'll stay here then!' He slid his hand down the front of nightgown and stroked her breasts. She lay there, calm and relaxed, and gave herself up to pleasure. She knew that it was nearly over, and was determined to enjoy herself to the full. Once she returned to Edward she might never manage to get away again; at least she would have these memories to sustain her. She moved closer to Adam.

After breakfast they went down to the sea again, and walked hand-in-hand along the shore line. Laura noticed how young Adam looked when the breeze blew his hair back off his forehead. It was possible to picture him as a boy for once, and she felt protective towards him. She hoped that he appreciated the danger of his situation now, and searched around for some way of warning him.

'After we go back,' she said slowly, 'you will be careful of your thoughts when you come to the house, won't you?'

'Of course. I'll be very circumspect!'

'He'll be trying to find out what's gone on.'

Adam remembered his night-time vision. 'Yes, I know he will.'

'If he does find out, because one of us makes a mistake for a few seconds, then I think he might be dangerous.'

Adam stood looking out to sea, remembering the quality of the hatred that he had witnessed last night. 'Don't worry, Laura; I shan't underestimate him I promise you.'

She stood beside him, needing to tell him while they were still alone.

'I want you to know what a difference you've made to my life, Adam. Not only because you understand, but also because of this weekend. It's made a big difference to me, and I'm very grateful. Even if I never see you again I will remain grateful. I feel a different person thanks to you.'

Adam glanced at her out of the corners of his eyes. She looked very slender and frail as she stood next to him, and he wished that he could promise her more, but they both understood how tenuous his ties of affection were.

'You will see me again, Laura. We haven't reached the end yet.'

'It won't be like this again. This has been perfect.'

He took hold of her shoulders and swung her round to face him. 'I'm grateful as well. It's been something special for me, something that will stay with me long after we've parted. I want you to believe that, Laura; it's all that I've got to offer you, but it's the truth. You are something special, remember that.'

He took her hand again, and they walked on, but in silence now. It was as though they both sensed that by their actions this weekend they had changed the future irrevocably, and now they were appreciating the difficulties that lay ahead. Their interlude was over.

After lunch Adam came out to see Laura drive off. He struggled for cheerful words, knowing how apprehensive he would be if Edward were waiting for him.

'Good luck,' he said as he pushed her case into the boot. 'I'll call you Tuesday morning, about 9.30.'

Laura climbed back out of the driving seat and put her arms round his chest.

'I'm afraid,' she said, 'very afraid.' He held her tightly, there were no words of comfort that he could utter. After a moment she found the courage to release herself, and put a cheerful smile on her face.

'Right then, off I go! Drive carefully, Adam; you've got a long way to go.'

He raised his hand as she sped away from him. He thought that she was very brave.

As soon as she pulled into the driveway she could feel his rage. It surrounded her like a heavy fog, making clear thought impossible. She rang the doorbell, and saw with relief that only Nicholas and Belinda were standing there. Nicholas was openly relieved that she was back on time.

'Good journey, Laura? Not too much traffic?' She took her case from the boot and followed him into the hall.

'No, a very clear run really. Hello, Belinda, darling, where's Edward?'

'Upstairs,' said Nicholas. 'He said that he had a headache. I think really he was missing you.'

'I'll go up in a minute. Everything was all right, was it? No crises?'

'Everything was fine. Look, I'd really like to get off now if you don't mind, Laura. Could I ring you tomorrow evening for a talk?'

'Of course. Don't worry. I've decided to be sensible about it all.'

Relief showed on every line of Nicholas's face, and he smiled gratefully at Laura.

'You won't regret it, Laura. I'll make sure that you always have everything you need.'

'I'm sure you will, Nicholas.' She took Belinda's hand and together they waved Nicholas off. Once back inside Laura felt very tired, but she knew that she had to see Edward. Leaving Belinda in the kitchen helping her grandmother get the tea, she climbed the stairs.

Outside his bedroom door she paused, trying to fix some image in her mind. She decided upon a large horsechestnut tree, its branches blotting all the light from the sky. With that thought firmly entrenched she opened the door. Edward was reading, but looked up as she entered.

'Did you have a nice time, Mummy?' His expression was carefully neutral, his voice quiet.

'Very nice thank you, Edward.' The chestnut tree, she reminded herself, think of the tree. Edward looked at her, puzzled.

'Where did you go, Mummy?'

204

'To the seaside. I stayed at a hotel.'

'On your own?'

'Yes, on my own. Did you have a nice time with Daddy?' He ignored her question, and she knew that he was trying to work out the significance of the tree. Afraid that she would weaken she walked over to his window, keeping her back towards him.

'Did Daddy take you out?'

Edward did not reply. She turned to look at him. His eyes were closed and there was a look of concentration on his features. She saw how tightly his hands were clasping the book he held. The tree. Think of the tree, she urged herself. She heard him begin to hum, softly at first, but then louder. The tree began to dissolve; she had increasing difficulty in holding its image. She tried to walk away, but her feet were rooted to the floor. All that she could hear was the humming. Dimly she became aware that someone else had joined in, there were two separate sounds now that were trying to break her concentration. She thought of chestnut leaves, of the conkers falling in the autumn, but it was no use. She could no longer recall how the branches should look, or what shape the leaves should be. Sweat broke out on her top lip and on the back of her neck. An image of Adam threatened to appear and she fought desperately to bury it, but to no avail. Hard as she tried he would not be kept away. He came slowly into focus, and she knew that she was losing.

Edward was standing up now, his eyes were still closed and his face was calm. He could tell that he was winning. Laura watched in horror as Adam came to the forefront of her mind. Not just Adam, but Adam naked and masterful. She was with him, on the bed, totally abandoning herself to him. It was an obscene image, the truth but distorted. She had never been so

205

wanton, Adam had never leered as he was leering now. The image was wrong, spoilt, tarnished by an outsider. She screamed and the scene faded away.

The room was quiet. Edward was again seated on his bed, his dark eyes watching her thoughtfully. She could not meet his gaze and stumbled towards the doorway. Belinda was standing there, her blue eyes bewildered by what she had seen. Laura stopped by her daughter for a moment.

'So it was you who helped him!'

Belinda continued to stare. Angrily Laura brushed her aside and then half ran to the safety of her bedroom. She had failed. Despite her determination and increased self-confidence she had failed utterly. Edward could no longer be overcome; he had grown too strong and had reinforcements. She cried from fear and guilt, and stayed in her room until she heard Heather running Belinda's bath. Then she went downstairs and had a cup of coffee.

Somehow she made herself go and kiss the children goodnight. They both appeared the same as usual, but her knowledge of what they had seen embarrassed her and made normal conversation impossible. She did not offer to read a story, and neither of them reminded her. As she went down the stairs she heard Belinda getting out of bed, but she could not be bothered to stop her. What was the point? They could communicate with or without her permission these days.

She wanted to call Adam, but even if he was home there was nothing that he could do, and he might well feel that if she couldn't manage for an hour then he was better off staying away. She still needed him, and was afraid to take the risk. She went to bed early, and hoped that a good night's sleep would give her more strength to oppose the children. It had to be 'the children' now. However unwillingly, Belinda had joined her brother, and was giving him much needed support.

It was three in the morning when she awoke. She stretched sensuously, feeling again Adam's firm hands on her body. She knew that he wasn't there, but enjoyed the memory. After a few minutes she became more fully awake, but the memories and the sensations persisted. She could feel too her body's responses, and quickly sat up pulling the neck of her nightdress closely round her. For a moment the feelings stopped. Then, as she sat in solitude they began again. She knew that she had to take action, that something was wrong, but she couldn't quite grasp what it was. Her treacherous body urged her to enjoy herself, to indulge her fantasy a little longer.

With a shock she realized that it wasn't a fantasy, she was being used. It was the most terrifying thing that had happened to her, and her reaction was instinctive. She pulled on her dressing gown and flew along the landing to Edward's room. He was lying on his back, and turned his head to look at her as she burst in.

'Stop it!' She was screaming, but didn't care. 'Stop it at once! You mustn't do that! It's wrong, can't you understand that? It's completely wrong!'

'Go away,' said Edward. 'I don't want you in here. Go back to your room. I'm trying to sleep.'

'Leave me alone,' shrieked Laura. 'I'll kill you if you ever do that again. Do you hear me? I'll kill you!'

There was the sound of doors opening. Behind her faces peered round bedroom doors. Her mother-in-law, Heather, and finally Belinda. She turned round on them all.

'Go back to your beds! I'm talking to Edward privately.'

Ruth approached her slowly. 'Laura dear, come back

to bed. You're distraught, you have had a bad dream. Come along Laura.' She twisted herself free, dimly aware of what an hysterical figure she must appear to them all.

'He's a wicked boy,' she shouted, 'a wicked wicked child!'

'Come along, Laura, or we'll have to call the doctor.' The soothing tones warned her, and she tried to calm down. Her fury was fuelled by the fact that she had responded, had allowed him to prolong his experiment after she was awake. She heard him chuckle softly as she finally turned away and was led back to bed. Once in it she accepted a sleeping pill and then waited tensely for it to work. Apparently he had tired of the new game for she was left alone until the pill took effect. After that she had no way of knowing what he did.

In the morning both the children behaved perfectly normally. Belinda had started school as a rising five after Easter, and she was often a little tearful in the mornings now. As she sat grizzling over her cereal Laura glanced quickly at Edward. Dressed in his uniform he was eating his toast and looking as neat and composed as ever. The scene the night before might never have taken place. As soon as they had been taken to school she hurried to the telephone. She had to talk to someone, and there was only Adam. Hoping that he hadn't already left for work she dialled the number of his flat. She let it ring for five minutes, but then admitted that he couldn't be there. Replacing the receiver she was overwhelmed by a sense of desolation.

Suddenly the telephone rang loudly, and she jumped in surprise. Hoping it was Adam ringing her from the hospital she grabbed the receiver. 'Hello!' Her voice was eager.

'Laura? It's Nicholas. I wondered if you could manage lunch with me today. I haven't gone to town; Vicky isn't feeling too well.'

'I am sorry. Where did you have in mind?'

Arrangements were made, and Laura felt relieved that at least she wouldn't have to spend the day brooding. She would meet Nicholas at 1 o'clock in a small local restaurant. Until then there was her unpacking to keep her busy.

At 12.30 she changed into a linen suit and left the house. Heather and Ruth had kept their distance during the morning, but she had tried very hard to appear relaxed. Hopefully they would decide it was the strain of the weekend that had caused her behaviour, for she had no intention of starting the round of doctors again. She knew that in future she must be more careful; however much she was provoked she could not afford screaming scenes in front of witnesses.

Nicholas was waiting for her, polite, friendly and attentive. It was as though they were going out together for the first time instead of the last. They made small talk until the main course arrived, and then over their steaks Nicholas asked Laura if she had meant what she said about the divorce.

'Yes, of course. I'll go and see Mr Able this week if you like.'

'That would be best, Laura. He's very reliable, and will make sure you get everything to which you're entitled.'

'I'm sure that he needn't worry, Nicholas. I trust you implicitly.'

She did, in this respect. Nicholas would never be able to live with himself if he tried to cheat her out of her rights. To her surprise Nicholas flushed.

'The trouble is, Laura, there isn't only me to consider. As you must realize I have to think of Vicky and the baby. I can't just give every penny I earn to you and the children.'

Laura kept her eyes on her plate, determined to be reasonable about it all.

'I know that. However, Victoria does have a job, and I imagine that she intends to return to it once the baby's born?'

'Naturally. The point is, Laura, there are rules covering this sort of thing. You get about a third of my gross, less anything you earn, of course. Talking of that, now Bee is at school, you are able to go back to work really, wouldn't you say?'

She lifted her eyes to his. 'Nicholas you are a wealthy man, this pathetic penny-pinching conversation is quite ludicrous. If all you're going to do is repeat Victoria's monetary policy to me then I'd like to go home now. I think you would be the first to admit that Edward and Belinda are quite demanding, and I have no intention of returning to work until Bee is at least seven, if at all. It wouldn't be fair on any of us. In any case, I cannot believe that this is your feeling on the subject.'

'Plenty of women like to go back to work,' he said sulkily. 'Others don't have any choice if their husband's income is insufficient to maintain them.'

'Exactly. I however do have a choice, and I've just made it.'

Nicholas cleared his throat.

'If you like Edward could come and live with us.' Laura's fork froze in mid-air. She couldn't believe her ears.

'Edward? Come and live with you? Certainly not!'

'But you've always found him difficult, haven't you? We thought you might like the idea. After all Vicky's always got on splendidly with him.'

'Would she like my house?' Laura's voice was icy.

'Or Belinda, too, perhaps? A ready-made family for you both? My God, you've got a nerve!'

Nicholas was embarrassed, but he had given his word that he would mention it, and the thought of Vicky spurred him on.

'Well then, don't come whining to me when you can't manage. I've given you the chance of less to cope with, and you've turned it down. Fine, that's your right, but please don't come complaining to me the next time Edward gets a bit high-spirited!'

Laura thought of Edward last night and had a hysterical desire to laugh. High-spirited indeed! Nicholas was as blind now as he had always been. She looked at him, trying to recall how she had felt about him when they got married. She supposed that she had been in love, but it had never been like it was with Adam. She had settled for too little, but out of ignorance, not laziness.

'I won't complain,' she said crisply. 'Now, somehow I don't feel very hungry any more. Would you excuse me if I went back home?'

Nicholas wished with all his heart that he had kept Victoria's ideas to himself. She had become totally unreasonable about Laura and Edward lately. He put it down to her unwanted pregnancy, but it was still difficult to live with. He stood up.

'Of course. I'm sorry, Laura.' She turned a cool smile on him.

'That's all right; I understand. You should hear from Mr Able shortly. Goodbye, and thanks for the lunch.' He took her hand in his, and held it for a few seconds too long. Her eyes were thoughtful as she pulled gently away from him. Then she turned and left the restaurant, looking more elegant and composed than he had seen her for years. Regretfully he turned his thoughts towards his new home.

211

As soon as she was home Laura tried to contact Adam, but again without success. Then she rang Mr Able's office and made an appointment for the following morning. Finally she buried herself in a book until it was time to collect Belinda.

Belinda came out of school in the middle of a crowd of giggling girls. She wasn't nearly as bright as Edward, but she was far more popular. Laura was glad that they were at different schools; it gave Belinda her first opportunity to develop as a person in her own right. Already she had been invited out to tea a couple of times, and now she was anxious to return the favour. Laura hesitated only because of Edward. She didn't want him spoiling things for Belinda too soon. Now she noticed afresh how relaxed and happy her daughter was when alone, and how striking in appearance. The deep black curls and bright blue eyes were an attractive combination. She was a small dainty child, and her movements were naturally graceful. Laura wondered if she would grow up to be a good dancer or sportswoman. It would be nice if she did, for she was unlikely to shine academically.

In the car Belinda chattered away. She did this every day, getting all her news out before Edward was collected. After that she became comparatively silent.

'So can Heidi come to tea, Mummy? Tomorrow?' Laura looked for a place to park near the school gates.

'Not tomorrow, but soon,' she promised. 'I'll speak to her Mummy about it.' Belinda jumped up and down on the back seat.

'Thank you, Mummy. I do love you!'

'Cupboard love!' Laura laughed, but she was touched. How happy she would be if there was only Belinda.

By contrast, Edward came out of school alone.

Other boys pushed by in scuffling groups, but Edward walked slowly and with dignity. One or two smaller boys rushed past him shouting; most took care not to cross his path. They all remembered Douglas.

In the car he became talkative. He asked Belinda what she had done, then told her about his day before she could reply. He enjoyed boasting to his sister, knowing full well that she would never manage her work with ease, and enjoying the suppressed resentment that he picked up from her when he indulged himself in this way. He was still talking as they all went indoors.

At the sound of the telephone Laura hurried towards it, almost slipping on the rug in her haste. She snatched it up.

'Laura? It's Adam.' Her legs felt weak with relief. Even the sound of his voice gave her fresh courage.

'How super! I hoped you'd call.'

'Is anything wrong? You sound a bit disturbed.'

Edward hovered in the doorway, casually eavesdropping. She released a blast of rage at him, and took pleasure in his answering look of fury. He moved away and up the stairs, not yet ready to battle with her.

'It's been a bit difficult,' she admitted. 'When can I see you again?'

'That's the trouble, Laura. I've got to cover for a colleague of mine who's had a car accident. I'm going to be hellishly busy for the next few weeks and I just don't see how I can get down to you. Is there any chance of you coming up to town for a night?'

'I don't see why not. Oh Adam, I'm so confused. It's much more difficult than I expected.'

'Why? Is he playing you up?'

'I can't explain over the 'phone. Look, I have to talk to you soon. I have to!'

He could hear the desperation, and his heart sank. He was too busy for her emotional storms. His work schedule was beyond belief, yet he knew that he had to try and help her.

'Can you come up Friday night? I'm off Saturday morning so we could have a lie in.'

'Yes, yes, I'll be with you then. I'm sorry, Adam, but when I tell you you'll understand.'

'Of course,' he soothed her. 'Just take it easy. Try not to get in a state; it won't help.'

'I know that!'

She saw Belinda come into the room, and guessed that Edward had sent her. 'I have to go,' she said swiftly. 'Goodbye.' She hung up without waiting for his answer.

Belinda tugged at her hand. 'Who was that, Mummy?'

'A friend. Haven't you got changed yet?'

'Which friend?'

'Your Uncle Adam. Come on, let's get you out of that skirt.'

'I knew it was him!' Belinda looked delighted with herself. 'I saw him when you were talking. I did, really I did! I can do it too!' She ran up the stairs, overcome by her skill. Laura followed slowly. She felt like a stranger in her own home, and was grateful for the presence of the other two women. Not that they could help her, but they lessened her sense of isolation.

Belinda was in the nursery playing with her Tiny Tears. She still looked excited, and her cheeks were flushed. Laura walked into Edward's room, and found him standing by the window. He didn't bother to turn round. Laura remained by the door.

'You heard your sister? You know what she did?'

'Yes, I know.'

'I hope you feel pleased with yourself.'

He didn't reply. 'Auntie Vicky's going to have a baby,' he said at last.

'I know. Did your father tell you?'

'Not exactly.'

'But you heard it from him?'

'Yes. Why is she?'

'I suppose she wanted one.'

'Are you going to have one, Mummy?'

Her cheeks went hot, and she remembered that she still hadn't got a prescription for the pill.

'I hope not. Why?'

He shrugged. 'Why not? I saw what you did.'

She kept her voice down. 'Do I really have to tell you that spying on people's thoughts is rude? You'll see far too much, and you'll get confused. Don't you understand what you're doing?'

'I used to get confused, when I was small. I don't any more.'

She looked at the square set of his shoulders, the confident tilt of his head, and she knew that he was right. Somehow at six he had accumulated enough knowledge to make sense of all that he saw and heard. She wondered how on earth she was going to keep anything from him again.

'You can't,' he said without turning round. 'There's no way.'

Laura began to tremble, and hurried away from his presence. For one fleeting moment she pictured killing him, but then she pushed the image away. It was too horrifying, as yet. In his room Edward's eyes narrowed in surprise. He hadn't expected that. He was grateful for the warning. She wasn't ready yet, but one day she might be. Now he was on his guard.

*   *   *

Ruth made it plain that she wasn't exactly overjoyed at being asked to baby-sit for Laura.

'You've just had a weekend away. Where are you off to this time?' Laura ignored the querulous note in the older woman's voice.

'I'm going to London. I shall come back on Saturday morning; surely you can cope for one night.'

'I can cope, of course. I just don't like you driving when you're not well.'

'I'm perfectly well thank you, Mother.'

'So you say. I know better; you've got all the signs of bad nerves.'

'I have not got bad nerves,' shouted Laura, and slammed out of the room.

Once she had heard from Adam the children seemed to settle down. Edward went resolutely about the house, making no attempt to interfere in his mother's affairs. Belinda reverted once again to being a normal happy little girl, and on the surface life was pleasant. Laura wasn't impressed by all this. She knew that Edward was waiting until the time was right before he showed his strength again. He could afford to wait, time was on his side.

Adam's flat was a haven of tranquillity. She sat in the living-room drinking a strong gin and tonic and watching as he moved about in the tiny kitchen.

'That was my week,' he concluded, deftly mixing salad dressing while he talked, 'so tell me about yours.'

Laura did. She even managed to tell him the entire truth about the night of her return. Adam continued to prepare the dinner, his face tightening as he heard the details. When the gammon steaks were cooked he took them into the living-room.

'Let's eat in here, off trays. It's much more relaxing.'

Laura picked at the food, only managing half of the salad and a few forkfuls of gammon.

216

'I'm sorry Adam. It's delicious, but I'm not hungry.'

He glanced over at her. 'You're looking a bit thin. Aren't you eating properly at home either?'

'Not really. I'm too strung up.'

Adam forced himself to eat; at least it gave him time to consider what he should say. After the coffee he stacked the dishes in the sink and left them.

'Right then. What are we going to do about Edward?' Laura gazed at him, her eyes beseeching him for constructive advice.

He cleared his throat. 'Laura, have you considered letting Nicholas and Vicky have Edward?'

Her eyes widened. 'Certainly not. That's what he wants, to get away from me. Don't you see, he'd be free there. Free to do what he liked. He'd never be stopped once he got away from me.'

Adam leant forward and touched her lightly on her shoulder. 'Laura, do you believe that you are going to stop him? Ever?'

'Yes. I know that I can. I have to.'

'How Laura? Be sensible. How are you ever going to make any impression on him at all? Don't you think that for your sake, and for Belinda's sake, it might be best to let him go? That's what he's after now, his freedom. If you're going to have any life of your own you have to give him up.'

Laura was shattered by Adam's suggestion. How could she let him go? She knew his potential, knew how evil he could be. In all conscience she could not hand him over to two well-meaning but completely ignorant adults and unleash him upon their lives. He was hers. She was responsible for the fact that he existed, and she could not shirk that responsibility.

'No, Adam. I can't do it.'

'Then you might as well give in now. Every day he

217

takes over a little more. Once it was picking up your thoughts, now he can force thoughts upon you. You've had him for six years and you're losing the battle. You've tried, Laura, but it's hopeless. Let him go.'

'I can't let him go.'

Adam looked her straight in the eyes. 'Do you love him so much?' A look of wry amusement crossed her face.

'No Adam, it isn't that. I don't love him at all any more; quite the opposite. This isn't a maternally possessive streak coming out. I simply couldn't live with myself if I gave into him.'

'Have you allowed yourself to think how it might end?'

'End?' She looked confused. 'I suppose there won't be a proper ending. He'll just grow up and leave. But at least I will have done my best. I have to fulfill my obligations.'

'You aren't worried that he'll take you over? Make you his puppet too?'

'No, Adam, I'm not afraid of that.'

'Perhaps you should be.'

When Adam went into the kitchen to make more coffee Laura sank back into her chair. She hated trying to look into the future, the present was bad enough. Of course it was sensible of Adam to take the long-term view, but day-to-day existence was her main problem. Somehow she felt that the future would take care of itself.

Waiting for the coffee to perk, Adam cursed under his breath. Laura was quite hopeless about the boy. He felt sympathy for Nicholas. If she would hang on to the child then she couldn't expect to keep running to people for assistance.

It was nearly midnight when they went to bed. They

both felt self-conscious once they were lying between the sheets. Laura remembered how Edward had duplicated the sensations so well, and Adam hoped desperately that the boy wasn't able to see what he was doing. It did not make for abandoned love-making, and it was the most unsuccessful and frustrating encounter that Adam had experienced. After he slept Laura cried softly, not because it had been bad but because she realized that it might never be good again.

In the morning Adam was brisk and in a hurry. 'I do have to work at 11 I'm afraid, so I haven't as much time as I'd hoped. I'm sorry.'

'It doesn't matter. At least I've been able to talk to someone.'

He didn't want them to part like this. It might be weeks before he saw her again, and the atmosphere was tense and strained.

'Laura, think about what I said. For all our sakes.'

She put her hands on his shoulders and kissed him on the chin. 'Don't worry about me. I'll be all right.'

He sighed. 'I'll ring you as soon as I can. That's a promise.'

'I've lost him,' thought Laura as she drove home. 'When I refused to let Edward go, then Adam gave up.' She tried to be sensible about it. After all, how could she expect him to understand. If it was his child then he might feel the same as she did. Guilty. She felt incredibly guilty that some mix-up of genes had produced the strange child who was her son. In order to appease the guilt she had to try and fight him, protect society from him. She was beginning to realize that there was only one final solution. The question was how long should she wait?

*   *   *

As May gave way to June and the weather became warm and dry, Laura managed to develop considerable expertise in the art of concealing her thoughts. Despite the fact that the divorce was now under way, and she had not heard from Adam since the end of May, she remained calm and outwardly tranquil. She took pride in blocking Edward whenever she could. Sometimes she even managed to extricate Belinda by removing her from the house and sending her to play some miles away. The outside world became slowly less real to her. Her only reality was Edward.

Edward, too, was becoming an expert. He found his mother's attempts to control him vastly amusing, but as she persisted in her childish games he became piqued. There were times when he could not pick up a single thought from her, only a velvety blackness, and it exhausted him talking to Belinda when she was miles away. He could do it, but it was very tiring. He wondered why his mother bothered. Didn't she realize that he was all powerful? The whole world was waiting for him once he grew a little older. There would be nothing that he couldn't achieve. She was becoming a nuisance with her petty irritations. He suspected that Adam Castle had given her the strength that now sustained her, and he made his plans accordingly.

After the schools broke up in July Adam was less busy. Many of his patients were away abroad for weeks, and he decided to go and see Laura. As far as he could tell everything was under control in the household, and he felt that his visit would do Laura good. He packed an overnight bag and set off for a long weekend.

The first thing that he noticed was how Edward had grown. He was even taller and had broadened out. He had an adult air of self-possession and beside him

Belinda looked like a toddler. After both the children were in bed that night he tried to discuss Edward, but Laura seemed reluctant.

'He might be listening,' she said when Adam tried to persuade her.

It was the first time that he had stayed overnight in the house, and he wondered how he would feel knowing that Edward could be listening. For a few brief moments he felt self-conscious, but then as they made love avidly, both of them trying to make up for the weeks apart, he managed to dismiss it from his mind. He knew that he had to, or the child would ruin their relationship for ever. They talked for a time afterwards, gentle endearments and tender words that brought them even closer together. Later on they slept, Laura cradled against Adam's side.

He didn't know why he woke. For a few moments he lay still, trying to work out where he was. When he finally remembered he reached out for Laura, but she had gone. The other side of the mattress was cold. He wondered if one of the children was ill, and swung his legs out of bed. Before he stood up the door swung quietly open and he felt a shiver of apprehension until he recognized Laura. She was walking on tip-toe, obviously thinking that he was still asleep. He watched her, wondering where she had been and what she was carrying so carefully. She was taking tiny steps, hesitating after every one in case she disturbed him.

'Laura, I'm awake,' he called.

She did not reply. Quietly she moved steadily towards the double bed, then slipped silent in beside him. He was sure now that she had been sleep walking, and anxious not to give her a sudden shock he stayed motionless on the edge of the bed.

The swift downward arc of her right arm took him

221

completely by surprise. He couldn't imagine what she was doing. It was only when he heard the muffled thud, and saw how hard she had to pull before she could raise her arm again that he realized she had aimed a blow of some description, and aimed it where he should have been lying. His stomach muscles tightened, and he suddenly wanted some light. His fumbling hands found the lamp switch and by the light of the dim bulb he at last saw her clearly.

She was crouched on her pillow, her lips drawn back from her teeth and a snarl of rage on her face. Even as he watched in horror she swung her arm down at the mattress again, and he saw the sharp kitchen knife that gleamed in her hand. He threw himself across the bed and imprisoned her wrist.

'For God's sake, Laura, what are you doing?'

Her glazed eyes met his wildly. There was no recognition at first, but as it slowly penetrated her brain who he was she gave a high-pitched scream of fury.

'Get into bed!' Her voice was cracking with the intensity of emotion. 'Get into bed, you bastard, and let me kill you!'

Frantically he twisted at her wrist, trying to force her to release the knife. She had incredible strength and he realized that he was not making any impression on her. She jerked backwards and freed herself, leaving him sprawled over the quilt. With another demonic yell she launched herself at him, stabbing wildly in the direction of his back. Instinctively he rolled over, falling off the foot of the bed and hearing the muted thud as the knife met the quilt. Now, while she tried to release it, was his chance. He scrambled up and grabbed her from behind, pinning her arms to her sides.

'Laura! For Christ's sake, wake up! Laura!' He shook her hard, and felt her hand come away from the knife handle.

Now that she was unarmed he twisted her round to face him. Her eyes were dilated, and she wrenched one arm free and clawed at his face with her hand. Her nails just missed his eyes, and he felt blood trickle down his cheeks from the furrows they left. She was completely silent now, and fighting with the desperation of a cornered animal.

It was almost impossible to believe that she was actually attacking him, but he was aware that he was probably fighting for his life. Despite the extra adrenalin that the knowledge caused to flow he was scarcely a match for her. He wondered if anyone else had heard her yells of rage; surely if they had they would come and see what was happening.

Silently now they grappled, Adam trying to force Laura into a sitting position where he could keep her until she came to her senses; Laura trying to free herself and return for her knife. As sweat trickled down his shoulder blades Adam found that he was gradually winning. There was less resistance from her now, and slowly he could feel her rage abating. Reluctant to take any chances he dragged her over to the door and removed the cord from her dressing gown. Then he pushed her on to the dressing-table chair and tied her hands together. By the time he had finished she was sitting slumped in a heap, refusing to look up.

He tried not to think about how she had looked when she had stabbed at him, and raised her chin to gaze at her face. She stared dully back at him, exhausted and apparently uncaring.

'Why?' His voice was a whisper. 'Laura, why did you try and kill me?'

'It's all your fault,' she said, her voice strangely pure and child-like. 'You gave Mummy help. Without you she wouldn't dare oppose me.'

The hairs on the back of his neck prickled, and he took a few steps away from whoever it was who sat on the chair.

'Where's Laura?' he asked it.

Laura's mouth opened, her eyes tried to focus on his face.

'I'm Laura.' The voice was the same. Too light for Laura.

'No, you're not. You're Edward.'

'I'm not, I'm Laura!' The voice was stronger now, changing back to Laura's.

Suddenly he wanted to get away. He had tried. He had even warned Laura that something like this could happen. She had refused to listen to him, had been certain that she could cope. He was getting out. Going back to London and concentrating on his work. He didn't want to be involved any more. He couldn't afford to be; next time he might not be so lucky. Frantically he pulled on his clothes and shoes. He didn't bother with his case or toilet things; they were replaceable. As he tugged the jersey over his head he knew that he was behaving like a coward, but he didn't care. His one instinct was for self-preservation. With a final look at Laura, still sitting slumped on the chair, he opened the door and went out on to the landing.

The night-light gleamed softly. Everywhere was still. With one hand on the wall he stepped quietly to the top of the stairs. A board creaked beneath his feet, and he froze for a few seconds, but no one appeared. With a sigh of relief he put his hand on the banister rail and lowered his foot on to the first stair. In the few seconds that were left to him he had time to note with a peculiarly detached awareness that the steps appeared to have vanished. Someone or something had pushed him between the shoulder blades and he was undoubtedly going to die. After that he felt himself falling, falling into a dark space that had no end. When he finally crashed into the hallway his head hit the ground first and his neck broke with a sharp crack. He died instantaneously.

Laura felt uncomfortable. Her shoulders ached and her ribs were sore. She opened her eyes, and discovered that she was sitting on her dressing-table chair, and not lying in bed as she had supposed. When she went to move she found to her amazement that her hands were tied, and glancing down her surprised gaze met the sight of an old dressing-gown cord wound round her wrists. She frowned, trying to work out what had happened. Then she looked round at the bed while she tried to ease her hands free. The bed was rather crumpled, and something protruded from the quilt. She couldn't quite see from this distance what it was. There was no sign of Adam.

With a final tug she freed her hands. She listened carefully, but could hear no sound at all. Completely confused she walked over to the bed. As soon as she saw the handle of the kitchen knife she knew that something bad had happened. Something that involved Edward. Her mind was completely blank, she had no recollection of even leaving her bed, let alone being tied up, but anxiety swamped her. She hurried out of the bedroom, perhaps she would find Adam safe in the bathroom and he could explain what had been happening. She doubted it, but she had to hope.

The bathroom was empty. Taking her courage in both hands she went quietly into Edward's room. He lay sleeping, one hand tucked beneath his cheek in his usual fashion. She looked down on him for a moment, wondering what he had been up to tonight. Whatever it was it hadn't disturbed him, he slept the sleep of the innocent. Trying to dispel the fear that persisted she checked Belinda's room and the nursery. Nothing. Adam had disappeared. Terrified, but without knowing why, she tried to calm herself. He was probably downstairs, having a cup of coffee because he couldn't sleep. It didn't explain the knife, or why she was tied up, but that didn't matter. The one thing that mattered was finding him. Without Adam she couldn't go on.

She walked slowly down the stairs, listening for sounds from the kitchen. At the foot of the stairs her toes met something soft but solid. She pushed at the object, assuming it to be a soft toy left by Belinda. It refused to move. Her heart was thumping in her chest now, and she was reluctant to bend down. Gradually she crouched, stretching out her hands until they fastened on to what was quite unmistakably an arm. She gave a small moan deep in her throat, then rushed to the light switch. The hall seemed horribly bright. Adam lay on his back, his head twisted at an impossible angle with his eyes gazing at the opposite wall. She knew without approaching him again that he was dead. No one who was alive would lie like that.

For what seemed an age she stood there, whimpering to herself and trying to find the courage to move towards him. There was something that troubled her apart from the way he was lying, something not right, but her mind refused to function properly and she couldn't make out what it was.

At last she forced herself away from the wall and bent down by the body. She would not look at the face, the fixed stare from the grey eyes was too horrible to contemplate. She looked all over the body for signs of blood, terrified that he had been stabbed by the kitchen knife, but there was no trace. As she stood up and prepared to call the doctor she realized what was wrong with the body. It was dressed. Adam had got up and dressed in his slacks and jersey before tripping down the stairs. It made no sense. Nothing made sense any more. Still whimpering she picked up the telephone and dialled the doctor's number. After that she went up the stairs and woke her mother-in-law.

When the new young GP arrived he found Laura in a state of incipient hysteria, and her mother-in-law not a great deal better. He got Nicholas's telephone number from his mother and rang him. The women needed a man in the house for the rest of the night. There was nothing he could do for the body in the hallway except pronounce it dead. A broken neck obviously, but a post mortem would have to be held. He stayed at the house until Mr Wells arrived, and then left. Accidents in the home were always annoying. Most of them could be prevented with proper attention. He wouldn't mind betting that the stair carpet turned out to be loose or worn. It was such a waste of a life, and he sighed to himself.

Nicholas took command straight away. He put Laura to bed and persuaded her to take a sleeping pill with some warm milk. He checked on the children and pulled their doors closed. Finally he joined his mother in the kitchen.

'Did he often stay overnight?' He sounded annoyed, and tried to moderate his voice.

'Oh no, dear. This was the first time. He seemed a nice gentleman to me.'

'Yes. I didn't really know him, and I had no idea that Laura was seeing him.'

'Was it an accident, Nicholas? Do you think he slipped?'

'It's hardly likely that he was pushed, Mother.' She didn't answer him. 'Mother! What did you mean?'

'It just seemed strange that he was dressed, as

227

though he wanted to go home. Laura has been rather strung up lately, and I thought that if she had been annoyed with him, trying to keep him here, she might have . . .'

'Don't be ridiculous! For heaven's sake, Mother, don't go repeating that sort of thing to outsiders. This is going to be bad enough without you stirring it up! Do you honestly think that Laura . . .?'

'I suppose not. But, it did look rather odd. Why was he dressed?'

Nicholas stood up. 'I don't know, and I don't care. Perhaps he never got undressed. Perhaps he wanted a cup of something and pulled on his clothes in case the children saw him. There are masses of possible explanations. Masses.' He was trying to convince himself. He didn't think that he could contemplate the future if he had driven Laura into a breakdown by leaving her. Besides, she had been so composed of late; his mother was being ridiculous.

'Go to bed, Mother. You must need some sleep.'

'All right, dear. Good night.'

Poor Laura, thought Nicholas as he rubbed his eyes; now she was alone again. He hoped this wouldn't affect the divorce, and then pulled himself up for being so selfish. Of course it wouldn't, but he must expect Laura to be shaken up. Perhaps he should offer to take the children off her hands for a few days, give her time to pull herself together. Yes, that was the best idea. She could go away for a few days, get some sea air. He went into the drawing-room and slept on the couch for the few hours that were left of the night.

When it was all over, after Adam had been cremated in the Berkshire town of his birth, Laura refused to let the children go to Nicholas and Vicky. She was adamant.

228

'I'm better off if they're here to distract me,' she told Nicholas. 'I'd brood on my own.'

'It wasn't your fault,' Nicholas reminded her. 'The coroner said that his shoes were untied, he must have tripped over the laces. It was an accident, that was all, a terrible accident.'

Laura, who knew about the kitchen knife, nodded.

'I know that. I understand. I still miss him. I can't believe he's never coming back. I need the children.'

He gave in to her impassioned pleas, half-grateful that he wouldn't have their noisy games to contend with every evening.

Laura, all energy gone and every emotion drained, sat in the sun and nursed herself back to full health. She would doze in the day, drifting off in the sunlight and then waking slightly burnt and heavy headed. She no longer slept at night, she didn't dare. It was when she was asleep that she was most vulnerable. She knew that now, and so she adapted, slept in the day and read at night. Her body managed to adjust after a time, and although she was tired it wasn't as bad as she had feared. She was becoming stronger. She had to. She needed to become very strong indeed, otherwise she wouldn't be able to do it.

Edward too used the hot summer to re-charge his batteries. It wasn't easy to do what he had done, it had exhausted him. When he was older, more powerful, then it wouldn't drain him so much; now, while he was still a child, it was hard. He was grateful for the breathing space that his mother's self-imposed convalescence afforded him. He too grew stronger. Only Belinda, trapped in the middle of them and picking up random thoughts that made no sense, did not flourish. She grew pale and lost weight, wishing that it was all over.

*   *   *

At the beginning of September Victoria was now in her sixth month of pregnancy and in a bad mood.

'I just can't manage them both for a weekend. Surely Laura isn't too worn out to cope for a few more days. They go back to school next week.'

Nicholas tried to sound placating, his usual role these days, but he was also firm.

'Look, Laura has done everything she could to speed up my divorce, and is being extremely reasonable in her maintenance demands. In return the very least that we can do is take the children for forty-eight hours while she visits her mother. They'll be visiting us every other weekend once we're married, so the practice will be good for us. Besides, you like Edward.'

Vicky turned petulantly away from him. Life wasn't going at all as she had planned it, and knowing that it was her own fault did nothing to help. She had continued to work, and became over-tired and out of patience. There were one or two complaints to the senior partner, and she received a gentle reprimand. As a result she had to be on her guard all the time that she was working, which only left Nicholas to bear the brunt of her ill humour. Her vision of sweeping serenely through her pregnancy, admired by everyone and feeling on top of the world had long since vanished. Now she wondered why women ever got pregnant twice; once was enough for her.

Quite apart from her moods she had a second reason for not wanting Edward and Belinda. She was beginning to find Edward creepy. He had turned into a watchful child, and wherever she turned she would find his eyes upon her. He rarely smiled any more, and although he was always well behaved there was an air of superiority about him that irritated her. She couldn't admit it, that would be tantamount to supporting Laura and her daft theories. All that she could do was bottle it up and hope that Nicholas didn't notice.

'All right,' she said at last. 'I suppose we haven't any choice. Laura certainly looks peaky enough. Have you noticed how pale and thin she's become?'

Nicholas, relieved to get the problem solved without too much fuss, was hardly listening.

'She looks the same as usual to me,' he said casually. 'She never has much colour.'

On the Saturday morning Edward and Belinda arrived with Laura. Belinda carried two soft toys and a jigsaw, but Edward had nothing in his hands. Victoria groaned to herself; another two days of him hanging about in a desultory fashion with nothing to do. She opened the door to Laura, wearing the polite smile that they both used for the unavoidable times they met.

'Come in Laura. Nicholas is through in the kitchen.'

Nicholas looked up and greeted Laura warmly.

'Hello there! That's a smart suit, is it new?' In the background Vicky frowned. Smart clothes were another source of annoyance to her in her present condition.

Laura looked vague. 'I suppose so. You probably haven't seen it before. Here are the children's night things in this case. Bee has brought a few toys, but Edward didn't want to. He said that you might take him out?'

Edward stood by the table, his eyes flicking from one adult to the other. If he gets taken out, thought Vicky, then I shall demand an evening out myself later on. He never takes me out any more. She caught Edward's eyes upon her, and could have sworn that he sneered. Before she could be certain he had looked away. God, I hope my child isn't like him she said to herself. Edward's back stiffened, but he did not look round at his aunt. He was glad now that he had never come to live with her; she was pathetic these days. Always moaning about something.

'I'll be back Sunday tea-time,' promised Laura. 'If you need me I'm at mother's.'

'Sure thing. Why are you going there?'

'Since Bob died and her television series folded she's been very lonely. I thought I'd play the dutiful daughter for a change.'

Nicholas looked closely at her. 'Are you OK Laura? You look a bit tired.'

'I haven't been sleeping too well. All this hot weather I expect.'

As Nicholas went to the door with Laura Vicky glanced at the children. Belinda was cradling her doll, Edward was watching her, but even as Vicky looked they glanced at each other in unison and smiled. She put her hands over her stomach and turned away. She was becoming fanciful of late, and had an overwhelming urge to protect her unborn child. She wished with all her heart that it didn't have to grow up surrounded by Edward and Belinda. There was something strange about them these days. Giving herself a mental shake she started to peel the potatoes. No doubt once the baby was born she would feel quite differently, and see them as the normal children they had once been.

Laura drove fast and well. She was in a hurry to get to her mother's, mainly because it had been so long since they had met, and she knew that she might not have much more time to make amends. The house was in the heart of the Surrey countryside, set back from the road in two acres of ground. Leaving her car in the drive she rang the bell and then embraced the older woman warmly. Even to her mother's uncritical eyes she appeared drawn, and there were heavy shadows beneath her eyes.

'Are you quite well, dear?' she enquired over the water melon.

'A bit tired, Mother. I still find Edward difficult.'

'You should get your sleep. It makes such a difference if you start the day fresh.'

'Yes, Mother.' She pushed the half-finished melon to one side. Her mother should see her during the nights: lights blazing, endless cups of coffee, stimulating books to read. It was an endless battle against sleep. A battle that she dared not lose in case she went wild again.

After Adam died she found that by drifting into a half sleep and making her mind blank it was possible to recall some of what had occurred that night. Not all, but enough to see that she had tried to kill Adam, even if she hadn't ultimately succeeded. He had warned her, she could recall that quite clearly, warned her that Edward might take her over, and she had dismissed the idea out of hand. Now she knew better, and was determined not to be caught out again.

She only picked at the chicken breasts, and then forced down some fresh fruit salad in case her mother became too concerned. Over their cups of coffee, they chatted. Laura told her mother about the children's progress at school, and said how attractive Belinda had grown.

'She must take after you, Mother. She really is striking.'

'You're very fond of her aren't you?'

'Of course. Isn't that natural?'

'I don't know. I was a very bad mother myself. Sometimes I feel guilty over how much I neglected you.'

Laura didn't want that. She didn't want her mother left blaming herself if anything went wrong.

'Please don't be, Mother. I always remember my

childhood with great affection.' A blatant lie of course, but what did lies matter now.

'And Edward? Do you love Edward?'

She toyed with her teaspoon. 'Not as much as Belinda, but enough. He can be extremely difficult, Mother; sometimes I think he pushes me just for the sake of seeing how far he can go.'

'That annoys you?'

'Of course it does. On bad days I wonder that I keep my temper. There have been times when I could have really hurt him.' There, she thought. She'd said it. Her mother would remember that, trot it out as evidence of the strain she had been under. It would help, and she was going to need all the help she could get.

'I should see the doctor, get something for your nerves. It's bad for you living under constant pressure. I really think you look quite poorly today.'

After that Laura turned the talk to her mother's favourite topic, the old days. In the evening they played cards, and the next day they went to church together. Laura felt guilty about going, but didn't see how she could get out of it. Her mother had become quite religious since her last husband had died, and although she would doubtless grow tired of it when a new man came along and caught her eye, for the moment she was sincere. At the end, during the blessing, Laura wanted to get up and run out but she sat upright and tried not to listen. At last it was over, and she and her mother filed out into the September sunlight.

After a traditional roast lunch Laura kissed her mother warmly and left. She was pleased with the way it had all gone. However things turned out the visit wouldn't have been wasted.

At the cottage Edward and Belinda were already packed and waiting.

'Did you have a nice time? Were you good?' asked Laura, apprehensive because of the air of strain that was obvious.

'They were fine,' said Nicholas heartily. 'Vicky felt a bit off colour I'm afraid, so I didn't manage to take them out, but they seemed to amuse themselves all right.'

'I hope she's not too bad?'

'Oh no! she's been a bit busy at the surgery this week.'

'Of course. Well, thank you, Nicholas.'

'Any time, delighted to have them!'

Edward pushed past his father and took hold of the door handle.

'Bloody liar!' he muttered. Nicholas took hold of his collar.

'What did you say?' Edward wriggled, flushing with anger.

'I said you were a bloody liar. You kept wishing we were at home. Didn't you? Didn't he Bee?'

Laura tried to keep calm. Nicholas would feel guilty because his feelings were apparently transparent, but she couldn't tell him how Edward really knew. Nor did she want to any more. There was no point. Soon it would be finished.

Nicholas turned Edward over his knee and smacked him soundly.

'Don't you ever swear again, my boy, or you'll feel my belt on your backside.'

Belinda started to cry. 'I want to go home!' Laura gathered the two children together and shepherded them out. Nicholas, his face openly embarrassed, stood in the doorway and watched them go. As soon as the car pulled away he slumped against the wall in relief. He hoped that Laura didn't need a break for some time in the future.

Back at the house they all separated; Laura to her

room in order to unpack; Edward to the living-room where his books were; Belinda to the kitchen to coax some biscuits from the new cook. They all kept their minds carefully blank and tried to pretend they had nothing to hide. They were all skilled at self-control these days, the weeks of practice had seen to that. Even so Edward knew that the waiting was nearly over, and as he read he hummed softly to himself.

The children were back at school, and Laura stretched languidly in the mid-day sun. Mornings and evenings were cooler now, the summer was almost over, and she at last felt that she was ready. Her mind conjured up a picture of Adam; Adam at his best, the intelligent grey eyes alight with humour and love. She had taken his death with a resigned calm that would have been surprising, except for the fact that she knew he would live on. Until now it had been a secret, but as her waist-line slowly thickened she was aware that it would be impossible to hide it much longer. Adam's child, a tiny foetus whose existence might well prove the saving of her. The law looked with compassion upon pregnant women.

She moved indoors, running her fingers along the dusty window sill. The house was neglected these days, she had no interest in it. Her daily woman had left, and Laura did not trouble to replace her. All of her energy had gone towards this day, there had been nothing to spare for everyday life. Probably she was being talked about. Ruth was bound to have carried tales to Nicholas, but she didn't care. All that mattered was this final battle with her son.

Secure in the knowledge that he was miles away, seated at his school desk and his attention fully occupied, she went upstairs and locked herself in the bathroom. There she opened the medicine cabinet, and took out bottles of tranquilizers and anti-depressants left over from the days of doctors and psychiatrists. Carefully she opened up an assortment of plastic capsules and poured the powder into an envelope. She did not know how much would be needed, so she mixed the tablets thoroughly, feeling sure that a strong combination must be lethal for a six-year-old.

That done she took the bottles and hid them at the bottom of the dustbin, before placing the envelope in her handbag ready for the evening. Her mind was sharp and clear, acutely aware of her every movement. She seemed to stand outside of herself and watch as each step was completed.

The hardest part would come when she collected the children from school. Somehow she had to block out all that she had done and planned to do, and instead she must think normal, everyday thoughts. Her hours of solitude and rest during the past months had all been aimed towards this. She was sure that she could do it. Lately Edward had picked up very little from her, and his baffled frown had encouraged her to persevere.

It was still hot when she stood outside Edward's school gates. Belinda was already in the car, happily eating an ice lolly. I shall never collect him again, thought Laura; this is the last time that he will walk out of school and allow me to kiss him on his cheek. I will never come here again. She had a moment of panic, of terrible awareness, but she pushed it away. She breathed slowly and thought about the doll that Belinda wanted for her birthday next week. By the time Edward walked gravely towards her she was composed again. His eyes flickered briefly over her, with no more than his usual interest. She took his hand and walked him to the car, aware that his hand was still very small; he was after all only a little boy.

Again her mind closed the thought off, and she hoped that she was in time. Anything out of the usual would alert him, she must try harder. A quick glance showed Edward looking undisturbed, rattling the handle of the car door. Belinda let him in, and Laura moved round to the front. Despite the heat of the afternoon she felt cold, cold right through.

The children changed into play clothes and went outside. Laura busied herself with their tea, concentrating on the bread, the cakes, anything that took her eye. She was not nearly as strong as she had thought, but fear of failing drove her on. She could not afford to fail, for if she did he would be undisputed leader of the household and she would never again have such an opportunity. She heard the door creak, and spun round.

'Only me, dear; you are jumpy today!'

'Oh Mother, I was miles away. Could you make the tea for me?'

It was easier when there was another adult there, someone to talk to. She breathed a sigh of relief. It was nearly time, she only had a few more minutes to get through and then she could think what she liked. She would be free.

They came in quietly, not boisterous like most children, but they were never boisterous any more. They were grave, thoughtful children when they were alone together. Laura passed the plate of sandwiches round and then turned her back on them while she poured the mugs of tea. She sneezed, and turned for her handbag that hung on the back of her chair. The children were busy, they liked marmite sandwiches. Her mind was as

238

blank as a sheet of new paper. Automatically her hand tipped the contents of the envelope into Edward's blue mug, and all the time she repeated a childhood poem to herself. '*I wish I lived in a caravan*,' her brain was busy recalling all the lines. She put the mugs before the children and turned back to the sink. '*With a horse to drive like a pedlar man . . .*'

'Mummy, can I have a cake?'

'Yes, Belinda. "*Where he comes from nobody knows*" . . .'

'Mummy, did you sugar my tea?'

Oh God, did I? 'I don't know, Edward. I'll put some more in.'

" '*Nor where he goes to, but on he goes.*" . . .' There you are.'

'Thank you, Mummy.'

'*His caravan has windows, two, and a chimney of tin that the smoke comes through. He has a . . .*'

She turned back to the table. Her mother-in-law was bringing the mugs to her for refilling. She glanced inside them. All empty. Her legs turned to jelly, and she felt violently sick. She ran out of the room, and only just managed to get to the downstairs cloakroom in time. As she crouched heaving over the bowl she allowed herself to think about the enormity of her crime. She had poisoned her own child. Her firstborn, the much longed-for child of her dreams. I had no choice, she whimpered, no choice.

At last she felt a little better, but a quick sight of herself in the mirror made her start. Her eyes stared out from a bloodless face, the shadow beneath them indicated sleepless nights and ill health. Not that it mattered. It was probably better if they saw her like this. All the more people to say that she had appeared ill.

In the kitchen only Edward remained. He looked up, but his eyes were glazed and he peered at her.

'Mummy? Mummy, I don't feel well.'

She went over to him and felt his forehead. It was warm, clammy.

'You'd better go and lie down, darling. Perhaps you've caught a chill.'

'Mummy, I can't see properly.'

'I'll carry you up.'

It was worse than she had anticipated. Somehow, now that he was helpless and frightened, he became much more an ordinary small boy. His head pressed against her breast, and his hand clutched on to the front of her dress. Love such as she had not felt for him since he could walk welled up in her. She held him tightly; she did not want him to suffer, just to sleep. To sleep for ever.

She took off his top clothes and slipped him between the sheets. His eyes closed, and he sighed deeply. As she bent down he grasped her hand in his hot fingers for a moment, and tears slid down her cheeks. I had to, she whispered, please understand that I had no choice. He was breathing slowly now, and the lump in her throat threatened to choke her. She took one final look at the top of his golden head and then walked away. She loved him then, completely, as a mother should, for the only time in his short life.

Downstairs she went into a frenzy of activity. She cleaned every kitchen surface, put away every object she could find. Then she turned out her larder and wiped the shelves down. She went into the garden and dug the vegetable plot over, removing the weeds that had been there for weeks. She worked mindlessly, furiously, until the light began to go and then she stopped and checked her watch.

To her amazement it was 8 o'clock. She felt guilty. Heather must have put Belinda to bed and she hadn't even noticed. Before she went in to her she would check Edward. Surely by now it must be over.

She went quietly up the stairs, wondering what she would find. He might have been sick, might even have tried to get out of bed and call her, she knew that she had to be prepared for anything. Outside the door she stopped and listened. There was no sound. At last she found the courage to open it, and she pushed gently. It swung open at her touch. She took one step into the room and screamed.

Edward sat on the side of his bed, fully dressed and reading a book. He glanced up and looked at her cheerfully.

'Hello, Mum! Can I have a drink, I'm thirsty.'

She opened her mouth, but the words refused to come. She coughed, and tried again.

'Do you feel better?'

'Oh yes, I'm very well thank you. May I have a drink?'

Laura was shaking, but desperate to regain control. He must have incredible strength if he could look so alert already. But, did he know? If he didn't then she might be all right.

'What sort of a drink, Edward?'

He paused, thinking. 'Lemon I think; that would be refreshing. I haven't had a drink for hours. I let Belinda drink my tea.'

They stared at each other. Laura transfixed by horror, her eyes wide with disbelief; Edward solemn faced at first, watching, waiting. As he saw realization dawn on Laura's face he smiled. It was the warm all-embracing smile of his babyhood and it filled her with terror. With a cry she blundered out of his room and along to Belinda's. The bed was empty. She shouted her name, calling frantically, unable to believe that Edward had spoken the truth.

Heather appeared from her room. 'I can't find her, Mrs Wells. I thought she must be with you.'

'No. No she isn't!' It was a scream of agony, and Heather backed away.

Laura half-ran and half-fell down the stairs, flinging open the living-room door with a frenzied strength. Nothing. She ran to the dining-room, looking round in complete blind panic. Nothing. With increasing dread she reached the cloakroom, and noticed that the door was half-open. She walked slowly in, pushing at the door but anticipating its refusal to open fully.

Belinda was lying in a crumpled heap behind it. She had been dreadfully ill, the entire floor was covered in blood and vomit. Laura was moaning aloud, a terrifying sound, as she bent down by the little girl. There was no doubt at all, no chance of a mistake, Belinda was dead. Then Laura began to scream. She screamed and screamed, not aware when her mother-in-law tried to pull her away, not aware of Heather crying as she picked up the telephone, but painfully aware of Edward. Edward standing in his bedroom, alone and friendless, but expressing his rage and despair in the only way that he could. Every time that Laura took breath to scream she felt the shock waves from her son, and they increased her hysteria. She had failed, and now she wanted to die too.

The doctor and Nicholas arrived together, and they managed to remove Laura from the cloakroom and carry her to the settee. There they left her still screaming and hysterical, and Nicholas's mother kept watch over her. Soon the ambulance arrived, with two nurses and a doctor from the nearest mental hospital. A quick consultation, words whispered between the adults, and then they were taking Laura away. She seemed unaware of all that was happening, never looking at anyone, lost in her own grief. At the front door she lifted her head, pulling away from one nurse's grasp.

'It should have been Edward! I meant to kill Edward! Do you understand what I'm saying? For the love of God Nicholas answer me!'

Rooted to the spot by the horror of her words Nicholas could only nod, attempting to bring some measure of comfort to this deranged creature who had once been Laura.

With Laura gone and Belinda's body removed the house was horribly still. Vicky sat huddled in an armchair, a heavy cardigan wrapped round her shoulders. She thought of the Laura she had once known, the pretty fair-haired child who had only ever wanted to marry and have a family, and she cried softly to herself.

Nicholas climbed the stairs, trying to find Edward who had gone into hiding when the doctor arrived. He found him standing at his bedroom window, watching as the ambulance sped away. Nicholas put a hand on his son's shoulder.

'Your mother is very sick,' he explained gently. 'She didn't know what she was doing.' The boy's shoulders drooped, his head hung down.

'My sister's dead. Now I'm all alone.'

'Not alone, Edward. I'm still here, and Auntie Vicky. You'll come and live with us, and when the new baby comes that will give you another brother or sister.'

'It won't be the same. Belinda and I were special.'

'I know, old chap. But it will be something. Think of all the things you can teach it as it gets older.'

Edward turned his face to his father.

'I hadn't thought of that. I suppose I could try.'

'There, you see! There is something to look forward to.'

'Where has Mummy gone?'

'To a special hospital, where they'll try and make her well again.'

'She killed my sister, she should be killed too!'

Nicholas put his arms round the boy. 'We don't know that Edward. She didn't say that she did.' Edward stared at him, they both knew what she had said, but that was too painful to bring out into the open.

'I never want to see her again,' said Edward at last. 'Never, never, never!'

'You never will, I promise you that.' Edward smiled. At last he was free.

Laura was found unfit to plead, and sent to Rampton to be detained at Her Majesty's pleasure. Heavily sedated she withdrew into herself, refusing to talk to any of the psychiatrists and psychologists who attempted to help her. In early February the following year she gave birth to a baby boy who was taken into care and later found an excellent foster home. Laura never asked after him, and indeed never referred to him once he had gone.

For a time the small village where Laura and the children had lived was inundated with sightseers who wanted a glimpse of the house and the little boy whose mother had meant to kill him. Naturally they never saw him. He was far away living safely with his father and stepmother in their new home. Eventually the scandal died down, as scandals do, and the house was put up for sale. It stayed on the market for nearly a year, but then it was bought by a down-to-earth business man from the North who didn't in the least care who had previously owned the house. It was exactly what he had been looking for.

The months passed. Laura refused any visitors, and

spent her days alone in a barred room, sitting and staring into space. She took no interest in anything, and it became doubtful if she even understood when people did talk to her. One day Nicholas visited. He had been told to expect a great change in her, but he was still shocked. Her hair was lifeless and cut short, it clung to her head emphasizing the sharpness of her features. Only the eyes remained the same, large and brown, but there was no longer any life in them. They stared uncomprehendingly at him when he entered.

Nicholas talked of everyday things, reluctant to come to the point of his visit in case he upset her. Finally he knew that he had to speak, had to try and get a reaction.

'Laura, I wanted to speak to you about Edward.' Her eyes moved nervously, but at least he knew that she had heard. 'I wanted to tell you something. I don't blame you for what happened, I blame myself for not understanding what you were going through.' No response. The eyes were dull again. He pressed on. 'What I'm trying to say Laura is this. We're finding him very difficult too. Bloody difficult to be honest. He's a strange boy, and Vicky finds him very disturbing. I wanted you to know that it wasn't just you. He is pretty impossible at times.'

At first he thought that she wasn't going to reply, but then she turned to face him fully and she smiled gently. It was possible for one fleeting moment to see the Laura that she had once been.

'Finish it for me,' she said clearly. 'Kill him.'

Horrified at the emotion he had re-awakened Nicholas jumped up.

'It's all right, Laura; I didn't mean to upset you. I'll be going now, and we'll manage, don't worry. Vicky and I are coping very well.' He glanced back, but Laura was once again lost in her own private world.

As he walked out of the hospital Laura's chief psychiatrist came over to him. 'Mr Wells, they told me you'd come! Did she know you?'

'I think so. How is she?'

'The same, Mr Wells. I don't think we can expect much change after all this time. At least she seems content.'

Nicholas didn't want to tell him what Laura had said; it might cause trouble. They might feel that she was regressing. After all, it was his fault for raising the subject. He held out his hand. 'Goodbye, doctor. I'll always come if you need me.'

'Of course. Goodbye, Mr Wells.'

In the tranquility of her room Laura allowed herself the luxury of two small tears. No one had ever believed her except for Adam, and no one ever would. But at least here she was safe. Edward couldn't interfere with her here, and she had her memories. Adam, Belinda, the boy child. Many happy memories.

Epilogue

1975

Vicky sat at the pine-topped table in her ultra-modern kitchen and regarded her stepson thoughtfully. He was now eight years and two months old and she realized that he would probably remain with her and Nicholas for another ten years. Ten years! She doubted if she would keep her sanity. The thought was quickly rejected. A mere figure of speech, in no way connected with Laura whose sanity had forsaken her forever. It was simply that he was such a knowing child, she found that privacy had become impossible. Even if Edward wasn't in a room with her she felt his presence. Quite ridiculous of course, but an eerie sensation that she was finding impossible to overcome. She wondered how she could ever have been so fond of him. Had he changed, or had she? Sometimes she thought that as soon as he was securely settled with her he had ceased to exert the charm that had once enchanted her. It was almost as though she had been used.

Nicholas rarely discussed his son with her. They both knew that life was difficult with him around but to admit it openly would be giving credence to Laura's cries for help over the years. Neither of them was willing to face that possibility aloud. Vicky sighed. She ought to feel more compassion for the boy; after all he had lost both his sister and his mother in one terrible day, and had to live with the knowledge that he was the intended victim. Strangely it had left no visible scars. He appeared to have shut his mother from his mind and stepped into his new life with alert confidence.

The confidence had been a little misplaced. Last night, after baby Alastair was in bed and Edward in his bath, Vicky had told Nicholas that she wanted to get back to work. She could easily find a nanny for Alastair, a placid, happy eighteen-month-old toddler, but Edward would prove more of a problem. Nicholas agreed, and together they decided upon a small boarding school twenty miles away. He could come home most weekends, and Vicky would be able to spend more of her free time with her own child. The one problem was breaking the news to Edward. Nicholas promised that he would do it, and Vicky hoped that it would be soon.

The kitchen door swung open and her stepson walked in. They had been in their new house for six weeks, and Edward had made his bedroom into a den where he would retreat from Vicky's shouts or Alastair's interference in his games. Usually she had to call him down at meal times once he was immersed up there, but today he came purposefully towards her. It was a long time since she had seen him smile at her so pleasantly, and she felt a twinge of guilt over their plans. He stopped before her, and reached out to touch her dark hair.

'My Mummy had fair hair, didn't she?' He had never mentioned his mother before, and a prickle of unease ran down her back.

'Yes, she did.'

'She was pretty too.'

'Yes Edward, she was very pretty.'

He stared at her. 'You're not!' Vicky attempted a light laugh.

'No, I'm afraid I'm not.'

'If Daddy died no one else would want you, would they?'

The room seemed smaller, she felt as though he was backing her into a corner, so she stood up and moved over to the pine dresser, hanging some mugs onto the hooks.

'I don't know. Daddy isn't likely to die, so I haven't given it much thought.'

'It isn't very kind of you to want to send me away, Auntie Vicky.'

She stiffened; the wretched child had been eavesdropping last night. She was right to feel constricted by him, he scarcely even slept.

'Listeners never hear any good of themselves,' she said sharply.

He shrugged. 'That's a stupid saying.'

'Your father will talk to you about it some other time, Edward.'

He sat down at the table, and stared at her. 'He doesn't want to send me away. You do. I know it's your idea. Daddy wouldn't have thought of it without you around.'

'Edward, I refuse to discuss it with you. Now please move, I want to do some baking.'

He glared at her, and she found it hard to remove her gaze from the dark intensity of his stare. She stood with one hand on the dresser and tried desperately to look away, but she couldn't. His eyes seemed to grow larger and larger, his features blurred until only the eyes were clear. They kept her imprisoned, she felt a pain behind her temples and the room tilted madly. She caught the dresser top tightly in both hands, and then she heard a low humming sound in her ears.

All at once she was no longer in her kitchen. She was standing at a crossroads, looking at a line of traffic hurrying by. A child stood next to her, holding a ball in her hands. The ball was red with green stripes, and somehow she knew that it was important. With a chuckle the child threw the ball high into the air, and watched as it hit a lampost and bounced into the road. With a shout the little girl ran after it. Vicky screamed, and the approaching car hit the brakes hard. There was a confusion of sounds, the car wheels skidding, the girl crying, and then the shattering of glass. In slow motion she watched in terror as a shape came through the broken windscreen, bounced off the bonnet and then lay motionless on the road. A small, dark-haired shape in a bright green anorak and red woollen hat. A trickle of blood crept across the road, reaching out its tentacles towards Vicky's feet. She opened her mouth to scream again, but no sound came. She felt the earth move beneath her, and started to fall in a faint.

Her hands reached out instinctively to save herself, and her fingers met the cool pine of the dresser. She moistened her dry lips and looked around. She was still in her kitchen, nothing had changed. She blinked and shook her head, but everything remained perfectly normal. A chair squeaked, and she jumped nervously. Edward stood up, his face cheerful and pleasant.

'I'd better go then.'

'What?'

'If you want to do some baking, I'd better move.'

'Oh! Yes, yes of course. I must do some baking.'

Edward whistled softly between his teeth, watching her out of the corners of his eyes. She swallowed nervously, she had never been so scared in her entire life, and knew that her whole future depended on what she said now. In one moment everything was clear to her, and she spared a fleeting moment of compassion for Laura. Poor, misunderstood Laura. It wouldn't happen to her; she wouldn't allow it to. He could have anything he wanted, live how he chose. She would protect herself and her family at all costs.

'About school, Edward.'

He turned sharply, eyes wary, thoughtful. 'Yes?'

'If you really don't want to go, then of course I shall tell your father. The last thing that I want is for you to be unhappy.'

He smiled his golden smile, and took a sultana from the jar. 'That's kind of you. Thank you very much.'

'It's nothing, Edward. From now on I think it would be a good thing if you let me know when anything troubles you. I'm sure that I'll be able to explain things to your father if he's at all difficult.'

'That seems sensible, Auntie Vicky. You can be my go-between.'

She stretched her mouth into a parody of a smile. 'Of course. Now, I really must do some baking.'

'Right. I'll watch out for the car.'

Once he had gone she allowed herself to sink down on a chair, burying her face in her hands. It had been horrible, and she had no intention of enduring such nightmare visions again. He could have anything, anything at all, as long as she was spared that.

The sound of the car horn brought her upright. She must look normal for Nicholas. He must never be allowed to know. She smoothed her skirt down and opened the front door. Nicholas got out first, then opened the passenger door and lifted Alastair out. Alastair in his new green anorak, his red woollen hat clutched in his hands.

'You shouldn't let him ride in the front,' she said sharply, 'it's incredibly dangerous.'

Nicholas looked apologetic. 'Sorry! It was only for the last hundred yards, coming back from the post office.'

'You go over crossroads after that. If something hit the car he could go right through the windscreen.'

'All right, Vicky. I've said I'm sorry. Nothing did hit us, as you can see!'

She held Alastair tightly. He was everything in the world to her, and she would protect him to her dying day.

'Hurt,' he complained loudly, 'Mummy hurting.'

'Sorry, darling. I hugged you too tightly. Come on in, I'll give you a drink.'

In the hall Edward waited, tossing a red and green ball from hand to hand. Alastair stretched out his arms to his half-brother. 'Carry,' he pleaded. 'Eddie carry?'

Edward reached for the child, and Vicky instinctively tightened her hold for a second before releasing him. She saw the look of protective care that was on Edward's face.

'Anything but that,' she thought. 'I could never let him have Alastair.'

In the kitchen she stood the percolator on the stove, and made fruit juice for Alastair. Nicholas was cheerful, talking all the time.

'I thought I'd have a word with Edward before lunch, just to sound him out about boarding school. Not that I plan to give him a choice, but at least I should prepare him gently.'

Vicky kept her face averted. 'I've been thinking about that. I'm not so sure that it's a good idea.'

'For Christ's sake, Vicky; you've been on about it for months!'

'Don't shout! It's just that I'm not sure we're being fair to Edward. We'll talk about it later.'

'We talked about it last night. My mind's made up.'

'No!' Her shout startled them both. She tried to laugh. 'I'm sorry, but I don't want to upset him again. He's been through enough, poor child. When you remember Laura, and Bee . . .'

'You knew about them last night, Vicky. Nothing's changed. Still, I'll wait if that's what you want. I shall never understand women, never.'

She knew that he was annoyed, but she didn't care. Let him think her hysterical, unable to make up her mind, that was a small price to pay.

She carried the baby mug into the living-room, Nicholas behind her. The room was very quiet. Alastair and Edward were sitting side by side in the middle of the floor, their backs to the doorway. Edward was rocking gently from side to side, humming as he did so. Alastair sat as still as a statue, his hands clasped together on his chubby legs, his head tilted to one side, listening. . . .

By the year 2000, 2 out of 3 Americans could be illiterate.

It's true.

Today, 75 million adults... about one American in three, can't read adequately. And by the year 2000, U.S. News & World Report envisions an America with a literacy rate of only 30%.

Before that America comes to be, you can stop it... by joining the fight against illiteracy today.

Call the Coalition for Literacy at toll-free **1-800-228-8813** and volunteer.

Volunteer Against Illiteracy. The only degree you need is a degree of caring.

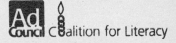

Ad Council Coalition for Literacy

Warner Books is proud to be an active supporter of the Coalition for Literacy.